Penguin Books

Birthmarks

Patrick Roscoe was born on the Spanish island of
Formentera in 1962 and spent his childhood in Tanzania, East Africa. He was educated in England and
Canada, and later lived in California and Mexico. A first
collection of short stories, *Beneath the Western Slopes*, was
published in 1987. Patrick Roscoe currently lives in
Sevilla, Spain.

BIRTHMARKS

Patrick Roscoe

Penguin Books

PENGUIN BOOKS

Published by the Penguin Group

Penguin Books Canada Ltd, 2801 John Street, Markham, Ontario L3R 1B4

Penguin Books Ltd, 27 Wrights Lane, London W8 5TZ, England

Viking Penguin Inc., 40 West 23rd Street, New York, New York 10010, USA

Penguin Books Australia Ltd, Ringwood, Victoria, Australia

Penguin Books (NZ) Ltd, 182-190 Wairau Road, Auckland 10, New Zealand

Penguin Books Ltd, Registered Offices: Harmonsworth, Middlesex, England

Published in Penguin Books, 1990

1 3 5 7 9 10 8 6 4 2

Publisher's note: This book is a work of fiction. Names, characters, places and incidents either are the product of the author's imagination or are used fictitiously, and any resemblance to actual persons living or dead, events, or locales is entirely coincidental.

Canadian Cataloguing in Publication Data

Roscoe, Patrick, 1962-

Birthmarks

ISBN 0-14-012016-5

I. Title.

PS8585.082B57 1990   C813'.54   C90-093098-5

PR9199.3.R657B57 1990

Acknowledgements

The following have been used by permission:

Excerpt from "First We Take Manhattan" by Leonard Cohen. © 1987 Leonard Cohen. Used by permission. All rights reserved.

Excerpt from "Shadows and Light". Words and music by Joni Mitchell. © 1975 Crazy Crow Music. All rights reserved. Used by permission.

Excerpt from "On the Nickel" by Tom Waits. © 1980 Fifth Floor Music, Inc.

Excerpt from "The Ballad of the Sad Young Men". Lyrics by Fran Landesman. Music by Tommy Wolf. © 1959 Frank Music Corp. © Renewed 1987 Frank Music Corp. International copyright secured. All rights reserved.

Excerpt from "O Very Young" by Cat Stevens. © 1974 Cat Music Limited. Administered by Westbury Music Consultant Limited.

Excerpt from "The Three Great Stimulants". Words and music by Joni Mitchell. © 1985 Crazy Crow Music. All rights reserved. Used by permission.

Excerpt from "Gypsy" by Suzanne Vega. © 1987 AGF Music Ltd./ Waifersongs Ltd. All rights reserved. Used by permission.

Some of these stories first appeared in the following publications, sometimes in a mutilated form: "My Lover's Touch" in *The New Quarterly*, "Rorschachs II: Mutilation" in *The Capilano Review*, "A Child of Man" in *Event*, and "Dying to Get Home" in *The New Quarterly*, and "Rorschachs IV: Night Train" in *Grain*.

This book was written with the financial assistance of The Canada Council and The Ontario Arts Council, as well as with the help of less legal bodies.

**For Joni Mitchell,
The Great Stimulant**

Contents

Contents

BIRTHMARKS

Other Voices
and the Real World I

I'm guided by a signal in the heavens
I'm guided by the birthmark on my skin
—Leonard Cohen, "First We Take Manhattan"

birthmark a mark or blemish on a person's skin
—*The Random House College Dictionary*, 1973

One of the most difficult things to do is to paint darkness which
nonetheless has some light in it.
—Vincent Van Gogh

Every picture has its shadow
And it has some source of light
—Joni Mitchell, "Shadows and Light"

UNBORN CHILD HOLDS LIFE FOR OTHERS
"Pediatricians feel it would be difficult to take organs from a
living, crying, wiggling child. . . ."
—*USA Today/International Edition* 12-19-87

dark 1. having very little or no light 2. radiating, admitting or reflecting little light 3. sombre in hue 4. evil, iniquitous, wicked 5. destitute of knowledge or culture, unenlightened 6. silent or reticent
—*The Random House College Dictionary*, 1973

light 1. something that makes things visible or affords lumination 2. the radiance or illumination from a particular source, as the candle or the sun 3. a particular light or illumination in which an object seen takes on a certain appearance 4. to come to rest; fall or settle upon; land
—*The Random House College Dictionary*, 1973

"I haven't been in love," answered Prince Myshkin as gently and gravely as before. "I . . . have been happy in another way."
—Dostoyevsky, *The Idiot*

Grandmother
and the Pygmies

Grandmother and the Pygmies

He was tall, at least. A tall, well-built prairie man who knew where she'd come from and what had brought her to where she was now. Although Fred was well into his seventies, with little strength behind his size, Eva married him. She hadn't spent most of her life turning a sow's ear into a silk purse for nothing, so down they went to city hall one drizzling afternoon. There was scarcely time for Eva to change out of her house-dress into something decent for the I-do's, never mind any loving or lolling, not with her having to fix supper for the boarders. They would begin to fuss and moan if the potatoes weren't mashed by six o'clock, be it the Queen's own wedding day.

Fred's my brother-in-law and husband, she said, always in that order, as if the first relationship were more important than the second. True, he had been married to her Elizabeth once, but that was years ago, back in Saskatchewan. A rambling man then, Fred had wandered away west across the plains, shrinking out of sight long before Elizabeth had any idea of dying. Oh, Eva knew what her daughers said. Mother is getting lonely and old, they said. She can't be choosy at her age, she takes the pickings from her dead sister's plate, they said. Maybe she's hankered after Fred all along, maybe she's tired with globe-trotting, maybe she's bored playing the part of Ms Independence, they conjectured. If wishes were horses, beggars would ride, was Eva's only answer to that.

You pays your money and you takes your choice. Life knocks on the front door one day when you're in the middle of the dishes, sets its foot quickly inside so you can't slam the door in its face, and says: well, here I am, let me in, why don't you.

After returning from her world-wide travels, Eva had stayed with one of her daughters for a few years, until she tired of biting her lip to keep silent at the sight of another woman's poorly run house. Wanting her own place again, she took what was left from the sale of the old land and bought a house in Nanaimo. It was a big barn of a building, sitting high above the cracked sidewalk on Kennedy Street and fronted by a deep, dark porch. She took in roomers to fill it up a little. Finicky, middle-aged single men, they mostly were, who should have had wives or, better yet, mothers to look after them, with their fussy ways and little secrets no child would care to know. They made a lot of work, but what was new in that? Feeding a dozen heads three good meals a day, keeping twenty rooms presentable: she'd done it before and she could do it again. She got the rent out of them, you can bet your last nickel on that, but it was hardly enough to meet the mortgage and pay for groceries, and the place cost a fortune to heat, those damp Island winters, being drafty as a sieve. Filling up a horde of men with plain, hot food, she might have been back on the farm again, except there was no joy in it now. The colour of these strangers' blood ran a different, paler shade than hers. They were prissy little men with delicate health and cautious, indoor jobs, like desk-clerking and filling out forms in triplicate. These men weren't about to use her food to raise up barns, bring in crops, build a country from scratch. Cooking up a big meal, a woman likes to see it eaten with some gusto. Well, there was precious little of that, only twelve pale men poking at their potatoes with sour expressions in the big, gloomy dining-room. Eva tried to liven up the table some, bringing up the damned Socreds and that crook by the name of Trudeau. She mentioned the hockey scores and the price of wheat, but those boarders' jaws just moved up and down like steel traps snapping open and shut. They fixed their eyes on her roast, manoeuvred to get the choicest bits into their bellies, and flicked out tongues to catch stray drops of gravy at the corners of their mouths. Eva talked about her fascinating travels

around the world, all the strange places and sights she'd seen. But
these half-men wouldn't even prick up their ears when she told
them about Africa.

Well, then Fred turned up. He needed a room and heard she
had one. So it's you, she said, facing him on her doorstep for the
first time in twenty years. She didn't have to go on like a Hollywood actress how glad she was to see him — he was almost her
people, wasn't he? It was a relief to have him around. Eva hadn't
admitted even to herself what strange thoughts she'd had in her
bed some nights, listening to those twelve men in the rooms
around her. Careful, stealthy steps, creaking bed springs, midnight coughs. She gave Fred the east room, a pretty good one.
Wouldn't take money from him, though he did receive the
measly old-age pension the crooked politicians were kind enough
to give the people who'd worked and slaved to make this country
a place where they, the fat cats, could sit on lard behinds in fancy
offices and wink at skinny secretaries while the whole land went
to pieces. Don't get her started on *that*. She only wanted what was
rightly due herself and her generation, after all.

Fred was a clean-living, quiet man who listened when she
yarned over people they both knew back on the land. He wasn't a
talker himself, but he sat evenings with her. During day he
brought out his tools and worked around the place, which could
certainly stand a little fixing. The sound of his hammer and saw
reached her when she was baking the bread and stirring the
gravy. Well, how's it going? she asked sharply, looking down at
Fred pondering one of his little odd jobs. You couldn't say he was
a quick worker, you couldn't quite say that, but he was careful.
Even if what he got done hardly amounted to the Lord's labour,
Fred did try. And that's what counted, wasn't it?

Soon after the wedding, Eva threw up her hands and sold the
house out from under the boarders' dripping noses. While they
whined and wondered where they'd roost next, Eva pushed her
glasses higher up on her nose, took measure of all the old, heavy
furniture she'd gathered around her over the years, and figured
out a way of getting it moved. She and Fred went to live up Island
in a trailer court on Nanoose Bay, pooling pension cheques to
cover rent and whatnot. Fred's daughter and son-in-law lived
next door to them in the park. However, Muriel drank and Mel
knew exactly eight stories not that interesting to start with and

downright dull on repeated hearing. You've told us that one, Mel, she'd say. He'd pause, then go on to another. I guess we've heard that one a few times too, she said. Finally, she just gave up. Oh, it was a pretty enough place, with the trees and the bay, but her furniture was meant for a big house. It wouldn't exactly fit into the trailer, and she couldn't part with it, though it wasn't actually antique or anything like that. A little cramped, she had to say. Still, there was a body beside her in bed again, and although usually they just slept, Fred could surprise her sometimes, he could. Then his allergies started acting up, wouldn't you know, so on the advice of the so-called doctors they moved down to the Lower Mainland, into an apartment in the suburbs.

Meant for a miniature mouse, Eva said, but those small rooms were all they could manage. The stores and everything else were miles away; of course she didn't drive, had no car if she could, and the bus service was awful bad. Plus, Fred's relatives lived nearby, and you'd think they had no home of their own the way they were always coming around. Behind Eva's back, they switched Fred into a Jehovah's Witness. *Watch Tower* and *Awake!* cluttered up extra space when there was none to begin with. Eva didn't believe Fred had the first notion what the Witnesses stood for; he was just too easy-going to contend with his people, who knew a quick convert when they saw one coming. Eva tried to talk some sense into their heads, but she'd learned sixty years ago that to try to blow out a grass fire is a waste of breath. She let them say their piece and cart Fred off to the meetings. That one Christmas they just dampened to destruction, the big bunch of them bleating their beliefs when all she wanted was a nickel's worth of good time, a tasty turkey, her annual glass of sherry. She nearly walked out then.

But she stayed.

She'd married Fred knowing he had the cancer. She'd take care of him until he died, seeing there were worse things she could do with her time. For years the cancer sat stubborn and still, like a mule that won't move forward or back, and won't budge to the side either. Spreads slow in old bodies, said the quacks. She just hadn't counted on so many years in that mousehole of a basement, too far from her own friends and family to do her any good. Of course, her girls knew she didn't like them to come meddling around, and they certainly didn't want to hear her honest opinion on how they lived. She'd taught them to speak their minds like she spoke hers, so when they did drop by there were always words. She did manage a few trips back to Saskatchewan, before Fred got bad. She went in early October, for those several weeks between hard summer and hard winter.

But her eyes were going. She'd always been a reader, liking most those long historical novels with facts as well as fancy to them. You learned something. And she'd always worked her hands, making something you could use, like a blanket or a quilt. Now she felt her mouth turning down in the corners from night after night before the TV. She and Fred watched the hockey games best they could, favouring rival teams. Each claimed his own men were up a point on the other's, and while arguing the subject they missed the announcer speaking the score. Next day on the radio Eva'd hear two entirely different teams had been playing. Their own weren't even in the game, never mind win, lose or tie.

Fred's health failed. She wouldn't say it, but it was hard getting him to the doctor, filling the prescriptions, let alone buying groceries and keeping up with housework. When Fred began to suffer bad, she moved him into the next room. Nights he woke and wandered, falling down like a tall tree in the forest. He spoke other women's names; he wouldn't recognize her. Elizabeth, he sometimes called her.

If it wasn't one thing, it was another. Her own health quit on her. They called it a stroke, said a blood vessel burst in her brain. She lost her sight a while; it wouldn't do her much good again, she knew. While she was stuck in that hospital, her daughters decided it was high time to get into the act. They moved Fred into one of those extended-care places you never leave alive. Then cancer was found in her breasts. Well, they hadn't done her much good for years, shapeless and sagging as they were from all the feeding. Still, they were part of her, familiar. She woke to find herself carved up like a Sunday roast whose warm, savoury smell lingers in the air long after it lies in the stomachs of strange, small men.

A short, squat woman, she was, with a strong body built for hard work. The word for it in her dictionary was dumpy, especially after she started gaining flesh at fifty. She felt herself a different species from those fashion models in the shiny magazines who couldn't lift a stack of kindling with their twig arms, she bet. Though she didn't reach five feet herself, Eva'd always liked a man with some length to him. She didn't feel dwarfed by long men; instead, she felt something larger and taller herself, and believed the life she put into her men had some scope to it, could amount to something big.

Hans, her first husband, had been even taller than Fred. Here we go nowhere. Who was to know that, thirty years after marrying her, Hans would topple over under the hot prairie sun, falling like the last tall tree left on the plains? He'd gone back to Saskatchewan to bring in the wheat on the old land they'd left behind in charge of a second cousin fifteen years before. Eva had urged the move to the west coast when it looked like all their hard work on the farm would amount only to more hard work. They bought a beautiful piece of land on the Island. But wheat prices dropped, the old land didn't pay as it should, so they sold the pretty Cedar place, though the only offer they got was poor. With the money, Hans and Eva bought a combination gas station-café high up on the Malahat. There wasn't a good deal of traffic along that road those days and business was bad. Eva had to pump gas with one hand and flip hamburgers with the other, since Hans had settled into a decade of brooding. Over what? He'd always been a smiling, handsome, hard-working man, and now this: lying for years on the couch, his length covering the whole thing. Or he sat with those long legs stretching halfway across the room before him, like he wanted to trip anyone who came by. He didn't drink or smoke or show temper, but his silence and stillness sometimes made Eva wish he did. The girls were afraid of him, cautiously tiptoeing around in their long skirts and pearls while they waited for their dates. Eva stayed out of his way, too. His face turned sour and German, all the sun just left it. Now and then Eva couldn't stop from wondering if the move to the coast had been for the best and if it was quite right to wish for an easier life, especially when living a hard one was all you knew. She saw Hans sitting around in his prime, like there was no work large or worthwhile enough to lift him to his feet. Of course his heart gave out on him soon as he returned that last time to the farm, a big man no longer used to heat or heavy work.

Eva buried him, sold the Malahat business and the farm, then used some of the money to finance a year-long expedition around the globe. She'd always wanted to see all the strange places that were. At this time she started saying she wasn't German at all. She wasn't a grim, silent German, stolid from heavy food and unable to find pleasure in hard work or joy when it was done. No, I'm Swiss, she said. Wasn't her maiden name, Basler, certain proof she came from a tidy, pretty Swiss place such as Basel? Eva said she was Swiss in Japan, New Zealand and Tahiti, and in England and Scotland, too. She loved the British Isles! This history she'd read about for years now lay there before her own clear, grey eyes. Dating from that time, she never drank a drop of coffee again. It became tea-time morning noon and night. A civilized drink, a pleasing ritual, Eva thought, making it the proper way. She remembered prairie women drinking cup after cup of scalding, bitter coffee while they glared out their kitchen windows at the hard, glassy sky.

Next, she thought she might as well head over to Africa to stay with her daughter's family, while she was gypsying about. Ardis had dragged a husband and four small children all that way for no clear reason that Eva could see. Well, all her girls were strong, stubborn women, she'd given them that much. Maybe it was just coincidence that the six of them married men of slightly less than middle height, much shorter than their father, whom they would each and every one of them leave sooner or later, with flimsy excuses. What would Mr. Freud say to that? Eva wondered. But of course she didn't breathe a word, her girls were so touchy.

Touchy and headstrong. Soon as Eva arrived, Ardis announced she and Mitch were taking a trip south. Didn't know how long they'd be gone, a few months maybe. Eva could stay with the children in the house on the hill, couldn't she? A neighbouring American woman would do the shopping in the market, the kids would be no trouble, but make sure they take their malaria pills, and away flew Ardis and Mitch without another word.

There she was, somewhere in a country they called Tanzania, near some town she couldn't find anywhere on her map. She was sure it was a civilized place, in its own way, this college built around an old Catholic mission. The house was made of a few cement blocks, a tin roof, some mesh screens in place of glass windows. It wasn't because she was frightened that Eva stayed inside the house, although lions and snakes did wander across her mind, she couldn't fib. She just couldn't jump like Jane through the jungle, not with her hands tied by four children between the ages of five and ten she didn't know from Adam, and it was no surprise to her that Ardis ran a house sloppy as stew. First off, she told the black boy to take a holiday; she didn't hold with slavery and could set the place straight with her little finger, anyway. As far as the kids, she had scant practice with grandmother work. She'd raised her own children, done a good job of it, she might add, then felt her shift as mother was finished. All along she'd had the notion that children were adults of slightly shorter stature: if you spoke sense to them, they'd use their heads and listen. These four acted old as hills that have sat centuries beneath the sky, and Eva'd never known a mountain to move at anyone's please and thank-you. Maybe she'd lost her touch, but she couldn't do a thing with these kids.

It being the rainy season, there wasn't much chance for them to play outside — although she suspected they didn't hardly go out even in the sun. They sat inside with her, listening to the rain pound away on the tin roof, like a native drum calling. That rain fell and fell, unlike any she'd ever known. Endless silver sheets sliding past the screen windows, turning the hill into a mess of mud that slowly slipped downwards. And there was all that green. Every day the world turned a brighter shade of green that made even the wet west coast seem faded. That glassy green spreading under the grey sky made her want to scream, but she didn't.

When you can't put in order the whole world beyond your door, you turn your hand to what's inside. Straight off Eva saw the kids didn't know how to do a thing but read. They said they didn't go to school because there wasn't one to go to. Apparently Ardis didn't give much account to their education, and they'd be way behind if they ever returned to Canada. Luckily, Eva had a strong streak of teacher in her, liked telling people what they didn't know. Forty years ago she'd taught in the one-room district schoolhouse, driving her buggy through the winter drifts, facing up to those big farm boys and feeling she'd done a good day's work if she got any kind of learning into their heads, never mind a whole curriculum. Around the kitchen table Eva tried to give these grandkids the first idea of geography and arithmetic. They sat with their legs folded under them, like animals, until she told them it was their affair if they wanted to interfere with their circulation and end up midgets. Otherwise the lessons weren't a whole lot of success. The kids were quiet enough, but they gave each other sly, sidelong glances and fixed doubtful expressions on their faces when she said that two plus two makes four. They made her feel she was a raving backwoods preacher, or an enemy they had to oppose silently and steadily because God was on their side. We don't have a bedtime was what they said, amazed to heaven that such a mad thought could harbour in her head. She was outnumbered, too.

They'll need some social skills if they ever hope to fit into any kind of people, Eva decided. Giving up on capital cities and long division, she taught them bridge. They caught on all right, young as they were, though she would have been very surprised if any of her blood didn't run smart and quick. Right away, however, they commenced to bend the rules slightly, varying the usual ways of bidding and following suit until Eva forgot what a simple cross-trump could ever mean.

She started playing the record-player all day long, putting on *Camelot* and *My Fair Lady*. She explained the plots of the shows and how cleverly the songs followed them. The kids stared out the window at African soldiers marching up and down the road in the rain. My, England's a wonderful place, Eva said, wondering if the country was planning a war and hoping it'd be decent enough to wait until she left before starting the shooting. The kids replied that they'd already been to England, as if that was the end of that. Wouldn't you know it: the record-player broke, she didn't have a clue why, it wasn't her fault. Father brought that three thousand miles and you can't buy another one here, the kids said, looking at her for all the world like she was guilty, sentenced and condemned.

Well, she'd make each of them a patchwork quilt, then she'd have done her duty by them and could get on a plane just as soon as their parents returned. She had a mind to see India. Couldn't believe any cows were sacred enough to roam around while humans starved. Couldn't believe women would throw themselves in rivers and on fires when their men died — instead of arranging a decent funeral, taking account of what money was left, and looking to see what they could turn their hands to next.

Eva cut bright, quizzical shapes from old clothes and fitted them together like a jigsaw puzzle. After basting the pieces together with strong black thread, she stitched the whole thing onto a plain white backing. Eva recalled lying long ago beneath a quilt her own mother made her, and how, on those winter nights in Saskatchewan when the temperature would drop into the coldest hell, she felt that the patches upon her were pieces of all the people who cared for her, holding her warm.

Meanwhile, the kids marched soldier-style around the house, one after the other, tallest to shortest. They chanted Swahili words to keep in step and carried mops and brooms over their shoulders in place of guns. She couldn't stand to see them line up for inspection, all at attention and neither moving a muscle nor blinking an eye for a good hour on end. Then they'd float around the room, discussing people she'd never heard of. Are you mentioning those American kids down the road? Eva would ask hopefully, for it would do these kids good to mix with their peers. But, no, they were talking about people from books as if they really breathed. It would be no news to her if the four of them ruined their only pairs of eyes, poring over the same books time and again. Their eyes were like kitchen windows blurred with steam she wanted to rub clear with a good clean rag. Other days those kids just sat there, quiet as mice. Closed themselves right up, tight as oysters you can't open but only cut your hand on the shucking knife trying.

No wonder, these kids had been dragged too many places and seen too many sights for their years. Look at her: she'd spent sixty-odd years staring at the land she was born in before taking a peek at foreign parts. Look here, she said. The first quilt's done. It'll last until you get back home, I guess.

We *are* home, David, the youngest one, told her.

We don't use quilts, we're never cold, said the middle one. Donald, it was.

Before she could finish the second quilt, Ardis and Mitch came back, and not a moment too soon as far as Eva was concerned. They didn't bother unpacking. Said they wanted to show Eva the continent. Said they'd all head up to the northern country. Privately, Eva wondered about Mitch's job; he didn't do much teaching that she could see. Picture the seven of them and all that luggage squeezed three months into one of those small foreign cars. A white Peugeot, it was. Travelling those dusty flat roads where you didn't see a soul for a hundred miles or more. She didn't like to think what would happen if the car broke down. The country flew by, Mitch drove so fast; she couldn't see a thing with all the dust. Anyway, hadn't she lived most her life on flat, empty land? She tried to get the kids to sing show songs to pass time, but they preferred to doze in the dusty heat. Once in a while one of them would open an eye and look stonily out at the landscape. Of course, the scenery was very beautiful and interesting and so on, and there was all the wildlife, all kinds of strange animals she'd only seen pictures of before. But what connection did it have to her — or to the rest of them, when you came down to it? Eva began to have the idea she'd seen all this before: these gazelles were first cousins to the deer that had haunted the scrub in the back section; these buffaloes just carried fancy names to cloud the fact that they were not much different from the cows she'd milked with her own two hands more times than she ever cared to remember. It was just strange enough to make it seem familiar, this country, and sometimes Eva imagined she'd somehow slipped back onto the old land at a time before her people settled it. The thought of all the work needed to clear and fence this unformed land wearied her, and Eva felt the sweat of two decades' labour trickle down her sides.

North through Tanzania, Kenya and Uganda they made their way, stopping by the side of the road for desolate picnic lunches in the middle of nowhere, sleeping nights in lodges of game parks. The natives got blacker and wore fewer clothes the further they went. Ardis said they might as well try to reach the northern tip of Uganda, since they had come this far. Eva stared at a blank space on the map. Either she'd gone blind or there were no signs of towns or roads or even game parks up there. Yes, a little dangerous, Ardis coolly admitted. But very interesting.

So is hell very interesting, I'm sure, Eva thought. This is where I jump ship, she declared. At the last big town before the puny paved road turned into dust, she stayed behind in one of those big old colonial hotels where tea is served prompt at four o'clock. There was a little ill-feeling: Ardis suggested that her mother was old and cautious; Eva had to say that it was fine for adults to risk their necks if that's what made them happy, but their kids were a different kettle of fish. A hazy plan for the white Peugeot to pick up Eva on its way back south wasn't needed, as the cookie crumbled. Her first night in the hotel dining-room Eva met an understanding Englishwoman who offered her a lift back to civilization. Leaving a short note of explanation behind, Eva took the ride to Nairobi, where she caught the first plane back to Canada. She never did have the chance to have that frank talk with the Indian ladies, by the flowing Ganges.

"Grandma?"

She opened the eye that didn't have a patch on it and saw a young man standing in the doorway of her hospital room. It must be one of those wisecracking doctors fresh out of diapers, she thought.

"Grandma? It's me."

"Me's a pretty common name," she said. Which one could it be? Eva shuffled through the names of her grandsons like a deck of cards, realizing she was short the whole pack. Many of them she hadn't seen all the years she'd been busy with the boarding-house and then with Fred. Didn't know if they were alive or dead. Her daughters never spoke willingly about their children, as if they were ashamed of them. When Eva asked whatever happened to So-and-So, they had to think a minute. I guess Lynn's in Montreal now, Arlene might say at last, the place where her youngest daughter breathed being of little concern to her, it seemed. I think she had another baby, Arlene would lamely add.

What had happened? Somewhere along the line the family had scattered like unrelated spectators going their own ways at the end of a hockey game. Naturally, all those divorces didn't help. Funny, but after her daughters deserted them, her sons-in-law had come around more than her own girls. Mother Riecken, they still called her. She kept a case of beer in the fridge for their visits, though she didn't care for the stuff herself. They knew she was interested in the same things they were and had a good head on her shoulders to discuss them, too. Sports, education, the economy, the chances of the NDP in the next election. Her daughters had come by less often, the past ten years. They paid short, formal calls, chain-smoking and drinking black coffee and nervously jiggling their skinny legs. Once in a blue moon they'd bring one of their kids along, to prove it was still alive. She couldn't keep track of all those boys and girls, how they kept shooting up past her height so she had to look up at them like their eyes were sky. Sawdust cookies, she said, placing a plate before the kids. The recipe comes from my head. They'd sit there, not saying boo, eating one cookie after another. Well, they got no home baking at all, of course. Later they'd sometimes send her postcards bearing stamps from Mexico, the States, some European place. She never could make head or tail out of the messages. Wondered if they were deliberately cryptic, if the kids had never learned to write a simple sentence, or if she'd lost touch with the jargon kids spoke these days. All she knew was they switched jobs and countries the way people used to change socks.

"I'm Richard," said the boy. "You know, Donald."

And they changed their names at the drop of a hat, too.

She felt small and shrunken in that damned bed they were never going to let her out of. She pulled the covers way up to her chin, over her carved-up chest. The boy touched the blanket. "You never made me a quilt," he said. "You promised, but you never made it."

"I guess you don't need a patchwork quilt in Timbuktu, or wherever it is you call home." She studied the boy with her one good eye, which didn't really do her much good at all. Couldn't read or sew with it, or even watch the idiot box. She saw glimpses of Ardis in the face before her but no traces of herself. Suddenly her blood moved angrily at this visible evidence that it carried only so far. "Wasn't your hair dark?" she asked.

"The sun," he laughed, touching his head. His skin was tanned a brown colour hers had never been.

She didn't want to think about these young people. Didn't want to know what they felt or thought or believed. What drugs they took. Their sex lives. "At least you've grown taller than your father," she said. 'I've shrunk two inches the past ten years, not that I could spare them. Next week I'll be a midget."

The two of them were silent, waiting for enough time to pass until it added up to a visit. "I was looking into the photograph album," Donald said. "This one made me smile." He pulled a snapshot from his pocket and held it out to her. "Do you remember? The time we visited the pygmies?"

Eva closed her eye to clear it, opened it again. There she was, in living colour, standing between two black pygmy men both taller than herself. Ardis had taken the picture so she could show it to people and give them a laugh at her ridiculous mother. In the picture Eva wore a green dress printed with pink flowers. She had liked to throw up her own clothes then, believing she had a knack for making things as good as what they sold for the moon and the stars in stores. But the green dress hadn't fit quite right, she had to admit. Something had gone wrong. It made her breasts look larger and lower than they really were. The two pygmy men wore necklaces of teeth across their bare chests.

Ardis had heard about a group of pygmies living in an isolated place a day's drive off the main road. The white Peugeot pulled up to a clearing in the jungle, before three grass huts. Dark faces watched out through dark, open windows. Then the pygmies slowly emerged. The men passed an opium pipe back and forth between themselves. The women wore only skirts, showing off breasts that sagged down to their waists. A few naked kids sat listlessly in the dust, not bothering to brush away flies that crawled over their faces, their eyes. A sorry bunch, Eva thought. She recognized the blunt, blurred features that come from inbreeding. Incest, they called it. A close family, she'd thought, hearing a sharp, bitter voice speak in her head.

"Give me that picture so I can burn it," Eva said. "They weren't real pygmies at all. Just claimed they were, so fools like your parents would pay shillings and cigarettes to snap them. They must be five feet tall if they're an inch. Or I suppose it's centimetres now. This is the modern age, I keep forgetting. That conversion was just a trick by the government to make their elders feel out of date and obsolete. You can't know the true size or weight of anything these days. How can a woman tell the weight of a good chicken, the height of a real man? They don't want us to know everything's smaller, punier these times."

Eva heard her voice wind down into the kind of tired complaint she'd once have died before she made. "I'm in a tight corner, Donald," she heard herself say. "My back's up against the wall."

"Then push it down," he said loudly. At once his tone changed. "I hear Aunt Bev's bought a new house and you're going to live with her once you escape from here," he quickly said. "I like Aunt Bev."

Eva closed her eye and saw her youngest daughter. After divorcing two men, Beverly had a married a third. He'd dressed in a kilt and sung Scottish ballads while drinking too much scotch.

One night he drank a bottle of the stuff in the garage. The next morning Beverly opened the garage door to the smell of exhaust fumes. The car was silent, though the ignition was on, beause it had run out of gas sometime in the night. Now Beverly went to aerobics classes three times a week and square-danced on weekends. She came home with flushed cheeks and sparkling eyes.

Donald looked into his grandmother's eye as it reopened. It was small and very bright, like a hen's. "How's Fred doing?" she asked. "I haven't heard."

"I'm trying to do something big, Grandma," the boy said, then abruptly stopped. How old was he? She tried to subtract one date from another, gave up. His face was smooth and unlined. He wore jeans and a T-shirt, like a teen-ager. In the place behind her eye Eva saw a confused mass of young people scurrying from one place to another, milling about in uncertain circles. She saw them picking up things, then dropping them like hot coals. All the while their eyes darted fearfully up at the sky, for sight of bombs. She felt with all the heavy, inert weight of her body that the time for doing big things, such as raising up a barn or fencing in a big piece of land, was finished.

Eva stretched out her hand, holding the photograph to Donald. His fingers clasped it. There was a moment when she felt the two of them holding the same thing, and it wasn't clear who was giving and who receiving.

He slipped the photograph back into a pocket. "I'll miss my plane," he said. He hadn't mentioned where he was coming from or where he was going, and Eva didn't ask. As he walked away, the bones of his back appeared slight, small. But his shoulders were set straight and strong. He shrank from her sight, growing smaller and smaller, until her only eye blurred.

Rorschachs I:
The Black Hole

Rorschachs I:
The Black Hole

When you are six years old, you stand in the sky with a halo of white cloud encircling your head. You are at the top of a tall tree whose roots dig deep into the earth of America. The sweet, rich taste of cherries is already in your mouth, but more tempting fruit dangles all around you, and you reach toward a branch that cracks. Air roars past your ears as you drop faster and faster; the descent seems long and dark, though your eyes are opened wide. Your heart beats just six times before you land upon Africa. Your left arm is broken, and the white cast rusts in the same red dirt that nourishes banana and mango and papaya trees. When Dorothy fell from her grey sky, she learned how quickly everything can become completely different from the way it was before. In every Oz the colours are too brilliant and the smells too pungent, and light falls in angles unknown to Kansas. You stare at the scar on your elbow, which fades but never disappears; you will the misshapen bones to float until they assume again the perfect shape they formed before. Stars fall from the heavens, stones sink through the seas. Only magic can lift you back through time to the top of the sky, where from the greatest, safest distance you viewed the New World before the fruit was plucked.

The black hole lacks the dimensions of time and space, and it is without light or darkness, warmth or heat. Being inside the black hole is like sleeping, except there are no dreams or even night-mares to remind you that a solid world waits nearby. It is the vac-uum that exists between falling asleep in a pretty white house and waking in a cold, dark cage. After you are inside the black hole once, you are never free from it. (Back in the farmhouse kitchen, the Kansas dust drifts upon Dorothy, she looks out the window and across flat land, hoping and dreading to be torn away by a tornado again.) You will always walk cautiously upon the earth, peering at ground that can suddenly open like a hungry mouth — to swallow you up, then spit you out nearly whole beside the Sphinx, on the Equator, inside Hollywood, upon the moon. You turn a corner of a street to find yourself in a different city, an-other country, where people call you by an unfamiliar name: you are Rick or Rickie, Richard or Reeves. You learn not to seem sur-prised by any abrupt change: it has always been like this, it will al-ways be the same.

You tell yourself that there are certain weak places on the globe, like fragile spots upon a newborn baby's skull. You wake slowly in the morning, your eyes open with suspicion. What unfa-miliar room emerges from darkness into the plain light of day? Who is lying beside you, and do the lines and angles of his face draw the map of a continent you know and love, and where you belong? On your skin are new marks of damage, betraying the force with which you crashed to the ground this time. Beside the bed are clothes that fit you, that must be yours. You feel in a pocket of the jeans for the scrap of paper with a name and address printed on it; you've learned to hang onto this paper, you fiercely clutched the branch that cracked until you hit the ground. In another pocket are money and keys. You prowl around these strange rooms in search of clues; but you are no longer a hopeful spy, there will never be enough clues to solve the puzzle seamlessly. To tell precisely how and why you ended up in these rooms, in all the other rooms.

Take a taxi to the address printed on the piece of paper. Open a door with keys that fit a lock. Enter a set of rooms as unknown as the one you have just left. Home? Outside the window leaves spin in the autumn wind. Upon the white wall is a splotch of black ink. A mark. Look at it, then lean nearer, until you hear the sky whistling past your ears again. You plummet through darkness, you will emerge from the black hole as another explorer who has patiently been waiting to be born.

My Lover's Touch

My Lover's
Touch

One night, when I am six years old, I fall asleep in my bed in the house where my mother and father also live, but wake up somewhere else. I am naked and hungry and cold. The room is bare and dark. There are no windows, and the light socket on the ceiling is without a bulb. The door is locked. I know, as I am certain my heart will beat again and then again, that my mother and father will not unlock the door, and will not bring me food and blankets, and will not comfort me. They do not know where I am, they cannot come to me, they do not wish to find me: the reason is not important. It doesn't matter why I live in this room, and others equally dark and bare, for the next eight years.

My sense of time is imprecise, and marked only by the ticking of my heart. After waiting several days in darkness, I am old as the ancient man who has searched one thousand years for love. He has crawled across the world, and I between these four walls, to find the holy places where He might appear. Only the desperate are truly hopeful.

If you stood outside the door and listened through the keyhole, you would hear me say: sky is blue, grass is green, God is good. These are the old songs I croon, my arms wrapped around myself tightly, tightly. I wonder if anyone hears me. Listens but does not answer.

At the beginning I sometimes wish for a bed. On the cement floor I lie pressed against a wall, trying to warm the cold stone with the heat of my body. The stone soaks up my heat but offers none in return. I attempt to recall sensations of softness and warmth with such strength that there might appear beneath my head a pillow, against my skin a sheet of silk. The more frequently and vividly a vision is remembered, the sooner it fades, as though inside ourselves are stored, like money in banks, impressions which must be added to and not only drawn from. Or we become a vault as cold and empty as this room. Stone is hard and cold, I must repeatedly remind myself, while the darkness blurs all definition. What is soft, warm? I grope blindly around the room, until I realize there is only one such thing. I touch my bare skin.

My skin is porous, and as the chambers beneath it empty of old impressions of colour and light, darkness seeps inside to replace them. It fills me until, if you opened a flap of my skin like a window and peered inside, you would be unable to discern any difference between the outer and inner darkness. In this way my body, swallowed up by the lightless room, seems to float in a big black belly. I savour all feelings of pain and hunger and cold which suggest my continuing existence. I would be grateful for any touch upon my skin, no matter from what emotion it was born.

My ears learn to listen. I see sounds and hear shapes. Those that reach through my walls are never loud or clear enough to permit me to see a person, a car, a bird. They are indistinct as strangers' faces in the night. By their quality, however, I sense that somewhere there is day as well as night. Periodically a needle is sunk into my arm and I fall into deeper darkness, wake in another room. Except that its temperature is slightly higher or lower, air staler or fresher, sounds more or less muffled, the new room might be the old one. Then I discover countless minute differences between textures and flaws of this cement and that of my previous home. But the darkness is constant and may be relied upon. A thousand secret quirks in its character I alone know and cherish; like any true and loyal ally I will not reveal them, though you beat me. I will only say that sometimes I believe I have been taken to a room just beside the last one. At other times, sounds that come to me suggest I am now higher above the world or deeper inside it, nearer or further from the heart of a city. Yet there is never a line of golden light beneath the locked door, and without this crack of illumination I have no proof that the globe is not a black egg, twirling somewhere beyond the warmth of the sun, the light of the stars. The moves from one obscure void to another have no meaning or purpose I can discover, except to teach me: every room is dark and cold and bare.

Always the only article in the room is a bucket in which I expel my wastes. When it is not emptied for several weeks, the air I breathe smells so strongly of decay that it feels to me a heavy substance, both liquid and solid, into which I sink, like a swamp. I spit on my skin and try to wash it clean with saliva. The bucket makes me more thankful for the darkness, which conceals the tireless journeys of roaches toward and from their pail of food. When I am most hungry, I view my excrement with appetite. I drool.

Every three or four or five days footsteps approach my door. The sound is purposeful and loud, suggesting its source is a large body and firm mind. Sometimes the steps pass my door, fading into silence. Maybe they stop just outside, and if my heart were not beating so loudly I might hear through the inch of iron the sound of another's breathing. A body listens, then walks away in the direction from which it came. Or perhaps a key grates in the lock. What I call food is thrown inside my room; anyway, I eat it. Soon I begin to wonder about the hand that throws the food, then I become curious about the heart that throws the hand. My need to know consumes me, and on the first occasion that the mass of flesh and bones and blood enters my room, I welcome it as explorers greeted their original sight of a new world. I feel warmth and weight strike me strongly, and treasure the discovery. Like the wheel and gravity, the act of love has always existed, though upon finding it for ourselves we insist it is our invention alone.

As his footsteps draw near, my heart pounds more and more loudly, and in their rhythm. A thin, mechanical cry, like that of a baby bird in a nest, swells through my throat. I do not know if I will be beaten or fed, and my emotion is an equal measure of fear of hurt and hope for comfort. Slowly this feeling becomes one inseparable thing, and I find pleasure in pain. I take satisfaction from the blows of his fists and feet against the surface of my skin, and this feeling enters me more deeply when he fills my body's openings. His generosity touches me. Sometimes he feeds me after it is over, sometimes not. Eventually food becomes as unimportant as light and warmth; when my belly grumbles, it is calling hungrily for his hands, and the only taste I savour is the salty richness of my blood. If I were not hungry, he would not feed me, I realize. If I were not cold, his body would not warm me; if there were light, he would not illuminate the darkness. His visits are unpredictable and always expected. Over the years, I notice, they occur with gradually increasing frequency and possess a more intense, powerful character. I wonder where they will lead. Feel him push further into me, like a brave explorer daring to enter more deeply the dark labyrinth from which he might not emerge alive.

He has never spoken to me, nor have I heard him moan, grunt, cry. I do not know his face except as darkness made solid. If I were free and walking down the street, I would not recognize him though he bumped into me and apologized at length. I would look into every face that passed and wonder if it were his. Strangers would glance quickly away from the small boy with staring, starving eyes. I would believe every face his face.

Alone. Waiting for his next visit, I try to imagine him. I consider whether his face is lined or smooth. Is his hair dark or light or turning grey? By his strength, I know he is not old. But I picture his eyes as old, and sad. I conjure his presence until he becomes as clear to me as someone I have once known, but forgotten.

Does he miss me when he goes away? Ache for me as I ache for him? I see him walking from this room, straightening his tie, smoothing his hair, with his handkerchief wiping away a spot of my blood that trembles like a tear upon his wrist. He drives home, stopping at a supermarket to buy the loaf of bread his wife has asked him to pick up on the way. His blue car pulls into a driveway before a pretty house. A small boy is sitting on the front steps. He looks hungrily at his father, who tosses three pennies to his son as he passes into the house. The husband kisses the wife. The family eats supper. Afterwards, the man sits in the livingroom with a newspaper held before his face, like a shield. The woman gazes at the man, but sees only headlines that scream war, murder, accident. As she turns to him in bed, he moves away. I should check on Rickie, he says. He stands above the bed in which the small boy lies with closed eyes though awake. The father's fists are hidden in his pockets. He looks down upon his son's face, which is smooth and white as a fresh, unmarked piece of paper. The father does not touch his son, the boy's eyes do not open. When he sleeps at last, the boy sees things that make him wish he dreamed pure darkness.

He has been beaten and kicked until filled with pain completely, I know. My body feels his desperate attempts to free himself from this old and lasting hurt. There is anger and sadness when such release does not occur, and steadily growing violence in his efforts to achieve it. I feel inadequate when he leaves me, as troubled as he was before. I would like to kiss away every tear in his eyes, stroke his back with tenderness. I believe I can save him. But I find myself protecting my eyes and kidneys and other vulnerable places from his blows; however much I want to, I cannot give myself up to him completely. He tries to smash through my skin so he can curl his whole body inside my dark empty room, and float there like a fetus that knows only warmth and comfort. The words of love I wish to utter emerge from my mouth as a very high loud squeal, which resembles the noise made by a pig being slaughtered and which continues until he forces my head into the pail of waste or fills my mouth with some part of himself. When he is gone, the cuts and bruises left upon my body burn with warmth and I feel, in the cold darkness, a hot bright fire near to me. My skin throbs and aches, remembering my lover. I feel his touch still upon me and I am not alone. The emptiness of his absence, my room, is filled. Yes, I wait for him with longing and pray that when he returns I can heal him at last.

Three times an angel has appeared to me — or that is what I call her, since she resembles my memory of that ornament that stood on top of the Christmas tree in the pretty house. She floats down from the darkness above me and illuminates my room with her presence. My eyes are not used to such light. It dazzles, blinds. She wraps me in her wings, which are warm and soft as all feathers. Milk and honey are what she feeds me during long, sweet kisses. She kisses the sores on my body and they are healed. She bathes me in scented water and rubs my skin with fragrant oils, murmuring soft sounds which might mean: one day the darkness will turn to light; or, the darkness is not so bad; or, the darkness is for the best. Then, with a wave of her wand, she is gone. I hate her. Not because she doesn't carry me away on her strong wings; I do not wish to leave my room, and would not go with her if she begged. But I have been familiar with pain and cold and dark hunger. They were my good friends, and the brief visitations of my angel only turn them into bitter enemies whom I must fight until I am conquered. When I am beaten, they are on my side again and tell me, warningly: we are constant companions, we are not fickle friends, it is less painful to lie always in darkness than sometimes in light. We will win every war.

The time of waiting can pass slowly. I repeat my prayers: bless him, save him, bring him back. Dragging hours are filled by recalling his last visit. Replay that act of love over and over until it becomes a film in my head I can start at the flick of a switch. Crouched against the wall, I watch the same scenes recur. There are certain favourite ones. Play them in slow motion, make the pleasure last and last. Touch my skin and feel the unique imprint of his hand. The tender bruises. Happy.

But in the darkness my touch is sometimes clumsy. I fumble with the switch and by accident start a film I do not wish to see and cannot halt. I see a boy of five years sitting on the front steps of a pretty house. He sits there because the sunlight is warm. He wears a pair of short blue pants and a white shirt with short sleeves. He wraps his arms around his bare knees and rests his head upon them. Through the open window behind him floats music. His mother is listening to the radio while she cooks supper. Tonight there will be macaroni, baked soft and warm. The cheddar cheese will be melted creamily throughout, the blood-red tomatoes sudden bombs of flavour, the top a crust of golden crumbs. The scent of cooking food and the sound of music are ribbons that twine around the boy. He narrows his eyes until sunlight enters them like a crack of golden light beneath the door of a dark room. He is waiting for his father to come home from work. Then they will eat. The blue car will turn the corner and approach slowly down the street. The boy will watch it steadily, because if he glances away even quickly the car will turn into another driveway and his father will go into another house, pausing to toss copper pennies to another boy, who will bury them like pirate treasure.

After the wrong film plays and the wrong images fill me, I cannot feel my lover. There is no dark space inside me for him to enter. I see him brutally loving another boy, who is smaller than me. Who cries and cries. He still sobs after my lover leaves the room. Shut up, I tell him, because the sound irritates me and because I am jealous. The boy weeps until he melts into a pool of tears. I lap up the salty puddle greedily, and he is gone.

A month later I can feel my lover's touch again. His gentle, tender caresses. Afterwards I am surprised to find my skin sore, my heart bleeding. Two words twist and coil and wrap around each other in my mind. Love hurts.

My ears become more sensitive to sound the longer they are surrounded by immediate silence. I come to believe the muffled sounds that pass through my walls are cries of other boys who also await a consoling lover. They weep when he is with them and when he is not there. Every cry uttered through time and space is the echo of one voice, I think. Listen to my voice escape from a boy who walks the tightrope of the equator and from one who leans his back against the Great Wall of China. From one who treads on air, above the new moon. Their cries bounce between my four walls, echo in the hollow space inside me. Or is this sound the beating of my heart?

I hear the turning key. Although it scrapes in the lock, the door does not open. Footsteps move away, leaving silence behind. He

has not come to me in a week, my skin holds no stinging memory
of his touch. I need to feel him upon me, against me, inside me.
My fists hammer on the door and my voice calls out. I turn the
doorhandle. It opens. After one thousand failed attempts to open
my door, I believed it useless to touch it again. At once I know
that since the moment I ceased trying, years ago, the door has
been unlocked. The sound of a turning key has been, always, the
protest of my rusted heart upon his entrance.

I am afraid to leave my room because it is my only home, and for
a moment fear that I will lose it forever holds me there. But I
must find him. Suddenly, I doubt he will come to me again, for I
have failed to swallow all his darkness, so he is going to another
bare room where another boy waits hungrily. I leave, walking
down a long, dimly lit hallway. On both sides of me are closed
doors like the one I have just opened. They are scractched and
marked, but without numbers. Through them comes the sound
of crying boys. As my footsteps approach, the cries stop; and I
sense breath held, pulses racing in hope. When I pass by, the cries
begin again, in a higher key. I could open any of these doors, fall
upon a waiting boy, soothe him with my loving blows. But I need
such comfort myself and walk on in search of it. The empty hallway bends. I turn a corner, then reach a flight of stairs leading
down. I descend them to a door below, open it, and find myself
on a street at dawn. Night is leaving the world, a red planet is rising in the sky, I am falling into darkness.

Warm. Soft. White. I presume I am lying in the arms of my angel,
then see I am in a bed in a white room. The sheets are also very
white, and so are the bandages that cover various parts of my
body. A tube runs from a glass tank filled with clouded liquid and
into a vein in my left arm. My lungs cannot breathe this thin,
odourless air and my eyes cannot bear this bright light. My skin
cannot breathe beneath these bandages, blankets, sheets. The pillow and bed beneath me are not solid or hard enough, I am sinking into softness. Drowning, suffocating. I gasp and struggle until
hands appear to hold me down. They are not his hands. They
belong to bodies clothed in white, to faces bearing expressions I
do not remember how to read. Do they convey love? Hate?
Sounds issuing from their mouths speak a language foreign to

me. A needle sinks into my right arm, and I am filled with joy beause I will wake in another dark room, and my lover will come to me there. Before falling into blackness, I see the sky outside the window. It is white. The air that enters the open window stings my eyes and hurts my throat with its freshness. It flutters the white curtain, like an angel's wing.

I waken to the same white room, the same bright light. Disappointment. The light drains the darkness from me, illuminating the empty space beneath my skin, leaving me weak and weary and sad. I lie very still and silent, becoming familiar with the routine around me. I wait, but only women in white visit me. When they touch my forehead or wrists, their hands are as light as fingers of air. The tube is taken from my left arm, my right arm is injected less often. My hair is cut and I am bathed. Later the bandages are removed. I watch mouths open and close, sometimes suspecting the noise they make is meant for me. It has no meaning. I strain to summon sensations precious to me — cold, darkness, hunger — but the bodies that bend over me refuse to let me live in my former state of grace. They are enemies who plot to kill me with attention. No matter how tightly I close my eyes, some light seeps inside their lids. Even at night scattered lights glow around me. Wounds on the skin of darkness.

A man comes once each day. By my bed he sits and moves his mouth. I wait for fists to strike my body, which aches more painfully as each sore heals, each bruise vanishes. When the man does not touch me and when I remain silent, we are both disappointed. I wonder what wrong I am doing that he does not lovingly hurt me. I struggle to speak. Lay me on the hard floor and love me with all your strength, I will say when my clumsy tongue learns to move again. I make sounds and the man's head nods. The first word I correctly form is not the one I expected to say. Darkness, I beg.

They ask my name and age and place of birth. They desire to know what happened before I was found on the street. Who did this to you? What was done to you? Where? How long? I can only say that once there was a dark room and a man. Before that? I describe the boy who sat on the steps of the pretty house. Was

that you? I hesitate. Then I mention my angel. I say that one day
she will come to me again. Lift me onto her strong wings. Carry
me back to the dark room. Save me.

They move me to another room, also white. Sometimes I am supposed to lie on the bed, sometimes I am supposed to sit in the
chair, sometimes I am supposed to walk around a larger room
where other people, dressed in the same white robes I wear, also
walk. Eat this. Then go to sleep. Now wake up. I am obedient. I
speak and they make dark lines upon white paper. They look at
each other and exchange single words: shock, damage, trauma,
amnesia. The more darkness they put upon the paper, the happier they are. I learn to please them; it is so easy to know what
they want. Keep my eyes open and blink the lids. Look at people
when they speak to me. Pull the corners of my mouth upwards.
Don't mention my angel or my lover in the darkness. I please
them, but they offer me no reward in return. No love.

One day I ask for a pair of blue shorts and a shirt with short white
sleeves. They smile, giving me a pair of long blue pants. It's winter, they say, seeing my disappointment at the length of the cloth.
I would like to live with my mother and father in the pretty
house, I say. First they say that my mother and father can't be
found. Then they say that my mother and father are eagerly waiting for me to return to the pretty house. Now they exchange different words: hope, cure, miracle. They show me pictures of
things I have not seen before, and teach me the names for them.
One day I will learn to swim, to dance, to ride a bicycle, they
promise. I will walk beside the sea and the sun will turn my skin
brown. I will drive a blue car to the pretty house where my wife
and children live. My name is Richard and I am fourteen years
old and I am as good as new. By the window I sit in the chair and
close my eyes. Heels click, click on the hard shiny floor. Grow
louder, fade away. They never sound like his. A hand floats on
my shoulder, a voice wavers into my ear. It's good to cry, it says.
One day you'll forget, it promises.

The car isn't blue. The man and woman are not my father and
mother. This pretty house is not the one I remember. I sense that
these people are troubled because I pay them and their rooms

little attention. Feel them watch me carefully, nervously. This is your room, they say. I close the curtains, shut the door, lie on the floor against the wall. A knock. When I do not answer, the door opens. The woman's hand is so light upon my head I cannot feel it. The man doesn't touch me. Doesn't love me.

The woman always want me to leave my room and go out to play. You can go to the park or you can go to the river. You're free. The winter sun is cold, white. My eyes always hurt, I strain them looking for blue cars. The loud noises and sharp air and vivid world around me hurt, and I long for my lover's touch to hurl me into darkness. I am forgetting what I yearn to remember. I become dull with heavy food my stomach is not used to, it makes me hungry for sharp hunger. Have another helping, says the smiling woman.

I must go to school. In a small room I sit alone with a woman who says I can sit in a big, crowded room when I catch up. She teaches me this and that, sometimes I learn to please her. Then it's time for me to walk in the crowded hallways because a bell has rung. So many people. Several come up to me. You're Richard, they say; I wonder who told them my name. I answer their questions, I look into their eyes, I blink the lids of mine. They shrug, turn away. Their running shoes make no sound, they could be ghosts. Or maybe there is a squeak of rubber against tile. I think of mice scurrying in the dark, hunting roaches whose bodies they crunch with sharp, white teeth.

There is one boy who wears jeans of pale blue and a shirt with short white sleeves. I see his hungry eyes. Some other boys come by, his face changes. He smiles like them. They all pass down the bright hallway, marching in step to some beat I cannot hear. The boy's name is John, I learn.

The lockers I like. Everyone has their own, and they can be opened only by secret combinations. I watch them spinning the black wheels, hunting for certain private numbers. Then there's a click. A metal door opens, revealing a small dark space. Girls have posters of rock stars taped to the insides of their lockers. They take out small mirrors and pout at their reflections, puffing their lips and kissing red lipstick on them. Girls' lockers are as neat as dollhouses, but boys throw their books into a jumble of baseball gloves and running shoes and old lunches. After banging their lockers closed with dramatic gestures, boys always kick the door, making one more small dent.

My locker is number 267. I won't say the combination. I carry my books around with me or leave them in the small classroom. The inside of my locker is bare, except for the small figure of a toy soldier I found in the park. Someone lost him or threw him away. While the teacher draws white lines on the black board, I see the soldier waiting in the small dark room. He listens for my footsteps, but when only those of others pass he doesn't cry. It's all right to cry, the woman says to me. I am sitting on the front steps of the pretty house. My arms are wrapped around my legs, my head is resting on my knees. Watching cars pass up and down the street.

My angel will never come for me, I know. She thinks I do not need her any more, because I am in light. Sometimes she flies with white clouds through the sky, her long robes flapping. She sees me walking below and waves her wand in greeting. The clouds break, scatter, dissolve. My angel has gone to a boy who waits dark days in a bare room. My fickle friend.

My skin is white, smooth, unmarked. A good healer, the doctor says. There was never any lover, my blank skin mocks. I dig the point of the knife into a secret place on my body. Watch the blood rise to the surface of the flesh. It feels warm and tastes salty. I write a scarlet word on my arm. Love. Lick it up, swallow it away. The small wound burns like fire, but one that dies down too quickly. Too soon it becomes a pale warmth, equal in strength to the spring sun. Summer will come soon, the woman says. Then the sun will be hot. Then it will burn me and then he will brand me.

I say some boys and girls have invited me to the park down by the river that evening. We are going to roast marshmallows and hot dogs over a fire, then drink Cokes with them. Later, when the fire has burned into hot, glowing coals, we will sing songs around it.

The man and woman are pleased. They smile and ask if I have enough money. I dress in blue jeans, white T-shirt, sneakers. I walk past the empty park by the river, through the streets lined with pretty houses and into the city. Many cars pass up and down the big, wide streets. On a corner I stand and watch for blue cars containing only one man. Count cars until I pass number 267. When the fire inside me has burned into hot glowing coals and my blood is singing, a blue car pulls up to the curb. The driver reaches over and opens the door for me. I get inside. As we move down the street, I stare straight ahead, not wanting to see his face. His sad, old eyes. He wants to know my name and age and place of birth. Out of the corner of my eye I see him glancing at me. He is trying to discover if I resemble a boy who sat on the front steps of a house, waiting. A boy who was himself.

Turn off the light, I say. Then the room is dark. He pulls me toward the bed. The floor, I say. He strokes my arm. Soft, he says. His touch is light as air, without my angel's wings I am falling through miles of empty sky. Hit me, I say. Feel him freeze. Feel myself fall upon the ground with a force that jars me, breaks me. Don't speak, I say. Harder, I say. More, I say.

It is very late when I return to the pretty house. The lights are on because the man and woman are waiting up for me. I tripped and fell onto cement, I answer their questioning looks at my bruised arms and face. The man says he drove past the park, but saw no fire or anyone singing around it. It was too cold, so we listened to records in John's basement, I say. In my room and behind my closed door, I lie on the floor against the wall. Darkness. Muffled sounds come through the wall. For a long time the man and woman murmur words I cannot hear. I feel my sore body. The tingling touch of love is with me through the night. Alive again.

I bury the money the men give me in the sand down by the river. Beneath a black ring of charred wood, ash.

At school the teacher no longer speaks so often of the day when I'll catch up. I no longer try to please her, or the man and woman. Save myself for the ones who offer right rewards. One morning I see that John has left his locker open. Quickly, I take the toy soldier from my locker and put it into his. That afternoon I see a crowd of boys and girls gathered in front of John's open locker. They fall silent as I walk past. John lives in a house on Jasmine Street, five blocks from the house where I stay. I walk by it on my way into the city, but John is never sitting on the front steps.

I search for him once or twice a week, when I feel the mark of the last hand leave me. Now the man and woman do not ask me where I am going at night. They look at each other when I leave the house in T-shirt and jeans. In the city I discover certain corners where cars will more likely stop for me. I learn that if I do not ask for at least fifty dollars, the men are disappointed and do not take me to their dark rooms. I tell them this or that story; it's so easy to know what they need to hear. My name is John, I say. No, that's my name, they laugh. I might go into a red or black car, if no blue ones stop for me and if my need is strong. Maybe there are two men in the car, instead of one. Sometimes I meet men whose love is not strong and who do not want to love me hard. Their eyes become puzzled or frightened, they hand me some money and ask me to leave. Others like to use their hands heavily, and those ones seek me at the corner again. No thank-you, I say when they find me a second time. I do not want to learn their faces well, and a single time is all it takes to teach me they are not him. None of them love me strongly enough. I am searching for the only man who can.

One night a car stops. I get inside, look straight ahead as usual. Richard, he says. I turn and see the man who lives in the pretty house. What are you doing? he asks. I was too tired to walk back home, so I was waiting for a ride, I say. He drives in silence. His hands grip the steering wheel tightly, his face is hard and angry. For the first time I think he might be able to love me. At the house the man and woman say they want me to stay home and not go out alone after dark. That night I lie in my dark room and wait for the man to come to me. I have not been loved in a week, my skin holds no tender memory of a touch. The man does not open my door. In the morning I walk towards school, past it, and into the city. The man and woman will not look for me, I know.

I live in a hotel. The hallways are dim, because one of the other prostitutes or drug addicts always steals the light bulb. I walk down the dark hall, passing closed doors on either side of me. They are scratched and marked, but without numbers. I hear the crying boys behind the doors fall silent at the approach of my step. How they hold their breath, then sigh in disappointment when I do not turn a key in their locks. My own room contains a bed, a chair, a small table, a sink. I lie on the floor, listening to roaches scurry into and out of the corners. The curtains are always closed, and I have taped thick black paper over the glass. I am visited daily, and sometimes my door is opened as many as five times in one night. My skin is never empty of traces of love. I glow with warmth. Tomorrow or the next day my only true love will come to me. One or another of the men will be him. I will not need to see his face, because my skin's perfect memory will recognize him at once. He will love me hard and finally, so I will never crave his touch again. In pure darkness I lie and await the approach of his footsteps down the hall. They will march to the rhythm of my hopeful heart.

Angie, Short
for Angel

Angie, Short
for Angel

Angie, Angie, short for Angel, you found him lying on the sidewalk in the tough tenderloin every midnight where you were amid stalled cars and liquor stores and sad scarecrows with sawdust hearts hanging from rows of crosses. Sulky Sue and Beat-Up Annie hugged by your shoulders and slurred: Angie, short for Angel, leave alone that little boy who is broken and all busted on such mean cement with black tears bleeding from his eyes. A little boy, a beautiful little boy, spoke Angie in a tone of wonder, bending beneath red and blue bars of neon which opened and closed their tired eyes to say: rooms, rooms, ten dollars for a room. The feathers of your wings brushed against the boy's bruised cheek, Angie, opening his eyes to see you there above him, your face painted like some exhausted clown, and to wonder if Heaven were this vagrant one-way street.

You were coughing like it was no joke that last September, Angie; however much you ruffled your feathers and swore that being sick was just for babies, your so-called friends were frightened from you. Now Sulky Sue and Beat-Up Annie could sense a situation, so up they shrugged their shoulder straps and huffed: we got to make a million dollars more before dawn. They slow-danced away a little crowd of ducky boys who were gathered around and singing: Angie, short for Angel, don't jump-start that boy while he's still down. Then a flying wedge of drunks leaped over the body of the boy, like it was that famous crack that broke their mothers' backs, leaving those lame lonely women to wonder exactly where they'd gone wrong. Angie, didn't you see that neighbourhood dying all around you, that only echoes from the graveyard tattooed down those streets where on your highest heels, your brand new stilts, you stalked a giant of a child far above this world wheeling and whirling through quantums of dark space? How the boy's hair was ruffled by that warm wind which blew him and you and all the other hopeful ones to California, once a sweetest place that melted on your tongue like coloured candy. Yet Angie, short for Angel, irreversibly you pulled the boy's head upon the lap of your robes, once pure white before the blues dyed them scarlet and put those ribbons in your hair.

Remember how you took him in a taxi, and up those stairs you pulled tricks on other nights until tomorrow. To those grey spaces you were always planning to fix up with rainbows on the walls; to those roaches who were permanent uninvited guests in the kitchen where you never cooked, food being what your mother feeds you until you leave home forever. But it was cheap to live among the *cholos*, across from the old mission where Spanish priests collected souls in big black hats once upon a time. Now dreams tied to tickets watched through pawnshop windows as welfare mothers slowly waltzed by in the arms of Valium and sometimes Seconal. On the corners *cholos* cracked whips to tame their territory, but, Angie, you would prance up to squeeze the flesh beneath their smooth silk shirts, you would whisper: let's have some rough romance. Causing the brown-eyed boys to droop their eyes and mumble *shucks* in broken English. They would watch you walk away beneath a moon no longer yours since you had fallen from the stars to land upon these several streets where you were celebrated after midnight closed its fist around the city, holding all the loose ones tight in the side pocket of a pool game played for half a dollar and a kiss.

See how you sat beside the lost boy on the bed of the front room, beneath the window that stared out at Sixth Street. In a voice concocted from smoke and scotch you said: don't try to talk until you learn the words for it. Didn't you press the warm wet cloth against his cheeks and clean his cuts with stinging antiseptic, every nurse an angel making it OK? He watched you, Angie, until you passed a hand across your face and said that no one ever saw you by the light of day. It made you tremble to see his eyes the colour of your daddy's old blue shirts, hanging on the line to dry.

When six days turned to lucky number seven, you asked who did it to him. The boy muttered that there was a guy who was a little nice for a while. Oh, I am intimately acquainted with that gentleman, he's a famous character, you exclaimed, ejecting a stream of smoke from the corner of your mouth. He has many names and faces, but he always leaves you hurting in the very same way. You watched the boy's lips, how they came together to touch each other in longing, then drew apart again in fear. And you thought: once there was a grey place anyone calls Kansas, until a tornado twists inside our hearts and twirls us away from the dirt and the dust and the drab voices that say you can't do this, you can't do that, and don't go there. So all angels have no wish to go back home, however much they speak of heavens and weary of strumming heavy harps. In odd Oz-es they remain to add to all the foolish victims who move inside the eyes of every city like so much grit to cause these tears to fall upon the streets and run in petroleum puddles down the drains. There was Angie, one angel with no umbrella window-shopping in the rain, the only angel in this boy's eyes.

The Boy　　　I mean I hardly knew who she was except for how she said she was an angel with broken wings and that's why she didn't fly away but lived two flights above this bankrupt *bodega*. Don't look at me, I'm a mess, said Angie by the bed where my body was getting better. Again she started coughing on account of how the air down here on the earth was dirty compared to how it was up there. She turned her face away, so all I saw were yellow curls that held a silver crown in place of where a halo had once maybe floated. I would close my eyes to feel hers brush against my skin, like lips that kiss it better, or a breeze that blows you back.

All September I closed my eyes in Angie's front room, and what I saw was a picture of Mary. She could never be my mother. Leave the kid alone, Earl told her when I used to cry. Sometimes I saw Mary sitting up in one of the cherry trees, hiding from Earl who tramped his big boots through the long grass below. Little girl, little girl, come to daddy now, he said, the belt wrapped ready around one hand. From up there Mary could see across the orchard sloping down the valley, all the way to the rooftops of the town. It shone in the distance, like the Emerald City.

A million times Mary's mind walked her down the Main Street of where Earl would never let her go. She looked in the store windows, then went into the café on the corner. Always before the ice could melt in the bottom of her Coke, Earl would catch sight of Mary's flowered dress peeking through the leaves. Come down now, he'd say in a voice kind of soft. I was just picking cherries for a pie, Mary would mumble when no pail was in her hand. She would follow Earl into the dark bedroom at the back of the house. The door would close behind them.

Or sometimes Mary would mention: I guess I'll go down to the bottom acre and see how the peaches are coming on. She'd move through the high grass, holding the hem of her dress up with one hand, trying not to look behind to see if Earl followed, to walk very slowly like she had not one thought of leaving. At the end of the orchard was the wire fence with three shining, sagging strands, and once she bent through them Mary would start running down the road towards town. The truck pulled up along side of her. Get in, little girl, daddy wants to take you for a ride, Earl said. The door would close behind them one more time. Then would come another space of silence. I'd sit in the kitchen with my hands holding one another in my lap, watching the second hand of the clock that turned around and around but never got away.

Earl would come out from the bedroom, snapping the suspenders back up around his shoulders. He'd go out on the porch and make the rocking-chair creak over and over. Mary wandered into the kitchen to start supper, her long dark hair with the threads of silver in it now floating down around her waist. In bare feet she moved heavy across the cracked linoleum, drowsy as if against her will she'd fallen asleep in the poppy fields beyond the haunted forest. She would never look at me then, her face locked like the bedroom door, the key to it hidden deep in Earl's pocket.

After, Earl went out into the darkness to move the long lines of pipe that kept the ground soaked good. Mary and I stayed in the kitchen, listening to the cherry bombs explode around us. Each sudden sound made Mary's body jerk. That was when I wished to wrap myself around her and press my face into the soft cloth of her dress and feel her fingers in my hair. How I had a memory of this happening to a very smaller boy who was maybe someone else, not me, in a time before there was an Earl moving out in the dark with the crickets screaming at him. Mary sat stiffly in her chair, pondering the floor beneath her feet. When Earl's steps returned, she would look at me once, warning against I didn't know what.

Until one night I thought I heard Mary calling from way behind the orchard and even past the little town. She was calling from some place where her hand would touch my hair and I would feel her fingers the same size and shape as mine. I would smell the flowers sprinkled on her dress. I tiptoed into the dark bedroom and found Earl's pants folded on the chair. I took the money from the wallet in the pocket. As it moved into my hand, I saw that Mary was not far away and calling for me to join her there. She was lying on the other side of Earl, between the mountain of his body and the wall. I saw her eyes unlock. They were shining in the dark, they were watching me. Like two pools beneath the moon I could never drink from, no matter how thirsty was my throat.

And here was Angie, holding out the glass of water. It's short for Angel, she said, twisting her mouth into a poignant snake. She set her wand on fire, sucking its magic into her lungs, hollowing her cheeks until her face sharpened and made me wonder. She looked like someone I had maybe known so long ago, I couldn't think who. Not like Mary or any mother, not like that at all. More like the pieces of a jigsaw puzzle, when even after they are fitted together correctly you can still see the cracks in the picture. Sometimes all you see are the cracks, you can't see whatever beautiful picture is there before your eyes, just waiting for you.

Angie would catch my look, touch her body and her hair. Didn't I fix myself right? she'd ask. All the things I never knew until the end. Sometimes her hand would reach towards me, then something like a frightened deer jumped across her eyes; and her fingers caressed only air, or some invisible child she would never bear. She never touched me, you know. She never laid a finger on me, damn her.

The Angel   Darling, I sincerely believed that every broken boy has lost his baseball glove and lucky marbles, and that's why he rests a smashed cheek upon sidewalks of queer cities with which he has not the slightest acquaintance. (Listen hard, Bitch, you've never heard me talk like this before, and please watch your Royal Ass because in a twinkle I might just speak The Truth!) I Confess! I didn't ask his name, I didn't ask where he was from: alas, I remembered! After he no longer hurt, he was still severely exhausted, for your first journey away from home is always farther than from here to any star. (Please, don't Insinuate, it doesn't suit you, My Dear — and who doesn't know that you're the only Chicken Thief around here?) I told myself I only hoped one boy inside my rooms would make them no longer as hollow as the tombs where all our Darling Daddies hide. Why don't you stay for the meantime? I asked, before recalling who but Moi could never bear for anyone to see Her during day, when the ghastly light of this sordid city reminded me somewhat of that in Heaven; but here it was never dazzling, always weak, only strong enough to mock the celestial sunshine of Before.

How once that light was warm and soft, and I grew through it, in my own way. The way that made my daddy look at me with puzzles in his eyes and made my mother tell him to leave me alone. In the backyard of Before I stood beneath the leaves of the maple tree, wishing for a vision of the boy who lived next door. But the fence around the yard was so tall you could never see or climb over it. You could only hear his mother call and call him home to supper when the summer light was everlasting until ten o'clock. They called him Todd, but in long conversations he held with me inside my heart his name was a secret something else, and only we two knew that I was really Angie. A boy like that had private places where he went when the world was finally dark and all other children played hide-and-seek around a streetlamp they called Home. To me who could not follow, still lacking the wings some beings need for flight, he whispered that he climbed up the mountain inhabited by prowling bears, down to the river that liked to coldly sweep from sight bodies that it drowned.

Ready or not, here I come, cried little Karen Thom, always It because her short round legs could never carry her swiftly. She counted out loud the numbers that lay before the one that meant it was time to leave Home and search for others. I heard the screams of children coming out from hiding to dart through the darkness back to the circle of safe light.

I had no wish to return to any place of light haunted by someone with a body and name not mine; there was not room for both
me and that impostor there. I heard the children's tongues trip
over numbers as they quickly, easily counted themselves to and
from their Home. Those numbers were not my numbers. I
remained behind the bush of fruit that tasted strange and bitter,
the red chinaberries that appeared black in the darkness. The
other children did not find me, and away from light I waited with
the patience of a sphinx until they all went to their beds. I whispered numbers, counting them off like beads strung upon a
rosary of prayers, believing one miraculous multiple of seven
would bring a boy to part the leaves and see me crouched upon
the dirt. I found you, he would say, for the first time speaking my
real name out loud, and that would be the final end of being lost.

But he could never see me at all, even as the other children
teased me for the way I walked and talked. Something was wrong
with me. I didn't know what, I couldn't fix it. Then began the
time to stay inside, through the window watching other children
grow older in the world outside, still playing hide-and-seek, now
concealing themselves in pairs, not wishing to be found. Only my
mother saw through the opaque panes of my eyes, only she knew
always what would become of me. There was no choice but one
day to put on angel's robes and paint my face and on unfolded
wings fly out into a world that teemed with hidden souls only I
could part the leaves to find.

So I became the true self I had always been inside. Yes, God
sent me down to this exile and gave me strength to lift the lonely
ones to choirs above the clouds. I strummed my harp and eased
their ears, and this was my consolation for being forever unfound
myself. Angie, short for Angel, who confused the minds of mor-
tals by describing in a single breathless sentence a Home that was
always to be escaped, always to be yearned. Angie, who walked to
the terminal where boys and girls arrive on buses from wherever
they can not stay. Angie, who narrowly watched them descend on
this new world to look through each other's only eyes. Angie, the
one who turned away to tell the man who guards the Lost and
Found: there is something I misplaced, I can't remember what, I
offer a large reward for its return, I'd recognize it at once if it
were here.

This boy before me. How sometimes he looked at me as though

Angie were the impostor and the boy behind the chinaberry the real me. The fear that there was no going back fluttered my feathers. I wove my words into the most intricate webs, handled my props with the finest flair, performed all the set pieces which only to his new eyes were not sickeningly stale. Told him about the numbers, the lucky ones, the ones less lucky. Don't go outside until the numbers fall right, I advised. Always I prayed he would never go out there, for it takes the strength of an Angel to raise rain back to the watching eyes from which it falls.

And then, Angie, you ventured out one dusk to the rooms where happiness is bought and sold. I would like clothes for a boy, you stated, plucking clothes from racks, narrowing your eyes and frowning as you summoned up old photographs from the album of your heart. You discarded and chose red and blue and yellow, remembering what makes a rainbow call. I'll pay in cash, you said in your harsh voice, taking the fat roll of bills from your purse and making the damned clerk's eyes shut up. You also bought running shoes, a baseball cap, and books of coloured comics. Toy soldiers. And model planes that could be assembled by a boy who holds his breath and is very careful with his clumsy hands. All this pirate treasure you carried home within your wings, Angie, and then the ice in your drink chattered while you watched the boy try on his new clothes. He did not wonder how you knew exactly the size of clothes that would slip around his body sometimes tight, sometimes loose, always revealing. He had no idea how you made him look like some boy who is mean until you touch him in the right place, whereupon he melts. You could still wave your wand and make it Christmas any time, Angie, even as you counted your fingers and knew that you were running out of wishes.

Wasn't that the month of thirty rainy days when you stayed inside together, the boy and you, floating in your odd ark above the sick and troubled land? The telephone would ring ten times before it quit, and Fat Alice and Beat-Up Annie insisted with their fists against the door that a holed-up whore is forgotten by tomorrow or Tuesday.

Angie, you taught the boy to worship the television screen, upon which were projected numerous glimpses of the way stars once always shone white against a background of black sky. You communed with Bette Davis and Joan Crawford, those beautiful bitches, until the boy believed them your dear old friends who heeded your wise words to leave the guys because they weren't worth the tips of their little fingers. The boy listened to your voice drip with scorn when it did not melt with love, and he watched tears fall from your eyes as though those flickering scenes in fact were images escaping from inside your skin. Damn men, you rasped, throwing back your yellow hair, closing your eyes so no careless thief could climb inside to steal your few remaining secrets.

But darkness would come crashing down beyond the glass, the hands of the clock would point to holy numbers, your wings would ache to stretch. So you would swallow a round white pill to blur your face into a rainy window, to muffle the voices of all the empty ones who commenced their nocturnal cries to you. Then you retreated into your special room, the place where the boy could never follow, according to your only golden rule. Darling, I'm dead, you explained, leaving him in the front room to learn the language of stylized love spoken by the stars. Weren't you always careful to close the door behind your back?

Hold me tight and let me stay inside, you beseeched red velvet hanging amid many mirrors on your walls. How strange that you would worry about your own salvation at this late hour, and wasn't it also quite amusing that a single small boy could make you regret what you would leave behind? Angels can't afford to feel sentimental, you reminded your reflection grimly; but in the truthful glass you saw that your system of immunity was failing you in more than just one way. With thinning fingers you prepared the evening shot like the purest priest arranging mass. And then it was all right, Angie, you felt heavenly heroin singing in choirs through your blood. How you requested Billie to breathe the bitter prayers that would accompany your slow arcs around that perfumed space. Reading old love letters, touching ancient photographs, it was all another banal good-bye, my dear.

Still there was a boy who watched you emerge from your room with the jerky motions of a puppet controlled by uncertain hands. Who watched you nodding to the sandman. Watched you gazing at all the gone boys who were not named Todd, who were not grimacing up from the bottom of your bottle, who were not wondering where you were. Still there was a boy across the room who lightly touched the skeleton of a model plane that would one day really fly. You gave him the whole show, didn't you, you bitch.

The Boy   You see what happened was there was a night when Angie held her purse upside down, shook it, then swore that easy street had detoured by. She hummed an hour in the bathroom, performing many miracles with make-up, painting silver on her face, draping red satin on her body. Angie fixed the purple angel feathers upon her shoulders, making her ready to fly higher than any place before. Do I still look ugly? she sniffed, lining white powder on her compact mirror. I was reminded of the ladies inside the television who tossed their heads and snapped their mouths and threw their shoulders everywhere. Any of them would have looked as lost as Angie if they'd stepped from behind the screen into this front room without a carpet or much furniture or curtains on the windows. Like Angie, they would have inhaled something pure and white until a wonderful world shifted back into sharp, clear focus. Or suppose Angie was breathing in deeply as I used to do when clean new dew was sprinkled on the orchard grass. Then she would be ready to fly high like I was on those mornings. Already Angie was gazing towards the far places she would find, and like her famous friends inside the screen she didn't see me even when her eyes turned in my direction. Those ugly old who'es will have kidnapped my best customers, she fretted; and now her voice was different like I didn't know how, only maybe every word was instead of a scream. Her body swayed away, saying there was just too much inside it to trace a simple, straight line. See you in the movies, she called back, vanishing in a swirl of flowers and bluebirds and crosses.

They woke me when they fell up the stairs, Angie fumbling to fit her key into the lock. Something sad had happened while my eyes were closed, because the lady on the screen who had been laughing now was crying. Just call me Angel! she shrieked, dragging the drunken sailor by his tie. I rubbed sleepy stuff from my eyes and saw how glittering were Angie's, like the smashed glass of a robbed store. She took a pill from her purse, tossed it in the air, caught it with her mouth. I know plenty of tricks, she laughed, spilling whisky into a big glass then throwing it down her throat. Follow me and don't get lost along the way, she suggested to the sailor. Her eyes couldn't notice me there upon my bed, she was completely concerned with fluttering her wings. I could still hear them beating after Angie's door closed behind the sailor and herself.

It made me wonder extra hard when Angie's laughter stopped rippling from her room, leaving only the voice of the lady on the screen vowing she'd had enough and couldn't take it anymore. Then came Angie screaming so I thought she was attempting to call all the way to God, plus there were sounds of falling and breaking, as in glass. Later there were other things to hear, how people cry to themselves when it hurts and no one is around to listen.

The lady's face inside the screen turned proud and noble, though tears dropped from her eyes. You could easily tell her heart was swelling huge like the music at The End. Minus his tie, the puffy-faced sailor came from Angie's room and angled by me out the door. I heard Angie keep crying until she started coughing bad. Her friend named Billie was singing the same song over and over, like it was the only one in the world, or somehow she'd forgotten any others. She kept covering the waterfront and watching the sea. Will the one I love be coming back to me?

Angie must have thought I was sleeping when she went out again a few minutes later, because I felt like shutting my eyes while she passed through the front room. When I opened them, there weren't any more love scenes on the screen. Only patterns of shapes and lines I couldn't make sense of, repeating over and over. I went to the window and saw Angie moving down the wet street, her eyes turned to the sidewalk like there were footprints she could follow. Then the corner kids and bus-stop boys began to call her name all along Sixth Street, and Angie, short for Angel, lifted her eyes and looked for another someone she could find. Even when she was out of sight and fog turned the cold into a heavy hand, I left the window open. In case Angie's feet grew too tired to climb back up the stairs, in case she wished to fly back home to me.

The Angel　　　I didn't have to tell him anything, didn't have to explain a thing. The street insinuated I was teaching him the tired tricks of my trade, but for angels there is no course of lessons with a divine diploma at the end. It was a calling. A voice that reached you and spoke to you and wouldn't let you go. My voice? Sweetheart, I told you once and won't tell you again: I wouldn't wish these wings on anyone. Maybe there was more of a choice for him than there had been for me; but my insides were spilling into black pools behind the alley trash-cans, I was growing weak. It was becoming more than fun-and-games to save the strangers, never mind a familiar face that peered into the darkness, puzzled and alone. I couldn't tear off my brilliant disguise, nor abandon the painfully worn grooves scratched by dull needles into round black discs. Yes, I knew there was a line that lay between the ones who save and those who are the saved. I could have invited him within my wings and forever have placed him on the other side, separate from all us angels. But I couldn't let him inside my room. I couldn't. And, pray tell, where were you when he needed to enter a precious place like home, you wicked witches and false wizards? Tin men, cowardly lions, all of you.

It was always like that, Angie. You seemed determined to surprise the boy with the number of sailors and sad soldiers there were in the world. Late on mornings after, you would leave your room and lean against the wall the way you did, pointing your cigarette at things the boy couldn't see. Your face would be paler than usual, except you painted it pinker. Around the room you floated and sighed: so handsome, loving, tender. Every stranger is kind in the way he knows how, you murmured, bending over your number book and adding two or three digits from the night before into its pages. Every man you touched was one less to be saved, you believed. And when all of them had known your bed of blessing, the work would be done. You would unfold your wings one last time and fly away for good, presenting to the man who guards the Gate your list of lucky guys so he would let them in. I'm almost there, you muttered, gripping the glass of numbing nectar tighter, taking another sip to tinge the taste of blood you coughed. Angie, you pretended there was not a corner of your eye in which you saw the boy examine you, then turn to his own image in the glass. You told yourself that he would touch only toy soldiers, always, and never imitate your state of grace. Your walks on water, your gliding steps upon the sea of love.

The Boy   Sometimes I didn't know why they wouldn't like it inside Angie's room. An unlucky number would bust back out her door. And Angie, she'd have new colours on her skin, called purple and red and blue. He didn't leave a dime, not one wooden nickel, were words that set her face so still. Or some would leave her perplexed. That one seemed familiar, she would puzzle, has my touch so completely lost its magic they must be blessed a second time? Then Angie would sit by the window, squinting through the rain at the church that crumbled across the way. Some have hearts of stone, she might mourn, too heavy to lift to Heaven.

But most were very grateful for how Angie could heal them, and then we'd call a cab to take us to the Chinese café. Windshield-wipers slapped against the glass, the river of time flowed in numbers upon the meter. Another one down, smiled Angie, waving out the window to anyone at all. Those she sent above were so sad to be apart from her they cried, and every night of November was dark with rain. The cab carried us splashing down the nickel, wheeling us nearer the end of another lullaby. The driver sang along with Tony Bennett and Angie shivered. I bet you never thought California would be quite like this, she said, turning towards me in that space spiced by old tobacco. Then she leaned against the back of the seat and closed her eyes. She asked the driver to turn up the heat, she asked if we were almost there.

The Angel   There I was, Girl, meeting Mister Midnight on my Terribly Tragic corner, when I saw that little Boy idle by into a Bar. The clothes I had chosen fit him like a lucky charm; I barely blinked the beads off my mascara before he came out with a Hungry Wolf puffing at his heels, and they wound away like there was only One Way to go. Sulky Sue's little eyes grew bigger and she simpered: your Pretty Prize has found himself a Winner. Keep your cunt between your own legs, I advised, and continued counting the raindrops out from which the next Wet Wanderer would come for me to Warm.

It's just the Cold and how the fucking fog from that old bay climbs up my dress, I explained to Miss Misery, who glared at me as if I coughed expressly to disturb her Profoundest Meditations. My latest diet, I informed the Sidewalk Sirens, I live on Love Alone and lose five pounds a Week. Tough enough to win one winter Tenderloin without Bad Meat around, they fumbled, shuffling away from where I posed with my closest friend the Streetlamp and a wreath of smoke twined around my head. I felt all the Forsaken Ones rolling like lost marbles upon the tilted earth, which rose and fell beneath my feet until I reeled like one more Dizzy Queen who's lost her Cardboard Crown. Darling, I was Devastated, Too Destroyed to decorate the sewer a second more.

In Defeat I sat inside the Sad Café with coffee kept hot within styrofoam; but my human hands refused to warm. Shivers were shaking all the coldness from my bones, and for the first time my wings were Really Wet. Oh, they drooped, a sour, stale smell drifting from them. Once One Glance would have flattened the proprietor of this Plastic Palace, this Pig-Eyed Prince who knew I couldn't pay the price to sit an hour out from the rain, which yesterday or the day before I'd found as romantic as Frank Sinatra. December was Descending, my Time was tap-dancing away. My Dear, I was Too Tired to chase it. There was my Number coming up quickly and only so much more One Girl could do. Clear out, They'd say, and don't take Anything with you. And don't leave Anything behind. Ready or not, here we come, the Cruel Children cried. One two three, we'll find you now, four five six, abracadabra, seven eight nine, open sesame, ten eleven twelve, here's mud in your eye, thirteen fourteen fifteen, what to Do with the days that remain?

Use them wisely, go with grace, a fellow Angel whispered in my ear, stilling my silly heart.

I turned to see the boy beside me, looking like he'd learned something new and pulling three twenties from his pocket.

And then I really knew. Every angel can leave one thing behind when she is found a he behind a curtain of chinaberries or any other berries, and taken Home at last to where the Light shines bright. This was her unexpected salvation, her undreamed-of reward, unseen until now.

They could at least give you crisp fresh bills instead of these old dirty ones, they could at least do that, I said. Look, your halo's crooked, I croaked, reaching out to bless the seven points above his head.

Can I buy you coffee? he asked.

And so it was, Angie, that you took to your bed to lie awake all the hours of every night, no time to waste in sleeping. Water seeped out through the countless cracks in your rusted armour and you melted into one of any number of puddles that children splash through on their way to school. Billie sang you and herself forward through the darkness, the black sickness of the lost ones against whom you had refused to protect yourself. You waited for the boy to come running lightly up the four a.m. stairs. His knock on your door signalled a wish to relate new adventures you had originally undertaken several centuries ago and repeated beyond all numbers. I'm sleeping, you called through a quarter-inch of separation, then listened to his restless movements on the other side: switching channels of the television, dissatisfied with all movie queens; picking up the telephone to abandon it without calling even Information. It was never easy to fall back to sleep after they had woken you, was it?

The feathers of your wings fell from you one by one, drifting to the floor around your bed and lining it like the bottom of a nest. You were becoming lighter, Angie, you would need no wings to float finally away. How much did it cost to keep your back straight those infrequent times you crawled into the front room? Can you lend me a little? you asked when rent day came around again too soon. From the box beneath his bed the boy plucked several bills from among many crumpled others. His whistling was jaunty as he dressed himself, loving eyes embracing his own reflection in the mirror. Did he glance towards you when your hand picked up the arm of black plastic and your thinning finger dialled what you hoped was the lucky combination of an infinite number of digits. Mama, it's me, you said into the instrument, nervously clearing your throat. Angel, you repeated, maintaining the uncertain curve of your lips. You have the wrong number, you repeated to yourself, returning the arm gently to its cradle. The number was not right.

Go softly, Angie. You were silent when he brought his game to play in the front room. Go easy, Angie, you told him mornings after, when all you saw was someone else believing one more touch could prove him real. The power of love, the power of illusion: Angie, without your wings you were never really there. Surprise, surprise.

The Boy   Then Angie could not get out of bed until evening, or not at all. Oh, I'm so lazy, were her words when at last she left her room, the yellow hair all tipsy on her head. She'd seem surprised to find me there and herself there too. I'd hear her breathing like it was something hard to do.

She still squeezed big pieces of shining glass onto her ears and wore rings around every finger. Only Angie didn't look so much like an angel any more. The paint didn't look quite right on her face. I could tell her wings were really broken now, though sometimes she would flutter them within the walls, wishing they would work again. It came to me that someone smaller was inside Angie who every day was coming out a little more. Someone with lighter bones, a sharper face, and quiet eyes that hadn't learned to dance. Angie was shrinking inside her angel robes, her eyes were sinking into her face. One day there would be no day for her, I guessed.

Me, I could feel my own wings growing a bit more each time the funny men touched me. First it was like a weight on my shoulders that made it hard to walk quickly as in the orchard grass before. Then I learned how to use them. I became crazy about flying. I was always flying in and out of the place on Sixth Street, flying to where Angie must have flown many times before. Like up on the rooftops and way out to the islands in the middle of the bay. Flying for the fun of it, to everywhere far and near. I felt the air grow icy and saw silver angels in the bright store windows, lit up by electricity. Christmas is coming, I told Angie, who never asked me where I went or what special sights were there. She only wondered once if Fat Alice and Sulky Sue were still bragging on their corners, and if Beat-Up Annie was in the junkyard yet. It's nice to stay inside at last, she said, quiet in her chair next to the window.

Her eyes were turning to glass. They didn't blink even if I looked a long time into them. I thought they were each a crystal ball, where sights you wished to see or things you needed to know would appear. What did I see in Angie's eyes? There was Mary, looking right at me, inside me. I didn't let him touch you once, she said. Not a time, she said, you think on that. Then Mary faded away, I saw only myself pressed on each of Angie's eyes. Like there were two of me.

Angie stirred. Remember living in the hotel, way up on the top floor? she wanted to know. We could order anything we wanted from room service, we never had to go outside. That rug was so thick beneath our feet it was always like walking on clouds, and in that big bed we drifted through the sky. We were so rich! We threw ten-dollars bills out our window just to watch them float down to people on the world, who believed God was shaking the treasure tree in Heaven. Remember Mexico? asked Angie. Do you remember drinking beer on beaches, the Pacific foaming peaceful around our toes? Why, even I turned brown beneath that sun! That was when the sky was always blue and the flowers always blossomed.

Angie told me more about times before when we had always been together, except I couldn't remember any hotels or Mexicos. Sometimes I thought Angie was becoming mistaken about how things were, like believing she heard Susan Hayward when it was plainly Barbara Stanwyck speaking from the screen. The way she thought all the *cholo* boys ouside our window were named Todd, when every one of them was Juan or José. And like how she called me Angie now.

Then I wondered if maybe after falling asleep in the house among the cherry trees I used to fly away with Angie everywhere. If she had been with me from the beginning, always. I picked up one of the wands she didn't like to wave these days. Its fire burned inside me and smoke curled into the air, shaping into only lucky numbers. Suddenly I saw Mary perched atop a cherry tree, squinting against the sun to see the signs I made before they vanished into sky. I swooped down towards her, passing so close the tips of my wings brushed Mary's face, causing her to smile.

Angie, Angie, short for Angel, the first day of your true life dawned and you entered the room where you had never been before. A place for an angel to rest between her soaring, with many mirrors to remind her of the impossible image she had achieved. With drapes of heavy red cloth to filter the outside light and make this place inside the chamber of a beating heart.

On the soft wide bed lay the body of a boy who had grown old and tired with waiting to be found. His face was finally washed clean of the juice of bitter berries. On the nearby chair rested long locks of yellow hair.

Angie, you walked across the feathered floor to where angel

robes were hanging and you found the two pillows upon which tired men, climbing into the warm bed of your body, could rest their heavy heads. You fixed yourself, Angie, for the first time adding curves and curls to your lost boy's body, for the first time placing paint upon your face, making it no longer frightened. Making it right.

Angie, wasn't it just like you had always known it would feel? Look at you lighting your magic wands and see you tilting your mouth towards the liquid gold of gods inside the glass. Hear the stars lilting about love from the screen in the front room, listen to the angel's sister singing for the needy ones to take all of her. Take your lips and arms and eyes into the night, Angie, and give them generously. Soon there will be heavenly heroin and round white moons of pills to give you strength to put on ruby slippers and set out upon the road of yellow bricks. Into your big black book you will write the names of those you save, the list of all the ones allowed through the Gate and back into the Garden, where fruit hangs heavy and sweet from every tree.

It was Christmas, Angie, and a child of God was born again to man. You unwrapped the presents you had bought for another angel, you gave them to yourself. Through the air came the voices of a host of angels, their carols coming near. You watched them take the bones of a boy off the bed, to be planted behind a bush of bitter berries. A lucky number of boys would grow from them and one day you would find them and comfort them and shelter them, until some silent, holy night they would assume your wings for which they longed, Angie, short for Angel.

Other Voices
and the Real World II

What becomes of all the little boys
Who run away from home?
The world keeps getting bigger
Once you get out on your own
     — Tom Waits, "On the Nickel"

home 1. a house, apartment or other place of residence 2. the
place in which one's domestic affections are centred 3. an
institution for the homeless, sick 4. the dwelling place or
retreat of an animal 5. any place of residence or refuge 6.
a person's native place or country
     — *The Random House College Dictionary*, 1973

Homeless Move Beyond Urban Areas

"Police bring [the homeless] here because Evanston has a
bleeding heart. They're certainly not coming here for the
weather . . . ."
     —*USA Today/International Edition* 12-17-87

Sacramento, California — Gov. Deukmejian ordered National Guard to open armories to homeless during very cold weather. Counties may request use of armories for night-only occupancies when temperature falls to 40.
      —*USA Today/International Edition* 12-17-87

All the sad young men
Sitting in the bar
Knowing neon lights
Missing all the stars
      — "The Ballad of the Sad Young Men"

The goodbye makes the journey harder still
      — Cat Stevens, "O Very Young"

Rorschach test   a test for revealing the underlying personality structure of an individual by associations evoked by a series of inkblot designs
      — *The Random House College Dictionary*, 1973

Rorschachs II: Mutilation

Rorschachs II: Mutilation

The flies are drunk and drowsy in the African sun. Inside the house they bumble against the mesh screen all afternoon, fat and full of blood. They are content beside the web of wire that prevents them from having to vanish into the air outside. The small boy kneels on the floor of red tiles which his mother drives the houseboy to polish once a week; the scent of wax lingers in the air for days, like a reprimand. The small boy leans towards the window ledge. A pin is pinched between the thumb and third finger of his right hand. He contemplates the flies, discerning which is the fattest or biggest or most lazy. The fingers of his left hand hold the chosen fly in place and his right hand guides the pin into its body. There is a crucial moment when the pin must be forced through a thin but hard protective skin, then a sense of relief as the silver sliver eases into soft blood. The wings of the fly beat and buzz as red liquid drools upon the window ledge. With one finger the boy paints lines and shapes. He can draw numbers, letters of the alphabet or more elusive symbols. Recently, he has learned to spell his name.

The ants are always very quick. Before the blood can begin to dry, they are marching towards the tantalizing aroma of an easy prey. Tiny, efficient jaws nibble the body of the fly, tearing away choice morsels. Some ants are too excited by such bounty to decide if they should eat the food on the spot or take it to some safer place to savour. Some are insane with greed, piling more plunder upon their backs than they can carry. The boy watches this scene carefully, intently, now and then scattering away ants he finds overly voracious. Only once do his eyes look out through the window, and then they are overwhelmed by the sight of a world too much larger than the small one he controls. The southern sun hits his body flat and hard, like an iron. At the edge of the yard the houseboy and gardener are each holding one end of a thick, long snake. Their Swahili words twist and tangle inside the boy's head. He cannot remember the place that he is often told is his real home.

He decides to save this fly, for no reason other than this is what he wants to do. He withdraws the pin, then nudges the body away; it is surprising how after such an experience a fly can often limp away, apparently just a little more dazed than before. The other flies are unalarmed by what has occurred nearby: disaster is always far away, drones the sun and heat. Perhaps the boy will sever the head of the next fly with one quick slice of the pin. Or he will tear off only the wings, or only the legs.

He shifts his bare legs, which have grown stiff and sore against the hard tiles. He feels someone behind him. Turning, he sees Rogacion, the houseboy, staring at him with black eyes floating in pools of white. The dark skin is pulled very tightly across high cheekbones, the face appears without expression. It is set as still as when the boy's mother shouts because the housework is not properly done. The houseboy turns silently back into the kitchen. His feet make no sound against the floor.

The boy reverts his eyes to the window ledge. Suddenly he is sick of greedy ants and he is tired of flies that are so fat and easy to kill. He looks out the window again, down the hill that slopes towards the west. The dirt is red and hard and baked, and heat has cracked it. There are signs that the world has been broken, as if by earthquake.

There is no telephone in the apartment the boy moves into ten years later, when he learns the truth at seventeen. No one knocks upon the door, he does not see or hear other people in the building: it is very quiet. Occasionally he goes out into the cold to buy food and a few times a week attends a nearby university. He sits silently in the classroom, his face set still. Staring at the instructor, he makes no marks upon the white paper before him. He knows he is supposed to understand this language that marches into his ears; they tell him this country is where he belongs. At night cars ease down the street below his windows, their headlights crawl along the walls. He likes the rooms in darkness, when only a circle glows red upon the stove. He rests the blade of the knife against the element, bends his face close to feel the burning heat. When the metal is ready, he presses it against the skin of his arms. He must reheat the knife several times if he wants it to keep working; He applies it to various places on his flesh. A subtle scent rises to his nose. Later, when he switches on the light and the room jumps out at him, he will study the pattern of marks upon his arms, as if trying to interpret hieroglyphics. Often they will seem very near to possessing some meaning he can almost remember; he will hear a foreign language that is very familiar, nearly understood. Years later the marks will have faded into small pale spots, and when his skin is tanned they will be invisible.

At evening the young man lights three candles, the same variety that old Spanish women dressed in black burn beneath miniatures of the Holy Virgin or the Saviour. The thick tubes are encased in a skin of red plastic, and as the wax burns down fire fills the plastic with red glowing light. Three flames waver in the air that wafts into the room. It drifts inland from the Mediterranean, all the way from Africa.

On the bed the young man lies reading and drinking wine. A burning cigarette is pinched between two fingers of his left hand. His other hand continually and unconsciously worries the skin of his face, disturbing it, scratching it. When he turns off the light at last, Spanish voices reach him from other rooms, the hallway, the street. Although he understands this language well, years of living in foreign lands have taught him to flick a switch in his head, turning any words in the immediate air into mere sound. He allows the candles to burn through the night, beneath white walls bare of miniatures or photographs. Waking at morning, he looks into the mirror. His forehead is marked by perhaps ten small scratches where the nails of his fingers dug deeply into the skin. Today the scratches are disfiguring and red. The smell of wax is heavy in the room. He turns to see the three candles still burning. Carefully, he blows them out.

On his terrace the light is very clear, and the mountains to one side and the sea to the other appear in sharp focus. The November sun is almost hot. The young man leans back in a chair, tilting his face towards the sky. His eyes are closed. When they open an hour later, their vision is darkened for several moments; then sharp light forces itself painfully back into them. He looks again into the mirror. The red marks are still there, resembling the war paint of a native tribe; but they are vanishing already into the expanse of darkened skin. In a few days or a week they will be gone, and the young man will gaze into the mirror, trying to remember his name and age and place of birth.

The Ninth Life

The Ninth Life

Don't cry, cat. I know you're hungry, I'm hungry too. But there is
no food and no money, and there will be neither until I go out.
Soon. . . . First let me finish this little drink (they're never big
enough, Ethel would say), and don't cry, cat.

The old cat follows me around the room, crying. She entangles
herself in my legs, tripping me deliberately. When I sit, she lies
on my lap or feet; if I push her away, she slinks across the room,
to stare at me with eyes that are sometimes yellow, sometimes
golden, sometimes green. (My eyes are green on waking, hazel
some hours later, brown at midnight.) Or if I push her away, she
will perhaps swipe at me with claws grown long and dull. There is
no surface in this room upon which she can sharpen her claws
and I have neglected to have them cut. (My own nails I bite.) But
still they can draw blood, leave marks. More tracks upon my
arms . . . .

Her gaze is fixed on me, her eyes blink ironically. She is saying:
let's see you get us out of this one. Or: you left me before, you will
leave me again. Or: the end is coming, I am awaiting it; sometimes the time passes wearily, but such is life, alas.

How did we end up in this small third-floor apartment (they
call it a studio) in this cold northern city, the old cat and I? Why
this setting for this present life? There is one room that is not
very large; but coming after all the small hotel rooms and being
nearly without furniture, it seems quite spacious. The walls are

bare and white. The carpet is wall-to-wall and hard, as if tightly woven with iron threads. Small kitchen, small bathroom, small closet. A row of uncurtained windows overlooking the alley that runs behind Davie Street. A foam pad in one corner. A round metal table, white and flimsy and light, with two matching metal chairs. (They call it lawn furniture, and in catalogues it would be pictured upon green summer grass and surrounded by smiling people of obviously close relationship.) No dishes or plants or pleasant objects. Everything is temporary, for on any near night we might leap over a wall and vanish into the next life.

There have been worse places, smaller places, noisier places. Here it is quiet. No one knocks upon my door; I do not hear people in the apartments beside and below me (they are empty? inhabited by subdued souls? ghosts?); I rarely see anyone in the halls. Only infrequently do Lorraine and Robin call up to my windows from the alley below: let us in. There is no telephone, I dislike them. People calling in the middle of the night with unsolvable problems, I can't help them. Or else the telephone rings with wrong numbers, or it rings and no one speaks. Or it doesn't ring, you think it broken.

How long ago was it, cat, that I left this part of the world? Three years? It was a pity I could not take you with me when I departed from here then. It was certainly a shame I had to leave you behind with people who did not care much for you, but I was in a hurry: on your mark, get set, go. It was unfortunate also that on cold winter nights you cried on the steps and scratched on the door: let me in, let me in. Of course that life seemed endless to you, for how could you know that I was ever coming back? And the door did not open. Meanwhile I was in the sunshine, always warm and golden. California. Then I came back, running away from Rickie and Rick and Reeves. I believed they could be left behind in that grey room on the fourth floor (pay by the week or by the month), waiting for me to knock on the door. I thought I could leave them in the Gilbert Hotel, that haunted house in Hollywood where abandoned ghosts wander the hallways, wearing bare and forlorn paths into the carpet. They are waiting for a new stranger (for example, me) to arrive in town and to listen to old stories related afresh. These tales invariably describe a recent time when Rickie or Rick or Reeves was younger, stronger, luckier, and they always end with the insistence that good times will come back soon. Meanwhile, Rickie or Rick or Reeves will touch the newcomer's shoulder with bared bones of fingers, they will clutch at his sleeve. Rickie or Rick or Reeves will invite the unsuspecting stranger to their room for a quick drink, one they hope will last several lifetimes. . . .

What a surprise to find them here in this cold city! Rickie and Rick and Reeves followed me for a thousand miles north, trudging a million steps through the great states of Oregon and Washington. If I did not know them better, I might believe their long trek a touching testament of sincere affection for me. And what a surprise to find the cat still alive; you thought she would have died on one of those long winter nights, left out in the cold. I telephoned the house, then in a taxi went to bring her here. She shows all the natural bitterness of a once-abandoned soul and little gratitude at being reclaimed. She is frightened when she is not wearily ironical. Any day I might put her outside the door and not let her in again. Any day I might go away. She knows there will be no warning, you turn around and suddenly the room is empty. Or you come home and the door is locked against you. And no one opens it. I hear Rickie and Rick and Reeves crying at my door; they scratch the wood with their claws: let me in, let me in. I turn up the music. They are determined, and capable of any form. They can slip through the crack beneath the door or squeeze through the keyhole. (However, they prefer to enter humanly; they do not like to admit they are ghosts and will protest this fact endlessly.) In the mirror I see them staring at me through narrowed eyes. They are not pleased I wished to forsake them. I have no choice but to welcome them. Hello, Rickie, Rick, Reeves. So you're back again.

I force myself to prepare for outside.

There is a necessary ritual, a certain series of steps that must be followed exactly in order to take myself from this room to that corner. First, a little powder, folded in the corner of a small square of paper. There is not enough to sniff or swallow. Doesn't matter. I prepare a shot. My fingers are deft, quick, this is the one time they do not tremble. . . .

Let me do that, says Rickie impatiently. (He is convinced he can do anything better than I.) A boy named Slim is sitting beside Rickie on a bed in the Hudson Hotel. The noise of traffic on

Hollywood Boulevard, half a block away. Like this, says Slim. He is close beside Rickie, the youngest boy who has much to learn. His shirt brushes Rickie's bared arm. His dark hair falls across his brow as Slim bends over the eyedropper, the glass of water, the candle, the spoon. Slim is concentrating, this is the one time he does not smile. Quick and easy, in and out. . . .

There. Now it's simple. Shower. Shave before the mirror. MDA inside, just the right amount. Too much and there's a sense of falling fast, gathering speed as I drop (they call it gravity), hoping to black out before I hit hard pavement. Too little and I am not falling, but floating back to sunshine warm upon my skin, to fingers of breeze gentle in my hair. Not too much, not too little: this is right. I am still and calm as a pool of water upon which a reflection lies clear and perfect. My face in the glass changes as I change to go outside. My skin tightens, my mouth hardens, my eyes narrow.

Who will appear in the mirror? Rickie? Rick? Reeves?

It is Rick. Not the youngest boy, not the oldest. Rick, who worked alone on the corner and never spent half the money he earned. Santa Monica Boulevard, across from the Tropicana Motor Inn, that's where he stood, one figure waiting amid self-service gas stations, all-night liquor stores, grocery marts. He goes to the movies by himself, sitting in cool darkness all day long, watching the same scenes over and over until they become stuck upon his eyes. Then the corner at night, the headlights moving through cool darkness, look at them go: one, two, three. Like streaks of falling stars. Play those scenes over and again in slow motion, maybe one day or night they will come out differently. A happy ending. . . .

Yes, now I'm Rick, but the cat can see through my disguise. She knew me when I was ten years old and crying in the basement because of Ethel. . . . Lie still, Ethel said. This won't hurt a bit. The things inside me, it hurt. I stare at the pattern on the bedspread. Sailing ships. They float on the water, they never sink. Waves lap and slap their wooden sides, the salt stings. I'm floating on the bed, the stinging sea. It is wide and far and stretches all the way to Africa. . . .

The cat stares at me coolly: I know who you are. Then she begins crying again, louder now. She knows I am going out. She has not been outside once during the three months we have been together here and she would like to see some stars. We are in the middle of a city. Streets, cars. This is no place for a cat. If I let her out, the wheels of a car would quickly crush her. Or she would run until she was lost, unable to find her way home. She would tremble in the alleys, shiver in the rain, hiding from bigger city cats who prowl amid the garbage. The city would fill her with confusion and fear, until she could not recognize a familiar face. Until kindness and cruelty blurred into one suspect shape. And no one would open the door. Sometimes I am her jailor, this room her prison. You're lucky, I inform her. You are very lucky to be able to stay safe inside this cell and not have to go out there, where it is cold and dark and the eyes of stars all closed. The knives of eyes are sharp and cut you. They ribbon your skin into tatters that flutter as you walk. Wings that don't work.

Once upon a time there was a boy who lived in a small, ugly town huddled on both sides of a river that flowed coldly, swiftly, dangerously. Sometimes the river rose and flooded houses built on the lowest ground. Small children playing on its banks took one step too many into the current and then the game was over. A woman living at the end of the block finished her Tuesday ironing, then walked purposefully into the river. Pregnant girls. . . . The bodies were swept out of sight by the grey dirty water.

The reason for the town was a smelter built high upon a hill of black slag. Its tall towers reached far into the sky, piercing it like sharp needles and emitting clouds of brown and yellow smoke. Similarly-coloured water gushed from pipes into the river. The hilly land around the town was in summer dry and rocky and dusty, and green things did not grow easily. The winters were cold and long, with six feet of snow. The air in the sky hurt the boy's eyes, stinging them. It made him cough.

He lived in a small house high on the hill above the west side of town. A thousand old wooden steps, slippery during winter, slivery during summer, ran between the highest houses and the town below. Climbing them, Ethel had to rest often; she blew hard, her cheeks bulging, her face flushed. The boy lived with Ethel. Sometimes she said she was his aunt. When she drank from the bottle, she said she wasn't. They paid her to look after the boy because no one would do it for free. You bought me this bottle, she laughed, tilting it up to her mouth. Thanks a lot, sonny boy. In the dark bedroom she said she was a teacher. The boy would learn to be good, he wouldn't be like all those bad boys, Ethel told him. He lay floating, his face pressed into the soft velvet bedspread. It smelled of things old and musty and unwashed.

Every Friday the boy took the school-bus out past the edge of town, down the road between the river and the rocky hills. The music teacher lived out there, in a low sprawling house with a husband and six children. And cats. The cats were sulky Siamese, the colour of burned cream, with nerves tuned up as tight and taut as the strings of the boy's violin. First he played the piano. The teacher sat on a chair nearby. She lit cigarettes she did not smoke, leaving them to burn in a green glass ashtray. Smoke spiralled upwards in calm, still rings. Cats posed like statues around the room. Children played at the far end of the house. The boy touched the piano and sound washed through the room in waves. Sometimes the teacher left her chair to pace with closed eyes, listening hard. She was tall and young and had long dark hair. Standing behind the boy, she would lean over his shoulder and with her pencil draw a curve over a line of music. Shape, she would write. Her hair brushed the boy's cheek, smelling of all kinds of flowers. Shape, she said; and sound formed pictures that wavered in the air like smoke.

Ethel didn't like the music teacher. I don't want nothing to do with it, she said. The music teacher told the boy that the lessons were free. When he came home on Friday evenings, Ethel would be standing in the bright kitchen. What did she ask you? What did you tell her? The light made Ethel's face look sharp and her eyes looked frightened and small. She didn't want a piano in the house because of the racket, so every day after school the boy practised at the house of an old woman who lived up the street. Mrs. Nolan had a small white cloud of hair that floated around her head as she drifted through her house like air. The boy touched the keys, making shapes in the room; and there was Mrs. Nolan behind him, listening. When the boy stayed too long, the doorbell rang in two happy notes, the first higher than the second. Mrs. Nolan looked at the boy and quickly said: play something more. But Ethel was waiting with folded arms on the steps. She wouldn't come inside, with her hair full of sharp metal and hard plastic. Her fuzzy bedroom slippers wilted in the snow, like two pink rats huddling at her feet.

The music teacher gave the boy a small kitten that was not Siamese. It was black. Ethel said it cost a fortune to feed, and it had to stay in the basement because it stank. One day the boy came home from practising the piano and Ethel told him that the kitten was dead. She had taken it to the vet and he had charged her twenty dollars for nothing. The thing had still died and Ethel left it there. The music teacher gave the boy a second kitten, and this one was Siamese, white and golden, with dark markings. That kitten ran away. I don't know where it is, Ethel said one afternoon. I've got more to do than babysit cats. The boy wandered the hills of the town every day after school, until Ethel said: stop snivelling and don't be stupid, that kitten's gone.

The boy was given a third kitten, and the music teacher said that this would be the last one. Before it could die or run away, something happened. Ethel said the Holy Lord was dead and danger was outside. The black breath of the Devil rose from the smelter chimneys, infecting everyone with evil. Ethel had to keep the door and windows locked, the curtains closed. Neither she nor the boy could go outside. The telephone rang until Ethel cut the cord. When the doorbell rang and fists hammered from outside, Ethel sat very quietly until the people went away. Then she talked on and on about the Devil who had killed the Lord and about the bad boys who roamed around doing wrong. I know Ethel's eyes were crying, although I couldn't see her face because I was in the closet. It was locked to keep me safe from evil. Sometimes there was a thread of light at the crack. The rest of the time it was dark as a night without stars, and Ethel's voice kept coming through the darkness, crying because the dear sweet Lord had died and left her all alone. The kitten cried, too. Ethel forgot to feed the kitten and me. The closet smelled bad because there was no bathroom. There were crowding coats and shoes, and no space for me in the darkness. I couldn't breathe. I heard the kitten scratching on the closet door: let me in, let me out.

Then Ethel was gone, the small house on the hill was gone. The boy was living in a house in the new subdivision. They said they were his parents. They said there had never been an Ethel. The man and the woman always watched him. He went to a different school and wore different clothes, and the music teacher was someone else. There was a piano. And there was the third kitten. She was still so small, a ball of breathing fur that fit into the boy's hand. She was thin, like the boy, and her face was sharp and narrow. The boy looked after her carefully, so she wouldn't die or run away. She could also remember Ethel, the dark bedroom, the basement. She looked at the boy and they both saw old shapes in the air. When he played the piano, the cat sat on the chair beside him; when he slept, she lay at the end of the bed. The boy watched the black smoke rising from the smelter. He saw the grey river flowing fast. He grew older, the cat grew older, but they both remained thin. Then the boy left that house and that country. He left the cat behind. No green, yellow or golden eyes would look into his any more to say: we both remember the life that is gone. Good-bye, so long.

The first one came to me when I was floating on the bed with Ethel bent over me. I would look up from the sailing ships and see shadows in the corners of the room. Someone was standing there, watching. A shape. One day I saw it was a boy. He looked like me. He had no name and I didn't know where he lived. He would be there, he would be gone. That boy did not feel the stinging of the salt. He could stand in the shadows, out of Ethel's sight, and think about other things, such as what might happen tomorrow. I felt he was a friend, especially after he would float on the bed and feel the stinging salt and allow me to stand in the shadows and think about anything good that might happen the next day. Or the day after.

He came around more frequently. When I pressed the keys, I could create his shape. He lingered in the room until the last note vibrated into only air. He was there when the first and second kittens vanished. In the closet he was a shape less black than the darkness.

The other boy did not come to the house in the new subdivision. He didn't like it there. I shaped the music as the new teacher taught me, but his form would no longer appear behind me. Then the man and the woman asked why I stopped playing the piano.

When I stepped off the bus in Los Angeles, the boy was waiting for me in the depot. He had grown taller since the last time I had seen him, but I recognized those elusive eyes easily. In that city, his was the only familiar face. The place was strange to me, and I sat frightened inside the old hotel room. But the boy walked straight to the corner on the Boulevard, as if he knew exactly where to go and what to do. After he did it, he came back and gave the money to me.

That was Rickie. I could never know him well, for he liked to keep secrets and would not often answer questions. For instance, I did not know where he had been or what he had done since I had last seen him in the house on the hill. Those things he did tell me, I could not always believe; he was inclined to lie poorly when he wasn't bragging or pretending there was nothing he didn't know. I discovered quickly that although he knew how to stand on the corner, he had many other things yet to learn in the city. How to make the most money. How to fix the shots. How to mistrust strangers. At the beginning, when he was new on the street, it seemed that he was very lucky; only good things could happen to him, though he was careless and foolish too often. This was California, where the sun was warm on the beach at Santa Monica, and where the nights were warm, too. The stars were close. I can still see Rickie so clearly. On the corner that is his home he is standing with the other boys. He dances his eyes across the new land around him. He scuffs his shoe and kicks a pebble. Suddenly, he is twirling around a lamp post, like a world around its axis; and when he stops, the earth floats up higher than it was before. The lazy laughter of the other boys rises with cigarette smoke, and trails all the way down LaBrea Avenue.

Then there was Rick, who was one year older. Bad things started to happen. Rick wasn't fresh on the street, sometimes there wasn't enough money. Danger. Slim disappeared, and so did Frankie, too. Cats whined around trash-cans in the alley, where the torn pieces of boys are stuffed. Rick becomes silent, still, and the air feels colder when he is near me. He stands wary on the corner, alone. He goes to the movies, alone. He uses the needle too often. Sometimes he disappears for days, I don't want to know where he has been or what he has done.

Later, there was Reeves. Who was three years older and had been on the street too long. Who would rip off a drunk trick, an easy roll. Who carried a knife in his shoe. He knew I didn't like him carrying the blade, but he wouldn't listen. He knew I was often afraid of him. While he lay sneering on the bed, I had to clean off the blade and throw away the stained clothes, that last day.

During the final years in California, I never knew which one of them would walk through the door. Sometimes they would all be in the room with me, and then we laughed and drank and argued until dawn. But they were undependable. They stayed away from me when they were enjoying good luck or when I needed them most: it is three in the morning, the hotel is silent, the room is empty, the bottle, too. Then they returned when they were sad or lonely or in trouble, and usually when I wished to sleep or be alone. They press closely, touching me where I do not desire to feel a hand, in my ear whispering things I do not want to hear. They tell me things they've done.

In his runners Rick is as quiet as a cat in the night, and people are startled when he comes up from behind. Quickly heads down Davie Street, towards his corner. MDA a friend inside. Many Desperate Attempts. My Dearest Aspirations. Most Drugs Addict. Words play easy with MDA inside his head. Senses sharp and quick and sure. Feet know where to go. Uniform: T-shirt, jacket, jeans. He knows what they like because he likes it himself.

Turn behind Davie. Down a quieter, darker street lined with trees and apartment buildings. Pass boys on the corners, working in pairs. Hear them call out and laugh to each other to pass slow time, listen to them jeer and swear at tail-lights fading away. See their wild eyes and feel their high voices crack the dark like whips.

Walk by. Reach the corner. At the bottom of the street, away from the others. A big tree. A lamp post. No one else ever on this corner. Boys walk by in silence, or call out only: pulled yet? Signals say Rick is here alone. Wait, stamping feet to keep them warm. Cold in this city, not used to this cold that like an icy hand keeps touching. Here, and here. Only rain here by the sea, should be snow to fall and cover the ugly city, make it white again: frightened cries grow muffled, are silenced.

Watch with three eyes, hear with four ears, all alert. Cigarette burning between fingers, smoke something warm inside. Cars circle around and around the block, window-shoppers look to see what goods headlights display. Hunting for that rare bargain. Rick freezes in the searching lights. Sometimes squirrels or raccoons dash across the street, between dark shrubs on either side. Car approaches, animal stuck in the middle of the road, can't move. Metal machine comes closer, gets bigger. At the last second scared squirrels run to safety.

Car stops. Window unrolls, driver speaks. Rules of the game, price to play. All right. Inside is warmth and radio. Slouch in the seat. Car floats silently down the street, past other boys. And girls: look at Lorraine and Robin shivering on their corner. They don't see Rick, he doesn't wave: they will see each other when they need each other. What's your name? How old are you? Where you from? Been here long? Rick hardly answers. His words might not fit the picture of what the trick wants, the design of his desire: something goes wrong, car stops, get out, back into cold night.

Only a few more steps, Rick calls back. Game is huffing on the stairs, a little drunk. Good. Rick nears the door, the cat hears his step, begins to cry. The door opens. Rick kicks the cat away. The trick asks if the cat is Rick's. No, Rick says loudly. It belongs to Richard, he never looks after his fucking cat right, he should take better care of it. The trick sees the typewriter and mess of papers on the white metal table. Rick forgot to put them away before he went out. None of this is mine, he says. It's Richard's stuff. I don't live here, Richard does.

The cat is folded on the other side of the room, tensed and ready to spring. She hisses. The game doesn't want a glass of wine. He stands by the typewriter and reads the page in it. ". . . and the brats scampered away like mice." Then he reaches to touch Rick here, and here. Rick steps back. No, bills first. Three twenties slipped beneath the typewriter. The foam bed on the floor. Rick looks around the room, to remember where he is: not in California. The cat stares. Fuck, it must look pretty funny. Rick almost laughs. Careful.

Over. The jumped joker leaves quickly. Good-bye, so long. Rick does not think of the game walking down the stairs, still breathing hard, leaving a separate, secret life. Let me in, let me out. Rick doesn't think of him returning to his car, his hotel, his business trip. Rick looks at the clock. Thirty minutes. Quick and easy, in and out. And silent. This won't hurt a bit. More Deadly Actions. Marvellously Divine Affairs. The room feels cold. Hot bath, clean clothes. Out with one twenty to buy Nine Lives and cigarettes.

But the cat won't eat. She is old and perhaps sick. Even when Rick angrily sticks her face into the food, the cat won't eat. Now she sits across the room, crying softly. Why? Rick can never sleep after they leave (Reeves can), it is not easy to slip into the darkness where Richard waits. Four a.m. Soon the drug will wear off. Rick drinks wine and waits for morning. Can't remember his face, his voice, there comes a point where kindness and cruelty blur. Rick and the cat sit glaring at each other until dawn, just like that.

That's right, a one-way ticket to Los Angeles, California. And at what hour does the bus leave? A stopover in Portland, Oregon? Yes? Grant's Pass and Mount Shasta? Ashland, Medford, Redding?

What is Ethel doing awake so early and inquiring over the telephone? She is never up before I leave for school. Except for once a month. It must be cheque day again. That means I will stay home from school today, so Ethel can have someone to share the excitement with. My own excitement will be that of the person who goes to the station to see the traveller off, who cries bon voyage! and waves the bus away toward the wild blue yonder. Don't forget to write! Even a picture postcard!

It is early morning, but Ethel has already been working around the house for several hours. About her head is tied a polka-dotted rag, and she is humming tunelessly. She will try to make the place pretty for once. But it is hard to vacuum and dust when California lies just around the corner, and soon Ethel can keep her mind on not a thing except the Golden Gate Bridge and Beverly Hills. It's clean enough, she mutters, looking around the cramped rooms as if they were already receding out of sight; and at this moment I also become less irritating and burdensome to Ethel. This is one day I can be certain she will not stare broodingly at me, her expression becoming sad and troubled at the thought of how bad I am and how I must be taught good.

Ethel pours herself a little drink while we wait for the sound of the cheque slipping through the crack in the door. Ethel is going to put fifty of it into savings and not touch a penny of that, no matter how tight things get at the end of the month. She speaks and drums her fingernails upon the kitchen table and sips herself away. In no time at all there is more than enough for a ticket to California on the Greyhound. Of course, she will have to buy a few things for the trip south, she can't arrive in California dressed in these old rags. But once there, she will never come back. This dumpy little town, she says, her voice slurred with scorn.

Ethel knows all about California, although she has never been there in person. First, there are the movies. Nowadays the movies are filth, Ethel wouldn't go to watch them if they paid her. But in better days the movies were something, and all the old stars who aren't dead still live in California. People there have style, you can't describe it, you either have it or you don't. They know how to walk and talk and dress. A lady is treated right. Plus there are the orange groves, the sunshine, the Pacific, the Hollywood Hills. It isn't so much the exact things Ethel says as it is the way she speaks. Usually her voice is sharp, but in California everyone speaks smoothly, richly, slowly, and Ethel's voice takes on these qualities here in the kitchen. I can imagine her in California when she talks of Palm Springs. She makes shapes of swimming pools and Cadillacs and polo fields and Spanish-style castles in the air, and I am able to see these things rising clearly above our yellowed linoleum floor. On and on Ethel can speak without reaching the end of California. In the middle of Sacramento her voice stops suddenly: the mailman's footsteps tap on the sidewalk. The cheque has arrived.

Quickly Ethel puts on the flowered dress, the satin gloves, the hat with the veil. She wears these special clothes only once a month, because she is saving them for California, where they will be appreciated. She sets her hair hard and stiff with spray and mists the air around her with perfume from the golden bottle. We walk down the steps to town, Ethel clutching the cheque. In her excitement she always forgets to leave fifty in savings at the bank. Give it to me all in cash, she urgently instructs the teller. Once she has the money, Ethel scarcely notices me. I have become an employee like the chauffeur, who is well paid and not required to be addressed except when given orders; and my duties are to open doors, carry parcels, and in similar ways discreetly attend. Up and down Bay and Cedar Avenues we proceed from store to store. At first Ethel ponders before the glass windows at length, at once observing the displayed goods and her own reflection. While she attempts to transpose these objects from here to California, I in boredom hold the axis of a parking meter with one hand, and twirl around and around.

Slowly Ethel grows to despair of finding the things she wants in these few small stores, and her search becomes desperate. She stalks the aisles, bumping into other women and muttering: get out of my way. With the twenty-dollar bills in her hand, Ethel can stare back at women who stare at her. They don't have the slightest idea of what a real lady looks like in this town, she observes loudly. Look at that one over there, she points derisively. She is picking things off the shelves, then throwing them back again, shaking her head violently. Trash, trash, only shabby trash, she exclaims. I can't possibly find a thing that would suit me south.

By this time talking in a steady stream to herself and wringing her hands, Ethel walks in long strides down the sidewalk. I must run to match her pace. The money has become a thorn in Ethel's hand instead of a passport, and marching into the liquor-store she angrily pays for several bottles. In Kresge's she finds a number of small objects to put around the house. These will make me happier, she snorts, throwing back her head. I'll be in ecstasy staring at those walls now. She spends the money more quickly and carelessly, ridding herself of this reminder of failed power. At Safeway she pulls things off the shelves without looking at them, filling up the cart as swiftly as possible.

We must lug the stuff up the wooden steps. In the kitchen Ethel unpacks the bags, seeming surprised at what she finds inside them. She becomes very quiet. It all looks different now, she only says. All the bags are empty. If I make so much as a sound now, I will get it good. Ethel is worn out.

She changes out of her California clothes, and in the old housecoat opens a bottle. Disregarding the things she has purchased as substitutes for what she really needs, Ethel drinks quickly and quietly. I'll tell you what! she declares during the third drink. It's easy as pie! Fifty in the bank each month, and before you know it you're riding on that bus to California. Next month. There's plenty of work there, good jobs, too. Friendly people. She nods her head emphatically, looking fondly at the shapes which now surround her again. This is not the kitchen and I am not sitting across the table from Ethel. She is living alone on the second floor of a charming, carefully maintained building on Hawthorne Avenue. It is one of those stucco places built in the thirties, and like the immediately surrounding neighbourhood it is old, quiet and dignified. Ethel loves her three rooms, although of course she is hardly ever at home. She is forever out on the town, but when she is at home she sits for hours in the bay window. The light! The light! She can never get over the light!

Ethel never spoke about bringing me along to California. In all her stories she was a single lady in the sun, meeting men who were polite as well as considerate. They took her to nice restaurants, and afterwards there was dancing in fancy nightclubs. You turn around and around on the dance floor, and in the surrounding darkness small specks of light resembling stardust also twirl. You're spinning like any planet in space, any star at all.

Later, walking through the streets of Los Angeles, I always expected to see Ethel. She would come around the corner wearing a scarf and sunglasses. Upon vanishing from my earlier life, she had climbed on the first bus headed south, I believed. Perhaps she would not recognize me now, or I would see her as a stranger. In California her face is no longer puffy, and her eyes no longer red as with recently shed tears. She has coloured her hair and bought new clothes and is young and golden in the sunshine. She revolves with slow grace in every ballroom where stardust shines.

There is a place on Melrose Avenue which shows old black-and-white movies from the thirties and forties. The matinée audience is comprised largely of women who could have seen these pictures upon their original release. They usually attend alone, arriving on city buses from Silver Lake and Westwood. In the darkness they sit with spaces of empty seats carefully separating them from the intrusion of a stranger's sobs. They do not buy popcorn or soft drinks. Like pale moons their faces are turned intently to the screen, to the flickering images of shadow and light. The silver stars illuminate the fact that every life can last a thousand years without dimming and that each heavenly body can live a hundred different lives, now laughing, now sobbing, now in love, now alone. A thousand eyes can peer through the darkness at a single world turning. With my numerous eyes (I am Rickie, Rick, Reeves, Richard, and others too fleeting to be named) I watch the women who watch the stars. Any of these women is Ethel. They are all Ethel.

Or she sits in one of those small bars with much red plush located just off the Boulevard. Happy Hour lasts all day. She is among the solitary drinkers of afternoon, who perch on stools and lean across counters to reminisce with the bartender. He has worked this spot for twenty years. They were once connected to the studios, in costumes or make-up or props, assisting the stars to shine. The point of each story is that the stars were not really so brilliant as they seemed. The point too is that they once shone more brightly than now. *Look at what's happened to this town* is a standard closing line for these scenes. *All the garbage, the filth,* they say before the closing credits.

A switch flicks, a motor hums, a film runs: Reeves enters the doorway and pauses. Lately he has found himself coming often to these lounges where icy cocktails clink and tinkle in the darkness. Younger boys, such as Rickie and Rick, can still find pleasure playing in the sun, for their faces are smooth yet and able to withstand the scrutiny of bright light. Reeves cannot see clearly because he has just come out from the brilliant sunlight and these places are all dark. Ethel glances at him, nudging her neighbour. Then she slumps over the counter, her hand still clutching the glass. The filth, she slurs.

An hour later she has come to life. Reeves has bought her several drinks and is sitting next to her. She speaks with vivid intimacy into his ear, relating an episode which occurred at an indefinite time in the past and which concerned a woman who had several worlds at her fingertips. It is not clear whether this woman was Ethel or someone else. Reeves glances at the hand which rests beside his hand on the counter. Its fingers end in bitten nails partially covered with pink polish. The woman's voice still sliding steadily into his ear, Reeves stares directly into the mirror on the wall before him.

Now I am older. My skin is paler, my hair darker, and lines around my eyes say I have squinted too long into the sun. It is becoming harder. In six months I will have to stand a long time on the corner before a car stops. In a year I will have to wait all night, finally accepting a game played for stakes too low. Later, I will never score.

For now the money is still good. It would be easy to put some in a bank. Say fifty a month, and before you know it you're riding on the southbound Greyhound. But I do not make deposits at set rates of interest. The cash is there, then it's gone. In stores I pull things quickly off shelves, without looking at them. Then I say:

don't cry, cat. I know you're hungry, but there's no money to buy food. In a moment I will go out and get some. . . .

She is also becoming older, visibly aging day by day, it seems. Her coat is duller now. She walks more slowly across the room. Her claws have grown too long and they become stuck in the carpet, imprisoning her in place. She struggles to get free. One night Lorraine and Robin call up to my windows from the alley below: Let us in! Let us in! They have taken the night off and have a little coke we can blow. Not too much, not too little. The cat bites Robin when she tries to stroke her; she mistrusts even familiar strangers. She has a sore, Robin says. The cat has a small open sore on the top of her head, which I haven't noticed. Perhaps she has fallen and cut herself? I remember no accidents.

In the month before I left California, Rickie and Rick and Reeves would go off into the night, and their adventures were unknown secrets to me. Possibly they met up with unfriendly strangers, unkind acquaintances. Perhaps they drank alone in bars, then took a room in a strange hotel, where on the edge of the sagging bed they sat with sharp objects in their hands. Maybe they had accidents. . . .

During that period, I would wake up in my room at the Gilbert Hotel (pay by the week or by the month) after several days of unaccountable absence. What have Rickie and Rick and Reeves been up to? I see bruises on my body, cuts on my arms. More tracks. Were they walking the rails, waiting for a train? To take them east, north, south: away.

Increasingly, I take nights off. I do not go to the corner. Rickie or Rick or Reeves will not come to me; they hover at the corner of my eye, and flit away when I turn my head towards them. They are growing restless, for they do not like to stay in this or any city long, and they wish to leave. Let's go, they whisper. Now. It is a test of strength: if I will not take them to some warmer place, they will not take me to the corner. They will starve me into submission and make me listen to the crying of the cat, who is hungry because there is no food and no money to buy it. However, I hide a wild card up my sleeve: I do not care to have you near me any longer, please go away, Rickie, Rick, Reeves. The cat and I can cry when you are gone; we will be hungry always anyway.

I do not go to the corner or even to the movies. I stay inside and watch the cat. She does not sleep, it appears; or, she opens her eyes the moment I open mine, closes hers only when I close mine. She does not eat. Her crying has become mechanical, as if she no longer believes any easement of pain will answer it. As if it were a sound that will continue until the motor stops. The sound upsets, irritates, enrages. She does not often move. On rare occasions when she does, her stiff motions are accomplished with increasing difficulty and she cannot leap even the small distance from the floor to the chair now. Nor can she jump up to the ledge before the window. One month ago she would sit long hours there, hungrily staring at birds which perch on telephone lines strung above the alley. They sat not six feet from the cat, and often she tried to leap towards them, banging into the glass just before her in consequence. Then she learned. Not attempting to pounce, the cat sat still as a statue on the ledge, though she continued to watch the birds avidly. Her mouth opened and closed in silent cries. No sound.

We have nine lives, you and I. For this reason, we may have been careless or reckless from time to time, trusting in the ancient laws of Egypt. Now many stars have fallen from the sky and some old rules no longer hold true. We are growing cautious. We are not certain how many deaths we have already lived, how many new suns remain to rise inside our eyes. Sometimes we are afraid. Still I say: all cats must place faith in the ninth life. Still you are silent.

Later, I will say: she was old, sick, in pain. I will tell myself that there is always a ninth life, and it is always happier than this one. Probably I will believe it was Rickie, Rick or Reeves who did it; I could not do it; and they were each of them anxious to depart, and certain I could not again leave the cat to cry on the doorstep during winter nights: let me in, let me in. Leave her behind for good, they urged.

Possibly. Now, I have no reasons. A finger dials a telephone, a voice makes an appointment. Another voice, or perhaps the same one, calls a cab. It arrives quickly. Let's go, cat.

She is trembling in my arms as we leave the building. It is a clear day of pale light and spring might lie around the corner. She looks with anxious curiosity at a world she has not seen for months. It has become a strange and unknown place. Its scents have been forgotten, and unremembered too is this breeze that brushes her coat, on its way to spin dead leaves left over from last autumn. They twirl in the street. The cat shivers, she shakes.

That's a beautiful cat, the driver says. He soliloquizes on the weather, the hard times, the better days ahead. I hold the cat on my lap. Her coat has many colours, each hair a thread of silver, grey, gold. We reach the place. Don't wait, I tell the driver.

We are in a small white room with bare walls. There are no pleasant objects. There is a small table covered by a white sheet. A scent of antiseptic. Everything is very quiet, very clean. The man's hands are scrubbed pink and clean. I hold the cat on the table; even now she would attempt escape. She is quivering, but not crying. Her eyes are open wide. I feel her heart pounding in my hands, the big, strong heart of a lioness. The man explains. A simple overdose of sodium methylhydrate. A clear, colourless liquid. Quick and easy, in and out. Don't forget painless. And silent. The cat looks at me to say she has seen this coming from far off. The sailing ships are floating on the water. Waves lap and slap their wooden sides. The cat's legs crumple, she sinks. The salt is stinging, the sea is wide and far. Her body stiffens, becomes rigid, the point of her pink tongue sticks just outside her mouth. The white sails are growing smaller, they will soon be gone across the water, it stretches all the way to Africa. The man explains the process for disposing of bodies. I am fumbling in my pocket for money to pay for her passage.

The room (they call it a studio) is empty. There is nothing that cannot easily be left behind, nothing that will be missed. I find my works, my small supply. Quick and easy, in and out. This doesn't hurt a bit. Not any more. You become used to it, and grow even to anticipate with pleasure each small death that leads to the final great life. Ethel, thank you: for starting me on this forward journey. I lift my glass high to you. And drink to the day we meet in California. Beneath the palm trees, of course.

But where are Rickie, Rick, Reeves? They won't desert me now, when I need them. I need them after all. To take me in their arms. To carry me off to California. Shape, shape, sing and shape their forms into the air. There they are, yes. They have been waiting for the music to play once more, and see how they come to me now, so eagerly.

Wait. Is there enough money? Yes, for the moment. While I was with the cat in the room, they were on the corner, and there is plenty of money for today. Let's go. Good-bye, so long. Must Darkness Await? Might Dreams Awaken?

One of them walks on either side of me, and their arms are warm upon my shoulders. Reeves follows behind, with his knife protecting my back. They will harm me, they will help me, and I will do the same for them. Later, others will sidle up beside me with piercing eyes and perhaps they will be stronger, more dependable, less secretive. But for now, Rickie, Rick, Reeves and I are laughing. We are singing, and every wondrous shape we wish for appears like present stars above. We are moving forward. To try again. To reach towards the ninth life.

Shelter

Shelter

It's a fanciful child's vision of a haunted house, thinks Reeves, rather than the comforting place where he awakens relieved from strange dreams. Unknown and perhaps frightening things could occur inside this tall, narrow building, beneath this sharply peaked roof. There are faded awnings over the windows, like hoods over eyes, giving the place a closed, secretive look. A low fence of green meshed wire surrounds the small front yard in which a statue of a Greek god, male and nude and greying with damp and age, poses with proud inappropriateness. On either side of the front steps, guarding this entrance, recline sleek hounds also made of weathered plaster. Behind the house a scattered, overgrown rose garden is centred around a fountain; at night a switch can be flicked to make multicoloured spotlights play upon the flowing water. The house sticks out like a sore thumb from the more modest others of this pleasant working-class neighbourhood. People always glance curiously towards it as they pass, wondering what kind of people could live in such a place, what kind of life they might lead.

Pausing before the gate, Reeves shifts the heavy bags in which he carries all his possessions on his shoulders. In Chicago or Las Vegas or San Diego, running out of money and hope and courage, he bought a bus ticket and travelled as many days and nights as were required to reach this house. He has sent no advance warning of his arrival and wonders what kind of welcome awaits him. It is likely that the house will be empty of any sign of its owner for as long as Reeves stays in it. Or possibly it has been sold in his absence and is inhabited now by strangers.

He walks up the steps, pulls open a sliding glass door, and finds himself in some kind of small foyer. A richly red carpet is beneath his feet, heavy drapes of equally red satin hang before him, and on either side his image is reflected in many narrow, angled and connected mirrors. Multiple refracted versions of himself, lined up one after the other as though for inspection, stretch an indefinite distance to his right and left. Where am I and who am I and what is this place I have come back to? wonders Reeves, disoriented and tired.

Hello? he calls out, not expecting an answer, already sensing the emptiness that lies before him. He turns up the thermostat and wanders through the cold rooms, examining what changes have been made since he saw them nine months before. There are always walls with half their paper stripped from them, surfaces partially scraped of paint, stacks of lumber and sections of drywall, varnish and tools and paint. Each time Reeves returns to this house it is slightly different, partly unknown. It will never be finished, this house; a moment will not arrive when it can be pointed to as if to say: there, it is done, this is what it means and this is how it will stay.

And it irritates Reeves that the front door has been left open for anyone at all to enter. He feels robbed of a special claim on the house, a right to enter it before others. He checks to make sure no unemployed single mother is camped with several children in one of the bedrooms, as is often the case. I'm her son, he would explain, without asking the sad woman who she was or why she was there, then cautiously settling himself into a nearby room like a fellow inhabitant of a lifeboat.

This time the rooms are all unoccupied; Reeves unpacks in one of them. He inspects the bare refrigerator and kitchen cupboards. A bundle of letters waits for him on the counter, though they are addressed to someone else. There is no note from his mother telling whomever it might concern where she is and when she will return. Reeves considers calling long distance to his father; perhaps she is visiting him. *When are you going to settle down? Why don't you find a decent job? Jesus Christ, what do you think you're doing?* No. Reeves could call his brothers or sister, except he isn't sure where they are living now; in any case, they wouldn't know Ardis's whereabouts either. The plants have recently been watered and no stack of unread newspapers sits outside the front door. That must mean something. She may only be working late, she may come up the steps any minute, he thinks. Yet it seems unlikely: the house has the abandoned air of a body that has been left to wait empty and alone for its beating heart to return and warm it again.

It has grown dark early on this winter afternoon, and the inevitable Vancouver rain has begun to fall. Most recently, Reeves has been living in a warm, sunny land, in a room without electricity. Now he neglects to turn on the lights; his mother's rooms fill quickly with darkness. From the street the house must appear uninhabited, lacking the squares of warm yellow light that call children home. What did you expect? wonders Reeves. Leaving home at sixteen, disappearing off the face of the earth for too long, being safely buried for all anyone knew. . . . Then suddenly showing up one day as if you'd never been away. . . . Then leaving and returning from time to time without explanation, as though condemned to repeat this motion until getting it right. What kind of welcome do you *deserve*?

The house has been left open for anyone needing shelter. Don't be absurd, Reeves's mother would respond to a suggestion that, if she is going away for a week or a month, it might be wise to lock the doors. Don't be ridiculous, Ardis would say, as if the things she possesses could never be stolen. The address of this always open house is famous, having been passed from hand to hand in welfare office waiting rooms and shelters for battered women. A place to go when you have no other place.

This house has never been Reeves's home. He was not a child in it. There are few painful or pleasant memories for him within these walls. No sentimental attachment to certain objects, certain rooms. No scents that summon multiple memories from the past. No more subtle association with spirits.

How many years ago did she buy this place, nearly on impulse, with typically Ardis-like swiftness of decision? One morning she awoke to swear she'd had enough of living in rented basement suites beneath temperamental landlords. She had some money, a good job. Although few houses were on the market then, and their prices high, she closed a deal for the place on Tupper Street within a week. "My God!" she exclaimed to family and friends, initially revelling in its inappropriateness. "Wait until you see it!"

For years the house had been occupied by an elderly gay couple. One man had recently died in the basement, of an obscure, lingering illness, nursed to the end by his partner, who was then anxious to sell the house immediately and depart from its painful memories. After moving in, Ardis learned from neighbours that the couple had been spiritualists who held weekly séances in the room she decided would be her dining-room. The old lady next door, promptly dubbed The Queen of Tupper Street by Ardis, told of all kinds of comings and goings at any hour of day or night; the strangest people you'd ever want to see had vanished through the sliding glass door and many of them never came out alive, proclaimed The Queen. Good, thought Ardis, hopeful that by comparison her own irregular life would seem less worthy of the neighbours' notice. She discovered several windows cleverly blocked in and concealed beneath wallpaper, to keep light from the séance/dining-room. She also found out that the man who had died downstairs, James Wilson, had written a spiritualist text entitled *The Gift Within*. Mail addressed to him arrived at her door for years; presumably he hadn't sent change-of-address cards informing of his new home in Heaven. Or perhaps he felt that although he had died in the basement, there was no need for such a drastic step as moving from it.

A life beyond the one she was tensely living, or an invisible world coexisting beside the solid one she moved through with such determination, were things Ardis had never considered. If her children were to speak of the heart, the soul or the spirit, she would purse her lips and respond distantly, as though such concerns lay far beyond sight of her keen vision and were therefore negligible. Perhaps she would laugh shortly with embarrassment that things so inconsequential could be taken seriously. I don't know, she might murmur politely, in a way that suggested she really *did* know. What? That living is a somewhat complicated process without dragging gaudy rooms and ghosts into the picture. But, of course, no one would actually presume to broach such subjects to her.

After several days Reeves decides his mother has left the city for a distant place and an extended time. Frequently she banks many overtime hours at her job, then disappears. She has flown to work in the death camps of Ethiopia or she has travelled to Nicaragua with suitcases filled with medical equipment and supplies.

Or she has journeyed to a wet, green Gulf island and, ignoring winter, has pitched a tent beneath a tree, beside a shore. During the day-time she explores the woods or sits on a cold beach, her back against a log, a book in her lap. Her eyes wander between frozen words and moving water. At night she builds a fire and stares into the flames, watching coals grow brighter, then dim, then die. She kicks sand over the ashes, and in her tent lies listening to owls call, waves lap, branches fall. When she leaves the spot no trace will remain that she was there. I just went away for a few days, she would say upon returning to the city, if anyone asked. Then she would avert her grey eyes to a window, leaving an uneasy silence in the room.

Reeves sleeps long hours, listens to music, reads. Rests. He keeps the house ridiculously well heated, so he might almost believe this a tropical climate still. In afternoons he runs around the nearby park, then spends hours cooking enough supper for six; by the time the food is ready, he has lost interest in it, and carelessly wrapped leftovers accumulate in the refrigerator. Because he usually lives in a single small room, access to many is a luxury: he roams from one to another, enjoying the slightly different atmosphere of each, appreciating a sense of choice. Sometimes he takes naps in rooms other than the one he settled into; waking, he wonders where he is. All I need are several weeks of peace and quiet before tackling the world again, he tells himself.

Despite the changes his mother has made, the house's old decor still overwhelms. Throughout are thick carpets of ruby red or royal blue. The walls are covered with heavily embossed paper; their scalloped designs, swirls of gold or silver, are almost fluorescent. Impossibly ornate chandeliers — dizzying contraptions of dazzling drops of glass — provide the main source of light. Every door is actually a large mirror, so one is constantly coming face to face with oneself at the most startling moments. The hallways are dim and narrow and many. From the main floor narrow stairs rise steeply to a number of small bedrooms with enormous closets.

The house stands in a state of tension, torn between its old flamboyance and the clear, simple lines envisioned by Ardis. Why don't you sell this house to someone who could appreciate it and buy one you don't detest? Reeves has asked her. Facing the wall she is painting pure white, Ardis wouldn't answer. Reeves refuses to help her with the work. It's not a thing to be done lightly, tampering with the spirit of a house, he thinks. Despite its size and though he is presently its only occupant, Reeves soon finds the house cramped, oppressive, confining.

Reeves opens the letters addressed to James Wilson. Apparently, at the end of *The Gift Within*, readers with further questions were invited to write the author at his address. Ardis's address. Reeves hasn't read the book and doesn't know if it's still in print; it has never seemed important to find out. Vaguely, he imagines it as one of those books that floats around forever, passed from hand to hand, lost on disorganized, crowded shelves of dark, dusty second-hand stores.

The letters are from everywhere: Europe, Australia, all parts of North America. Reeves feels no hesitation in reading them; better that than tossing them unread into the garbage. Would it be cruel or kind to scrawl the word *deceased* upon the envelopes and have them returned? Is it right or wrong to allow troubled people to believe their words have reached someone they hope can help? Anyone who reads that kind of book, thinks Reeves, must be seeking answers they have failed to find in school or church, family or friends. They must have reached a state of desperation that only a magically gifted wizard could relieve. Clearly, it is ironic that the letters are intended for a saviour who in fact lacks even the power to breathe. Just as obviously ironic is that the letters are read by someone more lost than their senders. Someone in no position to offer calm counsel, wise words, soothing sentences.

The telephone rings. Dropping a letter with a guilty motion, Reeves lifts the receiver cautiously, waits silently. Hello? says his father. Reeves sees him sitting heavily in his chair four hundred miles away, dressed in his old orchard clothes, rubbing eyes beneath which another migraine is spreading. Before hanging up without speaking, Reeves hears the sound of a television over the wire. His father's house shines amid dark fruit trees now leafless, but each summer bearing extravagant crops. The rooms are stuffed full of old furniture dating back twenty years and all kinds of souvenirs and mementos that the old man can't bring himself to throw away. As Reeves reaches for a bottle of brandy, the telephone rings again, and then again. When it falls silent, Reeves sees his father move to a window and look across a field of apple trees, towards the Trans-Canada Highway that runs along his property. At this point it is an ordinary road of two lanes, and during winter it is frequented by little traffic. Reeves tells himself that his father's lonely house isn't haunted by children who in the middle of the night dance like raindrops upon the roof or brush like branches against the windows. His father doesn't waken to wonder if he has closed the windows against the rain and wind, if he has shut the chimney flue. And, Reeves must also believe, his mother's house is likewise free from spirits, not haunted by the man who died downstairs or by ghosts summoned in the dining-room or by the wounded women who pass through the upper rooms. Or by himself. He tilts the glass, and fiery liquid slides into his stomach at the same instant it falls into his father's.

Ardis moved into the house alone. Her children were grown and mostly gone by then and her husband lived in another town. She arranged to suit herself the odds and ends of furniture scraped together over years on her own. While perhaps she imagined this moment long ago, even as she gazed down at the babies who fed one after the other from her breasts, it had taken her ten years of visible, chartable effort to reach this point: her own house, her own life.

She began by taking night courses at the community college near the small, stifling town where she and her husband raised the children. Soon she also started working in the psychiatric wing of the local hospital, putting to use the nurse's training she had abandoned on marriage. The children and their father grew used to returning from work or school to an empty house, and to making dinner and doing laundry themselves, in a time and place in which this wasn't common. That poor woman, Ardis would exclaim on Christmas morning, rushing to the hospital to cover the shift of a single mother, leaving the family to stare at unwrapped presents beneath the tree. From the late sixties Ardis also involved herself in whatever environmentalist, feminist and leftist movements struggled for survival in the town. The children would tiptoe past the living-room where strangers were scattered across the carpet, raising challenging voices over bottles of red wine and Dylan's rasp. Out in the back yard their father bent over his garden, battling the weeds and insects and disease that threatened his plants. He became more quiet. On weekends the house was silent. Ardis would doze on sleeping-pills at its centre, then rise groggily to work the graveyard shift at the hospital.

At the time her children felt envious of cousins with mothers who baked and ironed and attentively followed soap operas. Only later would they see that, far from being the sole mad deserter of family, Ardis followed closely the blueprint of a certain kind of woman at a certain point in history. However, her choices seemed always highly personal, and she probably would have chosen similarly if the tide of social change had flowed against, not with her; anyway, that small interior town was untouched by such currents. She planned her moves carefully and stealthily, it would later seem, like a master chess player. Perhaps she meant to ease slowly and gradually from the family, so her absence would be scarcely perceptible in the end. Certainly, it was clear to the children that there existed more people in the world than themselves who needed Ardis's care, and that she was not prepared to limit herself to the nurturing of four children and one man. She has her life and we have ours, the children would try to tell themselves later, and they would see the mothers they had once yearned for without children to bake and iron for, now often thwarted or broken or lonely. At the time the children felt only neglected and abandoned. It was true that the small portion of time and energy Ardis spared her family meant that when she left for the Coast — suddenly, finally — there seemed little apparent change in the old house. She took all her belongings with her, leaving not even a ghost to sigh and cry on spring nights when her husband and children lay awake. Listening, waiting, hoping.

It is difficult to know, from reading the letters, exactly what kind of book James Wilson wrote. They are mostly scratched in handwriting difficult to decipher, and spelling and grammatical errors fill them nearly to a point of incomprehension. They do not discuss extensively matters Reeves considers "spiritual", although key words do recur: The Light, The Voice, The Peace, The Spirit. These nouns puzzle Reeves: they are so definite, so singular, conveying with such certainty that there exists only one light or voice or spirit, and that it is plainly known, obviously real. Like an object that can be held and felt and weighed. Something to grasp. Reeves holds the letters tightly and reads each several times.

He searches the house for clues. The rooms are neat and bare and fairly impersonal. Ardis said she would not bother to furnish them properly until the house had been renovated to her satisfaction. Only her bedroom, at the top front of the house, is finished: a large closet has been made smaller, a door has been positioned more conveniently, a slanting wall made straight, a window enlarged. Ardis has achieved a simple, roomy, well-lit space, furnished by a low bed of new clean pine, an old desk of refinished oak with matching chair and a plain bookcase made from dark, hard teak. Translations of Asian and Latin American novels lie scattered about. Cheque books and receipts and daily planners are arranged neatly in the desk drawers. She does not save letters or menus from restaurants or souvenirs of exotic places. There are no photographs or sentimental objects on the plain white walls to which her eyes can wander. No high-school yearbooks or family heirlooms or wedding-gown folded carefully within tissue. A closet filled with clothes made of cotton and silk. Leather boots and belts and shoes. Handwoven bags from Mexico. Fifty years.

What am I looking for? wonders Reeves. Proof that, for her, life is a long process of discarding distracting objects, of stripping away needless decoration, of paring off unessential layers of memory and association and context. To what point and to serve what end? To discover an essence of self, a spirit that stands alone, self-sustaining and strong?

Reeves is hunting for evidence that will explain why his mother left the family. And why, in turn, all four children left their father's house too young and unprepared to face the world alone. I never left home, Reeves sometimes shrugs. Because there was no home to leave.

If this were several years ago, Reeves could go downstairs to ask whoever was there where his mother had gone. Once the basement was a dark, unfinished place where homeless nieces and impoverished African students and Nicaraguan refugees bumped their heads against the low ceiling while waiting for Ardis to call down the stairs, asking if they were hungry. They would tentatively climb the stairs and with clinging eyes follow her brisk movements around her rooms. When the time came, she would write them a cheque and send them on their way.

One day, suddenly, she had the whole house lifted four feet, in defiance of building codes. After several months of plumbers and electricians, carpenters and chaos, the basement was a clean, bright, modern apartment which Ardis promptly rented out, ignoring another city by-law. She is usually cool towards her tenants and, perhaps trying to forget that she has unhappily haunted basements herself, appears oblivious to the fact that people are living beneath her feet. They remain strangers who do not pay the rent on time, who depart without giving notice, or leave the place in a mess.

Through windows Reeves watches the present tenants, a young couple, enter and leave by their separate, lower entrance. They are used to strangers passing through the house above them. They pay Reeves no attention. He searches their faces and clothing for signs that might suggest what kind of people they are, where they come from, how they feel. Their voices rise through the floor, but their words are indecipherable. How do other people live? Is there a secret? That is what The Queen of Tupper Street, peering through cracks between her frilly curtains, also wants to know.

He finds himself keeping odd hours. He wakens in early evening, lunches in the middle of the night. Rain falls steadily around the watertight house. The unanswered telephone rings from time to time, invisible spirits calling. Newspapers delivered to the front door are piled unread beside the fireplace. The existence of other rooms makes Reeves restless, and he is constantly climbing up or down stairs, passing back and forth along dim halls, moving in or out of doorways. It seems someone is waiting quietly in the next room, an impatient or capricious spirit who flits up the chimney or down the heating vents before Reeves can approach. Who?

He wonders if — and why — he is waiting for his mother to return. She might slide open the glass door tomorrow. Or Reeves imagines himself prowling aimlessly through the split personality of the house for years, listening for the approach of quick, light footsteps, waiting for the surprised voice asking when and from where he returned. His mother has never asked Reeves what he does in the places he journeys to. She never inquires why he has come back or how long he will stay. There are already too many questions with difficult answers, she thinks. Too many dark corners in her house.

A woman in Harlem, unemployed and unmarried, has a prostitute daughter, a junkie son, and several children already buried. What should I do, Mr. Wilson? Another letter describes a long, drawn-out case of a job unfairly lost, with supporting documents enclosed. What do you advise, Mr. Wilson? I have read your book and feel strong in The Light, but sometimes I have doubts and there is next month's rent to pay. Mr. Wilson, my wife has left me and I am trying hard to listen to The Voice, but it is difficult, I hear her voice instead. I read your words over and over, Mr. Wilson, in the time I have left, the doctors say there is no point in operating again, I can only wait for the end, or should I say The Beginning. I am afraid, Mr. Wilson.

At first Ardis thrived on the number of people in the city who believed in things she held important. After earning several university degrees, finding work as a public-health nurse and establishing herself in the house on Tupper Street, however, she ceased to attend meetings or to march in protest or to work on political presses. Her contact with people who shared her ideals lessened and her rooms were no longer filled with endless discussions of problems with no easy solutions. There seems little difference in the way things are now, despite the efforts of herself and others; her movement away from large issues appears to have been part of a natural cycle: she has done what she could, and now it is time for new people with fresh energy to take up the work. Yet it seems that these younger people have not come forward and the old movements have mostly collapsed.

Now she does what she can to create immediate change, however slight, on a daily basis. Her job takes her to homes and schools where she can perform certain positive functions. Sometimes at night her telephone rings, when welfare or immigrant women experience disaster: a violent husband, sexual abuse, sudden lack of money. Ardis puts on her coat, gets in her car and drives through the night, returning an hour later with a frightened woman and, perhaps, her children. They find shelter in one of the rooms for a day, a week.

Most evenings, though, she sits alone in her living-room, poised beside a newspaper she spends several hours reading. Her head shakes often in discouragement, in confirmation of her vision of a world ruled by increasingly oppressive governments. She sighs. Sometimes gentle relations or mild acquaintances drop by, and then she discusses the weather with apparent enthusiasm, almost eagerly; her embracement of talk she would once have labelled trivial often seems insincere and makes her listeners uncomfortable. An underground channel of thought and feeling seems to flow beneath the surface of her life, always more secretive, less often shared, further beyond reach. She climbs the stairs and sits at her desk, writing cheques she will send to South Africa and Central America. At midnight she goes jogging through the quiet neighbourhood, circling around and around the dark park. A small, thin woman of middle age.

Friends and family who have observed her over many years agree that she has never shown the slightest sign of fear even once. Don't be ridiculous, she would say if it were proposed that it might be reasonable, and even intelligent, to feel frightened in certain circumstances. Fear, doubt, confusion seem to be things she hasn't time for or frills she considers self-indulgent, like colour television. She drives her government car swiftly and expertly; her stride along sidewalks forms a quick, straight line. At lunch hour she takes an aerobics class; during weekends she attends medical seminars or intensive language courses. I'm so exhausted, so busy, she scribbles in notes she sends her children several times a year. It's been a real madhouse around here, she comments with pride and pleasure. An impatient expression appears on her face if it is suggested that she might occasionally relax. She marches off to tear down a wall that is in her way. She has always, it is inevitably recalled with a mixture of awe and horror, achieved everything she ever wanted, whatever obstacles were in the way. If she has failed to find certain things in life, or regrets some of the choices she has made, there are no indications. No one knows if she lies sleepless in her bed at night, although The Queen of Tupper Street will tell you that, whenever she wakens with some pain or other in the middle of the night, she always sees all the lights of Ardis's house blazing.

Reeves is not Ethiopian or Nicaraguan. He has been clothed and fed and sheltered as a child, fairly well educated and given examples of what can be accomplished with determination and effort. He has been provided for to the point where he can provide for himself, and there is no need for him to receive the kind of cheque his mother sends to people trapped by circumstance or history.

Still, he has no money and must make some if he wishes to leave his mother's house. If he works hard, on a good shift he can earn several hundred dollars between midnight and morning in the city of night. It takes a long time to ready himself for the job. Before his mother's mirror, a glass of brandy within reach, he tries on clothes until finding the costume that best suits the role of a very young man with something precious to sell. Often he wears something of his mother's for good luck: a T-shirt, a pair of socks. Her clothes fit him.

Stumbling back to the house in early morning of times before, he would pass his mother just leaving for work. Where were *you?* she would ask brightly, hurrying away. He would mumble a wordless reply, then crawl up the stairs to sleep. When he woke, it might be to hear his mother in the kitchen below and to smell the aroma of food he had never known her to make before. Dragging himself downstairs, Reeves would find Ardis dressed in colourful gypsy clothes, moving lightly between the kitchen, dining-room and living-room. She would set the table, light candles and pour wine for herself and the man who stood before the fireplace, stirring the flames with a poker. The man would usually be unknown to Reeves, usually younger than his mother. Would you like a glass of wine? Ardis would ask Reeves. No thanks, he'd reply, then climb upstairs to dress for going out.

Returning several days later to the house, he might notice his father's car parked before it. They would be reading newspapers and listening to the CBC in the living-room. Silent together. His mother and just another of the men she sheltered in her house, then with a wand waved away when they were warmed.

She saves the letters to James Wilson for Reeves, yet views his interest in them as odd. If she were to answer them, she would state to the man who has trouble hearing The Voice that there exist such things as hearing-aids, and she would probably enclose a medical report describing various recommended models. To the Harlem mother she would send addresses of social services available in that community, and urge her to contact them for help. Her advice to the unemployed man would be to seek assistance from a labour-relations board. Ardis would see no point in responding to the dying woman.

Clear common sense. Yet completely off the mark, not what these people need at all. Advice or money or support from some well-meaning agency or individual would never help; the only assistance that would serve would be divine: the sound of The Voice, the illumination of The Light, the concern of The Spirit.

The doorbell rings. Reeves wakens to find himself and the upstairs bed he is lying in soaked: he has left the window open and rain has come inside. The doorbell rings again, then a third and fourth time. Go away, grumbles Reeves. He walks to his mother's room and looks out her window. On the front steps below a woman is hesitating. She carries no umbrella, wears no hat, and appears soaked to the skin. In her arms is a heavily wrapped bundle that she holds like a baby. She stands there in indecision, then tries to open the door Reeves has locked. After ringing the doorbell several more times, she descends the slippery steps, leaves the yard, moves away down the sidewalk. Her head is bowed beneath the falling rain. Reeves watches her vanish around the corner. Then he climbs into a dry bed in a dry room. It warms quickly with the heat of his body.

At midnight Ardis changes into her oldest clothes to take up work on her house where she left off the night before. She bends over an electric saw, carries large sections of drywalling, reconstructs a wall, wields a paintbrush. For the most part the house is silent and brightly lit in the dark, sleeping neighbourhood. As she works, Ardis's gaze becomes more intent and focused upon the immediate task at hand, and the larger world moves several feet away from her. Her clothes become spotted with paint, her hair sprinkled with sawdust. The work is endless and seems to progress invisibly; but Ardis labours surely and steadily, seeing beyond the present disorder to a clear strong vision of a house with no murky corners or unnecessarily complicated lines.

She has stopped wearing make-up when she is alone at home,

and also when she goes out during day or evening. For years she dyed her hair various shades of blonde, red, light brown. Now it is mostly grey, and stands out somewhat wildly around her head. Twenty years ago she bought a wig and a fur coat, in a quickly aborted effort to blend in with the young matrons of the small town. Even now, without effort or artifice, she looks younger than her years; perhaps, in the same way, she appears stronger than she feels. At four in the morning she goes to bed, to sleep several hours before rising for more work. She is exhausted. While falling asleep, she listens to the house groan and creak in the dark. Complaining at change.

Dear Harlem Mother, Reeves might write. Dear Unemployed. Then what? I have my own problems too? . . . They are waiting for an answer. Reeves imagines one endless street, lined on both sides by an endless row of identical houses, running in a straight line across the globe. Every day, at precisely the same moment, someone emerges from each of the houses. With a simultaneous movement a million heads bend to peer into a million mailboxes. Then look again to make certain nothing is there. Still as one, they return disappointed back inside their little boxes, to wait until tomorrow. Hope is a drug that helps you make it through one more difficult hour, and then another. It is addictive and consuming, thinks Reeves. Anything that helps . . . .

They are hoping their words will be read and their questions answered. All Reeves can hope is that, however far away they are, these people can somehow sense that a pair of eyes is absorbing the account of their troubles. A mind is considering their pain, a heart is sharing it. Ridiculous, Reeves hears his mother say.

Anyway, does that help a little? Enough? No, of course not. There can never be sufficient help when the roof is leaking and a cold wind is blowing through cracks in the walls, and all the windows are smashed.

Three weeks after arriving at his mother's house, Reeves prepares to leave it. Either that, he tells himself, or I'll find myself tearing down walls and putting up new ones every night, trying to construct a shelter as functional as can be; for we need only plain, square rooms that keep out cold and rain and wind, rooms that don't ask much or give much but allow us merely to accept their usefulness then look beyond to find what we can do in this world.

Nothing has happened, thinks Reeves. There has been no definite occurrence, not the slightest precise detail that can be held onto like a symbol and invested with a lode of meaning: this is what took place the last time I was at my mother's house: see how clearly it reveals why I never went back.

Has he been strengthened or weakened by this time inside his mother's house? Either way, he is compelled to leave it in search of other kinds of shelter, his own kind of shelter. He tidies the rooms, wishing to leave them as they were before. He stacks the unread newspapers more neatly. He turns down the thermostat. Throwing away the untouched leftovers in the refrigerator, he knows that in a month he will be starving for this food.

The twenty-, fifty- and one-hundred-dollar bills he has earned are turned into travellers' cheques. The bags are repacked. What else? Should he leave a note, telling his mother he was here? No, that's not necessary. You can't help but leave signs behind. Some clue always demands to be dropped.

The letters. Take them with him or leave them for his mother to throw away? There isn't room in my bags, he tells himself, burning them in the fireplace. He watches smoke being sucked up the chimney and into the sky, where it will add slightly, so slightly, to the grey clouds that hang above the world.

He leaves the house unlocked and heads for the bus station. A ticket south will take him to a place where it is always warm and where cracks in the walls or holes in ceiling won't matter.

· · · · ·

Years have passed since I left Reeves and my mother's house behind for good. For better or for worse. I don't know if he still wanders through those always-evolving rooms, regretting the limited shelter they give him, wondering why he can't find more complete shelter elsewhere. Waiting, hoping.

I do know that letters to James Wilson continue to arrive at the house on Tupper Street, because I constantly meet people who send such letters. On the bus between Stockton and Modesto, between Ashland and Redding, or between any two points of fragile connection, they sit in the empty seat beside me. At once and without prompting they launch into their endless similar stories and they do not care to hear mine: to listen to another's troubles is one more luxury they can't afford. Most of us who ride the buses are poorer people without cars or the means to fly like birds through the air. We are related through our poverty and our hope — strong, stifling bonds that often make us look at each other with distrust. I sometimes consider giving the most desperate ones the address of the house on Tupper Street, but I never do. As the miles between midnight and morning slowly unwind they borrow my cigarettes, these near and distant relations, and confide in me about The Light that will come at dawn or The Voice they hope to hear tomorrow or The Peace that surely waits in the next town.

I still stay in the small rooms of boarding-houses and pensions and inexpensive hotels, paying for shelter by the day or week. Someday soon I hope to live in larger, more expansive rooms. A place with a pleasant view and familiar furniture and known objects to soothe my eyes. In the meantime, whenever things are too hard, I sit by my speckled window with pen and paper and look out across rooftops that stretch as far as my eyes can see. Do saints or murderers live beneath them? Dear Mr. Wilson, I begin. My problems are typical of every poorly sheltered being: there is not enough money or the bottle is empty; the room is too silent and the light bulb too dim or too bright. Dear Mr. Wilson . . . Only occasionally do I puzzle over the strange fact that I have seemingly gone out of my way to avoid the comforts of solid shelter. I muse on the possibilities of choice; it is always a theoretical meditation. Dear Mr. Wilson. I seal the envelope, address it to the house on Tupper Street, and drop it into a mailbox. Wondering if anyone will read it. Reeves?

Letters from my mother sometimes find me, though less and less often as time goes by and one impermanent address fades beneath another equally transient one. There is never any account of what she is thinking or how she is feeling. Instead she describes the work she is doing on her house. I learn that the Greek god, the hounds and the fountain have been sold and taken away. This wall has been torn down, and those small rooms have been made into a larger one. It seems she will never finish transforming her house into the kind of place that will give her peace. And this is not because she refuses to hire carpenters to finish the work quickly, nor because she insists on doing most of it herself. She will always be dissatisfied with her house; like any other, it will remain a place of uneasy shelter, for herself and for the strangers she takes in. Still, she grips the hammer tightly and with precision drives in one more nail, never hitting her thumb.

Rorschachs III:
Ventriloquism

Rorschachs III:
Ventriloquism

The tin can is large and heavy and, at the back of the furnace room, lurks in mute darkness. It is painted pale green, with silver showing at the dents. The tight lid eases off with a genie's sigh; an acrid scent of smoke rises from inside and mixes with smells of oil and dust. I dig deep into my inheritance: pale cat's-eyes floating frozen amid bubbles of trapped air; opaque agates. The globes of glass warm to my touch, then burn and moan and whisper. Beside me the furnace switches on and the earth trembles beneath my feet.

My uncle swallowed smoke before my birth, leaving behind hockey sticks and baseball gloves and a universe of stunted spheres. In photos his face appears pinched and peaked, unlike those of squinting boys who in springtime lay stomachs against muddy grass, push hair from whitened winter foreheads, send marbles spinning towards a target. *I got you!* they crow, hearing the click of glass on glass. My crystal eyes cloud beneath their breath, they make me twirl across the flat field until the world revolves dizzily, I can't see straight.

We never visit the cemetery on the hill where my uncle and grandfather practise patience. My father stares straight ahead as he drives us past; rows of white crosses blur by. The wiring of the Christmas tree lights was faulty, my grandfather forgot to unplug the cord that night. The old man and his youngest son were sleeping in the basement while empty rooms creaked and crackled overhead. (By then the woman had already dug herself into the earth; older children had also eschewed home.) The gaily wrapped presents beneath the tree turned brown, then black. Smoke stole down the stairs. They found the old man halfway between his bed and the window. The boy was posed in sleep, a lucky marble hidden in one hand.

They gave me his name. *Donald*, they say and his voice emerges from my mouth. *Dummy*, they say when he will not move my lips. My bed is in the basement, beneath the surface of the earth. The world twirls slowly; now I am older than he ever was. I grip a favourite marble and smell smoke. Without moving lips I chant a child's prayers; seven miles away they rise from beneath the graveyard's skin, muffled by snow as white and clean as the bones it blankets. I have passed through fire; I am as fearless as the phoenix.

There are years of cold winters and fiery summers in the small town split in two by a river that runs swiftly, icily, dangerously. From the bank I toss marbles into the watery mouth that opens, then greedily gulps. The empty can floats from sight. Finally I am free to twirl and spin across the world, the scent of smoke clinging to me always. I chip and crack. Indifferent hands warm me, roll me away to cool once more. *I never dreamed it would be like this*, the other Donald murmurs from my mouth as smoke from strangers' cigarettes curls knowingly into the corners of my cold hard eyes. At the bottom of a river marbles turn to stone. I drown with desire to be warmed by fire's hands, again and then again.

The Sacred Flame

The Sacred Flame

A curl of colour springs out from the darkness, in the window at the east end of the house. This is the room where the two girls sleep, my observations have informed me. Francie and Grace, they're called. Ten or eleven or twelve years old, I'm not certain; they are not the object of my focus here. The colour spreads quickly, like alcohol in blood, blotting out the darkness. The long year of cold darkness, this is the first time since last summer's fire that I have felt even slightly warm. Smoke puffs lazily into the sky. For the moment, in my hiding-place nearby, I am the only witness, except for the dozen glass eyes contained in my pockets. They become hot to my touch, they begin to whisper. Yes, yes. And my Father, who always looks over my shoulder, also murmurs with approval. Yes, yes, we softly sing. If I do not cry an alarm, it is not because I feel frozen, helpless. My vision is lucid, my senses quick. I notice how the flames soar thrillingly up a curtain, I see how they change colour according to the surface they encounter. The new skin they gave me — it has never fit, it has always itched — prickles in suspense. Will the fire move this way or that? Shift to the right or to the left?

I am familiar with fire, and though it is unpredictable, a fickle friend, I have learned to anticipate its moods. Each fire has its own character, and this temperament depends partly on the quality of the night — temperature and humidity of air, whims of wind. I take pride in my fires. They are good ones. Fast and strong. Full of vibrancy, spirit. Red and orange and yellow are the colours I take from my palette, though sudden swirls of purple, blue or green can make my artist's blood race. Especially at the start, when it is taking shape — finding its form, so to speak — I see the fire imprinted with my touch and responding to my special needs. My signature. Soon, of course, the flames will grow and go their own way, raging and storming like any stubborn child.

I am waiting for a first cry, a muffled moan, a scream. The two girls must now lie open-mouthed on their twin beds, and they will have sucked smoke down into their pink, tender lungs. It wanders freely through their throats, caressing, violating. In the next room the man and woman undergo similar transformation into one heap of char. I see their joined mouths. Possibly, there was time for her to waken and turn to him. She could have touched his shoulder, and given another moment he might have made it out of bed and half-way to the window, before my hot hand touched him and laid him down.

So far this one has been very silent, but that cannot last. A neighbour will be roused (I don't know what woke me, she will state in the local paper's interview, and repeat the same a hundred wondering times over coffee in various, similar kitchens) and will call the fire department, then the houses up and down the street. Lights will go on, and in pyjamas and nightgowns and slippers people will gather on the sidewalk. Half awake, stunned, uncertain, they will wait for the screaming trucks, the uniformed men. The futile efforts.

By then I will be gone. I have no wish to see my work ruined by water, turned into a soggy, ugly mess. Disgusting. That night, they told me I never saw the burning house, after I ran from it with wings of fire spreading across my shoulders, stretching beyond a span of six feet. They insisted I ran into the blanket waiting for me and did not hide behind the bushes, did not watch alone. The cloth folded around me, they swore, a white ring of pain past which I could not see forward, not see back. The first of their lies.

This moment is mine to cherish alone. (My Father understands my need to savour this scene undisturbed; He has fallen atypically silent.) The long time of waiting pays off here and now. All the details I have painstakingly impressed upon my brain serve at last. I see the pattern of the carpet, the grain of the wood. The particular combination of numerous ordinary objects which makes this house unlike the one next door. Familiarity has made it mine. My vision is searing. It devours with one fiery hungry gaze, refuels, then moves steadily towards its final destination. Below.

His room is on the ground floor, beneath the mother and father and sisters. Why do they put him alone down there, where in the middle of the night he wakens to hear the turning of a doorknob by a stealthy, gloved hand? The equally secret sliding open of an unlocked window? (They believe themselves so safe, the people in these small towns.) I have seen his face drawn and tired in daytime, from too many nights of lying stiffly, listening. He strains to hear the intruder's entrance, my step along the hall. Once I was in his room, lightly touching his model airplanes and wondering if they could really fly, when I felt his eyes upon me. Light from a streetlamp stole through the window and fell half upon him. His white throat, his face. He was watching to see what I would do next. I branded the air with the sign of my cross. Hello, Timothy.

Now he listens to the crackling above him. I wave my conductor's wand, and the sound changes from something dull to something sharp. Smoke creeps cautiously down the stairs. They better wake up before the smoke hurts their eyes, I thought. The smoke from Uncle Ivan's cigarettes always travelled straight to my eyes, stinging them. No matter where I moved, the smoke altered direction to follow me, as though my eyes held a special attraction. As though something about their clarity or colour asked to be clouded. How boys blow warm, wet breath upon their marbles for good luck, then send them to spin and twirl across the grass.

Timothy. The right name, the right age. As always, I have chosen carefully and well. The summer hay, the timothy. Hot scratches on my legs. In the middle of the field I threw a marble as far as I could. I wanted to lose it so I could find it. I searched for hours in the timothy. The itching of my hands, my arms, my new skin. Don't scratch. You'll only make it worse. I always find it, the itch is always soothed, for the moment at least.

Timmy, Timmy, the woman has called a million times. He thinks he hears her calling in the fire upstairs. He goes to her voice. The carpet is warm to his feet as he climbs upward.

Eighteen steps. At the top he can go no farther: fire fills the hallway on both sides, blocking his way. When he tries to push by, it
lunges back at him. Don't touch. Fastens upon his arms, runs up
to his shoulders. Sends him flying down the stairs, out the door.
The cool night is shocking. He doesn't see them waiting with the
blanket. (Later they will say: we saved you.) He is thrown past
them, is flung upon the grass. The wet dew. He rolls and rolls
across the lawn, as he has done all summer with Francie and
Grace. They got stains on their clothes, the green of the grass
rubbed off and marked them in July. I was gasping on the lawn, I
ran and hid behind the chinaberries, by the old fence with its
flaking paint. You couldn't eat the little red berries, you could
only throw them or squish them, exploding the skin and smear-
ing the inside upon your fingers, your face. Soft and wet and
warm.

No one else came running from the house. The door stood
open wide. The others did not fly down the steps with orange
wings fluttering from their shoulders. He watched the open door,
it was like the black mouth of a tunnel, it swallowed up his eyes.
Only when the big trucks came crying around the corner did his
eyes slip to the sight of the Thoms and Booths and Carpenters
milling on the sidewalk. Cash boxes and jewellery cases and
important papers were in their hands. Then the men in shiny
clothes and hard hats pointed the spouting hoses. They could
save only the houses to the left, to the right.

It will be an hour before the liquids and powders do their work
and the fire is controlled, quenched, killed. It will be another
hour before the four bodies are carried out. The boy behind the
bushes is shivering, it's so cold. Not until the first rosy streaks of
dawn, the first chorus of birds, will he come out from his hiding-
place, crying. (It didn't happen that way, they will always say. We
rescued you, held you, you weren't alone.) He has done something wrong and must be punished. First with questions. What
happened? What did you see? What do you remember?

I remember. All of it, now. Yes, yes, whispers my Father. The
memory fills me like marbles fill my pockets. It warms, strength-
ens, purifies. The shirt of my pyjama top is stained by the green
of grass. My fingers are covered with the blood of chinaberries. I
paint my face.

I believe in the sacred flame. When my Father asks me to spread fire, I obey quickly and without question. Ours is not to wonder why; we are here to carry out His commands. An aspect of my job is to make them clean with fear. At the funeral the survivors will look as though they have been shaken hard by the shoulder and they will never feel safe again, despite their televisions and Valium. Listen: heat destroys germs, disease. Pure and soft as my Father's touch, ash absolves the sin. Put it on wounds and sores. Set the match and set them free. Let them feel the flame, raise them with smoke above the troubled land, dissolve them in the heavens. Then my work is done and my Father allows me to leave. The shaken town will not notice I am gone; there is never a good-bye.

You would think my life a drifting, empty one. I say it is part of the larger plan. But during the months of cold that lie between one summer of fire and the next, the true purpose is sometimes hard to keep clear and strong inside. I steel myself against the crash of spirits, the plummet of mercury, that always follow a fire. Still, this winter seems longer and harder than any before, and the warm memory of the last Timothy fades too quickly. I wait through the frozen time in a room in the city. Lie low, instructs my Father. Behind closed curtains I turn the scrapbook pages. I study old, yellowed clippings. A thousand black and grey dots draw my face beneath the headlines. FIRE KILLS FOUR, ONE SURVIVOR! There are more recent clippings, the same headlines. A different boy's face stares back at me. Or is it the same thousand dots, the same eyes that have looked through the curtain of flame? FOUL PLAY SUSPECTED! bold type shouts. CAUSE OF BLAZE UNKNOWN! I smile. Their stupidity amuses me, when it doesn't make me sick.

Look: this is not a confession. I have done only right. You will not find the secrets of my method here, nor the keys to my art. Ask my Father, He knows. One day our famous Mounted Police will, despite their criminal incompetence, stumble upon me. They will lock me up tight and I won't resist. Pride will keep me silent, my deeds should speak for themselves. But I know our glorious fifth estate will pounce on my story, and in their usual fashion misconstrue, misinterpret, malign. They will try to lessen the glory of my achievement. So I leave behind these pages, these clippings, this record. My Father wishes it so.

And my souvenirs sustain. During the months between autumn and spring I become enraged by careless accidents. All across this cold land are strewn faulty furnaces, bare wires, live cigarettes in couches. FIRE CLAIMS FIVE! I weep with anger. Easy, easy, admonishes my Father. Such mishaps cloud the beautiful design of my work. And also conceal it.

Huddled beside the radiator, I envision the last Timothy. He walks beneath trees stripped of leaves, without realizing where his footsteps take him. He stands before the black, gaping hole. His new family says: don't go by there any more. They don't belong to him. Don't touch, they say, when in puzzlement he feels his new skin. It doesn't belong to him, it itches. He shivers. He never used to mind the winter, he hardly noticed it before. I could tell him it will get colder each year. Or is it only me? I know that above this earth the air is becoming warmer, smokier with time. Brown and yellow filth rises from a million factories. Grey exhaust trails from countless cars, buses, planes. We are racing anxiously towards the final fire. Our star will soon explode in flame once more, and scatter across the heavens.

But my own ice age seems unending, this season of suffering seems forever. I must stir to keep my blood in motion. I am the one you don't see walking alone down the city streets, head bent to the pavement. Your eyes glide blindly by my ugly clothes, my thin frame, my pale face. You also don't see me hunched over cheap food in plastic places. I shrink from cold, from the surrounding fear. This city is dangerous for me. I would not be effective here. The impact of my touch would not be felt among the random stabbings, rapes, overdoses. My hand would falter, slip. Go steady, He commands. I see young boys, already sick, polluting the corners. So many I cannot save. Soon, soon, promises My Father. I must take care not to be infected. A little longer, He tells me. I try to stay inside, safe. I turn the pages of the scrapbooks and count the small globes of glass. Each one is a prayer.

They are safe inside an old tin can that is dented and painted pale green. The full, heavy weight of it pleases me. Anchors me. I take off the lid and take out the coloured spheres. They warm quickly to my touch. I count them slowly, careful not to lose track even when the number becomes a large, clumsy object. I recount, again and again. There is only one holy number, I must be certain. By the time I have found it, the pieces of glass have grown cold. There are too many, I can't keep them all warm at once. For an instant, I panic. Then I feel His firm hand upon my shoulder. Patiently, I warm the marbles once more, one by one. We must do what we can.

I dream upon the pale flickers of colour caught within the glass. And the trapped bubbles of breath. In the street I keep my hands deep in my pockets (the scars are unsightly, people flinch) and feel the several special marbles hidden there. They stay warm. Like beautiful boys, they whisper when you touch them, soft moans without words. Hey! call the whores who shiver on the corners. I walk quickly from their drowning cries. They seek release.

When they let me out of the hospital, they said I was good as new. New skin on my hands, arms, shoulders. It's yours, they said. Another lie. Not mine, not anyone's. It was shiny and hard, something artificial. It still chafes, still itches like after the hay. Don't scratch.

And they gave me the large green can. Said it was all there was left, but I couldn't remember it from before. A lie. Everything else burned, they told me. The smell of smoke still clung to me, it wouldn't wash off, I saw the new family catch their breath. They carefully did not stare at my scars. He's the one, people nudged each other in the stores. I didn't listen, there was a kind of murmuring in my ears. That was when He found me.

In spring His sun uncovered the schoolyard from beneath the dirty snow. There was a month of playing marbles. Before and after school, at recess and lunch. The others were startled when I joined in the games, bringing twenty of the best marbles from the can each day. I sent them spinning across the field. The quick click when two marbles touched made me catch my breath. I got you! they crowed. The boys crouched down, getting the knees of their pants dirty in the muddy grass. They opened their mouths a little, pushed back their hair and squinted. Taking aim. Their faces were pinched and white from the winter. Mine! they cried when I let them win. I felt them roll my glass pieces between their palms, they made me moan. Then I narrowed my smoky eyes and won back all my marbles. The boys became bored with this game, they abandoned it for baseball.

My Father's voice becomes louder and more insistent with the lengthening days. He believes me too dreamy and nostalgic, and worries I will forget the grand scheme. The temperature rises. I feel heat reach towards me, but as something that has waned over great distance. I stretch like a cat, blink. My head jerks up from the glass worlds at the sound of His curt voice. All right! He snaps. Get to it!

There is nothing to pack but the scrapbooks, the old tin can. I go where I am told and learn from licence plates that this is Beautiful British Columbia. Another small town, they're all the same. One main street and two traffic lights. In summer the place is as complacent as a cat curled upon a warm ledge. I am the ball of fur that will stick in this town's throat and make it gag and choke and gasp for air. Until then, there are barbecues in back yards and picnics at the lake. Children are out of school and men take their three-week holidays. These people are so unsuspecting, I pity them.

My operation is swift, smooth, skilled. The waitress feeds me information while across the room her boss glares with eyes that pinch like little girls. Twelve thousand, work in the smelter mostly, pretty quiet around here lately. Good. Next the local paper, with its badly focused photos of the Kinsmen congratulating themselves at their annual dinner. The high-school basketball team, which will try again next year. Offers of used cars with low mileage for sale real cheap, announcements of auctions rain or shine next week. There it is: basement apartment, furnished, immediately.

The house is on one of the older streets on the east side of town. It has become too large for Gladys since the children have all gone and George passed away five years ago this fall. She tries to clutter it with big overstuffed chesterfields and photographs and doilies, but there is still too much empty space, too many rooms. At night she has lain awake in the big bed, one hand pressed between her legs, listening to the house shift itself. It groans, like all the hungry bellies she spent twenty years filling.

I rent the downstairs. I've met a dozen Gladyses from out here in the west clear across to PEI. I always stay with them. They never charge enough for their space and are eager to believe any story you hand them. Gladys stares openly at my hands, wrestling with revulsion and fascination. I know she wants to touch the skin just once, just quickly. The car went off the road and rolled, my world turned upside down, I softly say. Gladys's lip trembles and she apologizes at too great a length for the basement furniture, which was upstairs until they bought the new set ten years ago. When I start work, Gladys will creep down the stairs to pick carefully through my things. (The suitcase containing my history is locked, the old green can is hidden behind the furnace.) She wants to see if I've burned holes in the carpet or left rings of water on the table. She is impressed by my neatness, cleanliness; this is enough to make her like me. I don't smoke or drink, they're filthy habits. And I'm so quiet.

To further the necessary illusion of settling in, striking roots, I must work some job. It doesn't matter what, as long as it keeps me inside, safe from the big ball of fire in the sky that makes my blood roar, my fingers itch. (Summer has its own dangers for me.) Caution, says my Father. The high unemployment figures reported by the government are one more lie; I can always find work within a week wherever I go in this great land of ours.

This time it is a record store, a small branch of a large chain. Just call me Junior, winks the manager. He's another fool who would keep smiling if you told him his mother and father died last night. I stare at Just Call Me Junior until the two marbles in his face start rolling around like loose things. At once I see the store is badly mismanaged, and I explain to Junior the error of his ways. I make a report of these mistakes, but let Junior know it will not be sent to the head office. For now. He is relieved and grateful and also frightened. I smile because the big boys will soon smell this rat even if I don't toss him in their faces. He glances at my hands, gulps.

June jumps into July. Now I am set in motion, I can do no wrong, and temptation is easy to resist. Stay out of the sun, though its warmth attracts and I am always cold, because such heat is not enough to thaw me completely, it only makes me yearn for a stronger, final fire. Cool it, He advises. After work I stay in the dim basement, it is like being underwater. Submerged from the sight of boys dressed only in shorts, they are everywhere, their bare skin toasted by the sun, but not dark enough, I could make them burn. Relax, my Father chuckles, shaking His head in bemusement. Roll up your sleeves and loosen that tight collar, Gladys suggests. Lord, it's hot enough to make you want a holiday in hell. She is baffled by my formal attire, until she decides I keep completely covered from some kind of extreme respect for her. She purses her mouth and pats her hair.

At Sal-the-Record-Man's I straighten files and invoices, leaving Junior to take long liquid lunches at the Kootenay Arms Hotel. I breathe easier when he's not around, staring at the little girls dressed up like candy. They all come in here, the dollies and the dopers and the dumb dancing bears. Their heads bob to the music that always plays, as though their necks lack bones. They never buy anything, they just walk up and down the aisles, exchanging secret messages with their eyes. Can I help you? They see my hands and leave. I return the records they've pawed back to their proper places. The alphabet is holy. Work quick, work right, the true purpose running in seconds and minutes through the day, leading to the bright hour. The air-conditioner hums and blows cool air in my face. Outside the window Cedar Avenue wilts at one p.m.

The long evenings draw me back. I listen to the whirring of lawnmowers, the rumble of roller skates upon the sidewalks. The old sounds fold around me. I hug myself and rock back and forth. Gladys treads heavily above, like someone walking on my grave. My mother liked to go barefoot in the house, her step was so light I had to strain to hear her walking around the upper floor. Soon Gladys will call down the stairs, ask me to sit on the front porch awhile. The air has cooled and she has made a pitcher of lemonade. Again and again in a dull, droning tone she repeats stories concerning George and the kids; I listen very carefully, but fail to discern any significance in the banal, trivial events she elaborates. The way people speak about their families mystifies me. A dog barking at the end of the street interrupts her. In silence we watch occasional cars pass by. Gladys sniffles, her face looms like a splotchy moon. The tenth car will be a signal for me to commence my evening expedition. You don't want to sit around with an old dame all night, Gladys says half angrily. If I were not here, she would be slouched all evening before her television, staring at the cancerous images, at last to shake herself awake and wonder what she has been watching. Like the others, she cannot see.

Go on, stretch your legs, she waves me away. Now is the night time, the right time, my time. Black cats and I slink and prowl along the fences, our eyes glitter glassily. I turn a corner and fall into my neighbourhood, it always happens that easily. The place would hold no significance for you. Blocks of stucco houses, cracked sidewalks, maple trees. At ten o'clock children are still playing hide-and-seek. A lamp post is Home. The children scatter to hide up in the trees, inside the sheds, behind the chinaberries. One boy stays by the lamp post, holding a hand over his eyes as he counts to one hundred. He runs the numbers together quickly so he will be alone a shorter time. He uncovers his eyes and his face is frightened. He must leave Home to find the others, and they will try to steal back while he is away, and they will close the door against him. His face is familiar to me. He is a boy who lies awake at night, waiting, listening, fearing. With the other hidden bodies on the street I hold my breath. I think I have found my Timothy.

I am careful not to build premature hopes. He is the right age, the right size, but that is not enough. So many of them are spoiled too soon these days, most show signs of early rot before I can reach them. I patiently observe, note, study over two trial weeks. I see the two-storey house, the arrangement of the rooms, the two sisters, the mother and father. The chinaberries by the fence. It all seems fine. The main points are satisfied and I can overlook small details that do not match exactly. This is earth, not heaven, my Father drily points out.

Certain scenes bring me closer. His father is playing catch with the boy in the back yard. They toss the ball back and forth. The mother calls from the house. The father drops his glove and turns inside. The boy remains in the yard. He waits and waits for his father to return. At last he picks up his father's glove and tries it on, but it doesn't fit. And then at night I see him watch his mother put on lipstick. He is sitting on the big bed as she covers her mouth bright red. She leans into the mirror, leans into the reflection of the boy behind her. Are you ready? calls the father from the hallway, jingling keys in his pocket. The mother turns and brushes the boy's cheek with her mouth, leaving a scar he rubs a deeper red as the car pulls from the driveway.

Closer and closer. It is the seventh of August. I have ten days left. This time has the heightened quality of hallucination. The world around me is drawn with unusual clarity, everything is outlined and in very sharp focus. It is as though a layer of clouded glass around me is stripped away, and what appeared blurred by distance has come nearer. Meaning emerges from every action around me. Junior takes blondes to Christmas Lake every day at noon, leaving me to mind the store alone. Gladys places a bag of ice before the fan, there is a sad drip, drip all afternoon. She leaks sweat and swears this must be the driest and hottest summer in fifteen years. The town rations water, and grass on opposite sides of the street is soaked on alternate days. Sprinklers twirl like graceful dancers on the lawns, repeating the same spirals endlessly, perfectly. The forest service bans camp fires in the woods. From the beer parlour young men are enlisted to battle a forest fire raging a hundred miles away. I bob my head to the music in Sal's like other people do. I cannot comprehend what it is about the noise that makes bodies jerk, mouths widen, eyes tear. Really, I am nodding to my Father's instructions. Yes, yes, I repeat. Yes.

One midnight I drop ten marbles in the yard behind the boy's house, where I know he will find them. One for each soul I have saved so far, I feel their spirits with me. This boy will wonder whose treasures these are, where they come from, if they are missed. He will not mention his discovery of my marbles, but add it to his other secrets. With the eyes of a cat I roam around the dark house, and then inside. It is not alarmed against fire or human intruders. (Stupid faith.) I take exquisite pleasure in my caution, my daring, my perfect dancer's poise. This one is for you, I say, placing the eleventh cat's eye beneath his pillow. Upstairs, the man and woman are making noisy love. I dream another child's conception.

As the time draws nearer to the anniversary of my death, my birth, I find my momentum fading. The balance is so delicate, the slightest ounce of error can upset the scale. I don't know what is wrong, I say to my frowning Father. Usually I would be experiencing, these last days, what I suspect lovers feel while reaching towards climax. The pleasure in drawing out as long as possible the moment urgently sought. But I am only going through the motions. Explaining to Junior that my mother has died and I need a day off work to attend the funeral, I travel to the nearest large city to buy my materials. My Father's voice becomes louder, He demands and insists and urges. There is in His voice a tone of anger I have not heard before. It occurs to me that I am disposable, one of a large number of chosen subjects. If I am not willing, there are others who would be honoured to carry out this important work. And perhaps, I consider, I will be dispensed with when no longer of use. I saved you from fire, I can sacrifice you too, I believe I hear Him threaten.

In hope of re-igniting my spark, I study the scrapbooks and measure my accomplishment. It suddenly seems insignificant. Only one fire a year. (He will not allow more, He favours quality over quantity.) For one mad moment I long to take a torch and light a thousand fires at once — quickly, carelessly, desperately — and illuminate this entire earth with one splendid, joyous blaze. Stop! He shouts.

Then I see the photograph of the Timothy from five years ago. My favourite one. He must be fourteen now. I am filled with questions: how tall is he? how often does he study the globes of glass I gave him? how close does he sit to the camp fires they sing around in summer? I long to find him. To return to that town. To pass him a single time on the street. To let him see my loving eyes once more. No, it would be foolish. Look forward! shrieks my Father. They would recall you and recognize you. Strangers are still uncommon, and tragedies few and long remembered there. Stay away!

I feel so tired of the long war. I feel so weary of fighting the large world these ten years. Before me stretch longer and colder years, and as time passes it will become more difficult to warm myself with a single fire every four seasons. I will freeze as my scrapbooks fill too slowly. My glass universe will chip, break, shatter.

I picture a cabin by a lake. The scent of the pines is fresh and sweet. The breeze off the lake is cool. There is a mist. It hangs over the water like smoke, and when it lifts I can see them on the shore. Their limbs are thin brown sticks. Perfect and unscarred. They are daring each other to be the first to plunge into the lake; it is always cold, even in summer. They toss marbles in arcs through the air. The lake opens its throat to swallow with a greedy gulp. Then the boys are diving to find the coloured crystal that dances on the big bed below. The surface of the lake becomes smooth and blank, broken only by the bubbles of their breath. I hold my breath and wait for their heads to burst into the air above. Be careful! I call, too late.

Careful. Something is wrong. Always before, I would need no

sleep in the final week before the flames. There would not be enough moments to hover at the edge of the life I would soon touch. To fill myself completely with it. But now I cannot fight off sleep. Dreams. The kind that are so vivid and real you cannot believe it when at morning they are gone. I don't know what has happened to my Father, He has taken Himself away from me with no farewell, He is disappointed and disgusted. Now someone else listens to the intimate words He once spoke to me. I am forsaken and the pain of His absence is unbearable. I am not used to being alone. Then I hear new voices. Through the darkness I can hear Joan of Arc and the widows by the Ganges and the wise women of Salem. They are calling me. Come out from the cold darkness. Come to the light, it is warm, we will take you back to Him.

I wake shivering. I have slept too long, there is scarcely enough time. I try to hurry, but my cold fingers are clumsy, my blood has frozen into slow, heavy ice. I keep forgetting what to do next, and what after that. I keep thinking that at this moment Junior must be leafing through *Billboard* and nursing his morning hangover. He is not here to steady me with His voice. I stumble past Gladys, who is drinking cold beer and fanning herself with a piece of junk mail on the porch. I glimpse her startled expression at seeing me not at work so late in the day. Each moment of the following hours while I prepare the fire is a sharp sliver of glass; the pane has shattered open and I can crawl through the window, but the jagged edges cut me. I am not sure I have set the fire correctly.

Then I am behind the chinaberries once more. I twirl the marbles in my pockets, the world revolves dizzily. Dew has fallen on the grass, the children have been called home, screen doors have slammed for the last time this evening. The yellow light around the streetlamps is empty. I wait for the neighbourhood to settle into its big bed, turn over on the pillow, and fall asleep with one soft sigh.

For a moment I do not understand. Why are waves of red and orange licking the ground floor already? They should be flooding first the level above, where the man and woman and two girls sleep. Have my hands failed me? I glance down and see them smeared with the juice of chinaberries; it gleams wet and black in the darkness. I feel the boy's chest rising and falling evenly, and know his closed eyes see only a vision of tomorrow, the blue surface of the lake waiting to be broken by his dive.

I am running towards the house. Home. I trip over a sprinkler and go rolling on the lawn; and without looking I know my knees are green, as though I have been kneeling in prayer upon the grass. The marbles have fallen from my pockets, I feel them revolving across the lawn, scattering beyond my sight. Free of their weight, I am all lightness and am lifted to my feet, carried to the house. Bursting through the front door, I can hear one of the girls call above me: mother?

I have forgotten how hot it is. The heat inside is a shock after the cold place I have come from. It is so easy to push through the curtain of flame that flutters in his doorway. It is so easy now that my wings have returned to me, my ancient angel arms.

Timothy is fire. My Father's voice snaps and crackles around me, I ignore it, He has come too late. I am gathering Timothy in my arms, folding him within my wings. Already his eyes are fixed upon the kingdom above the smoke, and I must go with him there. I melt upon him, spill upon him, we are joined. We are soaring together, high above, away. This moment is so warm. This embrace so pure, so warm.

Other Voices
and the Real World III

Deep in the night
Our appetites find us
Release us and bind us
Deep in the night
        — Joni Mitchell, "The Three Great Stimulants"

                    How to Help Ethiopia
A United Nations convoy with food enough to feed 30,000
people for a month was recently destroyed by Eritrean forces.
And the other major insurgency . . . says it will not guarantee
safety of food trucks unless Addis Ababa halts its resettlement
drive.
        — New York *Times* 12-18-87

Raleigh, North Carolina — Attacks by hate groups on racial, religious
        and sexual minorities are up in state. . . . Attacks ranged from
        cross burning to physical violence.
                — *USA TODAY/International Edition* 12-17-87

Metheun, Massachusetts — 2 boys, ages 11, 13, . . . charged with
        attempted murder, assault, kidnap . . . are accused of throwing 4-
        year-old playmate into Spicket River, pelting him with rocks,
        sticks when he tried to climb out. . . . they "didn't like" youngster.
                — *USA Today/International Edition* 12-17-87

hate 1. to dislike intensely or passionately, detest 2. loathe, execrate, despise 3. intense aversion or hostility, abominate, abhor
    — *The Random House College Dictionary*, 1973

love 1. a profoundly tender passionate affection for a person 2. a feeling of warm personal attachment or deep affection as for a parent, child or friend 3. sexual passion or desire or its gratification 4. a strong predilection or liking for anything — tenderness, fondness, warmth, affection
    — *The Random House College Dictionary*, 1973

Night is the cathedral
Where we recognize the sign
We strangers know each other now
As part of the whole design
    — Suzanne Vega, "Gypsy"

Rorschachs IV:
Night Train

Rorschachs IV:
Night Train

The train stops somewhere in the middle of the prairie, sometime in the middle of the night. The young man wipes the blurred window clear and looks out at snow swirling in frenzies of white through the darkness. *It would have been cheaper to fly across this damned country,* he sulks; *as it is, I couldn't afford one of those sleeping-berths, never mind a private compartment.* His back is stiff, his legs cramped, and he has given up on sleep. *Only I would travel all this way by train,* he thinks in disgust. *Only a fool like me would choose a method of transportation so clearly outdated, inefficient and painfully slow.* After all, this is 1985, he reminds himself.

Yet flying is unreal: you step from frozen air into a compartment of controlled, pressurized air and emerge a few hours later into extreme heat, without feeling gradual changes in temperature or seeing slow alterations of landscape. You lack a conception of what joins two such disparate states. You miss the connection.

Richard is making the trip from Vancouver to Toronto overland with a vague notion that if he crosses the surface of the country he will reach some realization of what it's all about, what it means. He has never been east of Calgary before; and while many parts of the globe are familiar to him, this even, empty expanse of white is as exotic as the moon. This land is a mystery to him, one he is told he should understand. It's your country, they always say; yet he knows he has not paid the price of possession with the currency of time and experience and blood.

The landscape outside the window is flat and unmarked by mountains or valleys, buildings or roads. There is no station between which passengers and freight are moving to or from the train. Richard hasn't the faintest idea where he is — somewhere in Saskatchewan still? Or is this Manitoba now? There are no clues outside or inside the train. The carriage is quiet, the lighting dim. Few passengers are riding this part of the train; looking at them, Richard has no notion what kind of people they might be or why they are making this journey with him. Their faces appear inscrutable and withdrawn, their clothing obscure. Farmers? Businesspeople? Vacationers? Richard fears that if he addresses them a torrent of Chinese or Swahili will flood his ears. Some doze fitfully, restlessly shifting limbs in search of sleep; others hold silent vigil with cigarettes glowing red in the dark. Surely they could keep the train moving even in this snow, Richard wonders impatiently. They must have ploughs and all kinds of modern equipment to cope with just this situation. If they can send men to the moon. . . . This is 1985, not 1943, he tells himself again.

The train sits stubbornly, as if it had lost all desire to move forward or had just given up. Richard tries to avoid thinking about what will happen, tomorrow or the next day (or at Christmas, at this rate), when he disembarks at Union Station with one battered trunk, not enough money, and no job or friends or place to live. Another happy trip, he frowns anxiously.

The snow gusts erratically, and it is impossible to discern if it blows more from the west or more from the east. It screens the world beyond the light of the train before darkness can. At times the snow seems to fall in patterns of an old-fashioned dance, like a mazurka or a gavotte. My parents were born somewhere out there, Richard realizes suddenly, as though he had never known this fact before. He watches a photograph develop in his mind: the negative images darken quickly, become clearer and more vivid by the second. He sees a young woman with a closed face clasping a baby tightly to her shoulder, apparently frightened someone will try to take it away. Another photograph, also black-

and-white: a young man, with very clear eyes opened wide, wearing a soldier's uniform, an obviously unfamiliar costume for an unpractised role. Grandparents who never grew old. I'm already older than either of them ever were, Richard thinks. There is something wrong when we have never seen our grandparents and when our own mother and father have never spoken of them. Some necessary link between the past and future is missing, Richard's mind protests. Like the ties between these railway tracks. Something that holds together a means of moving forward.

Somewhere out there it happened. When and why and with what long-lasting effects? Just another story, one acted out upon flat land. Did that make it a smaller event? Or does the blankness of the background emphasize it in greater relief? The window of the stalled train is blurring before the young man's eyes, the photographs are dimming, and outside snow dances like static upon a television screen.

The girl rests the sleeping baby against her breast. She enfolds both baby and herself within the dress and the coat, the shawl and the scarf. Snow sifts with steady silence out in the night, like flour falling into the big yellow bowl when the old lady makes another cake no one will eat: they harden to stone until the girl chisels them into pieces she can feed starving birds. The old man and lady rock in the next room, creaking away time and listening to static fight war news on the radio. They are waiting patiently for their son to return from the troubles across the sea, when he will take this girl and her baby away. She doesn't look at names of the killed, wounded and missing printed in the paper, already knowing he is not coming back. Since the day she mentioned this fact to the old couple, they have politely avoided looking at her whenever possible. City girl, say their eyes in one more silent exchange. You're not going out in this snow? the old man asks as she slips on high boots. You're not taking the baby? wonders the old lady as the girl moves across the room, as stealthily as when she used to slip out to meet a lover. When she opens the door a gust of cold air throws snow inside, and in a flurry she is gone.

A sea of phosphorescent light gleams beneath a dark sky. The girl's heart quickens to battle the cold and it wakens from a stupor of slow sadness. She has not been outside since the storm started three nights before; the old man and lady insisted upon doing the milking and feeding themselves, believing winter was never like this in the city. The air is a sharp blade cutting the inside of the girl's throat until her warm breath can dull it. Only an hour ago the world spent its violence and calmed into a Christmas card; and now flakes fall large and soft and slow from the exhausted sky.

The girl moves forward as quickly as she can, passing the barn where horses and cows snuffle thickly and stamp hooves. She can just see the rise of track three fields away. When the snow rises livestock sometimes stumble over barbed wire strung along the rails; each spring the old man receives a cheque from the railway amounting to half the value of what the trains mow down. The girl hugs the baby more tightly, and feels it part of her like at the beginning.

The 8:19 sounds its whistle in the distance and the girl makes her way swiftly, strong muscles lifting one leg, then the other, a foot and a half out of drifts that have changed the prairie into a strange, slanting landscape. She turns once to see poisoned light from the farmhouse leaking yellow into the night. Her breath puffs around her face and she tastes cigarettes smoked in Regina streets, at Rotary dances. Her face pressed against the rough cloth of his shoulder, her eyes unable to see a thing. Turning round and round in darkness while the music played. Just when she could fall asleep joined to him in the bed, his cap was waving out the window with a hundred others. She turned away before the train pulled out of sight, walking quickly towards the buggy where the old couple waited to take her home with them, her own mother and father having gone west to warmer, easier times. It's your choice, they said when she stayed behind. There's no choice, insisted the baby inside her. We have to pretend to wait for him to return, we owe him that at least. But not much more.

She feels the weight of the baby grow heavier, feels the small warm breath blow through her skin into her heart. Why do you have it sleep with you in bed? the old lady wants to know. You'll crush him when you roll over in your dreams. The whistle blows again, and the girl blinks lashes frozen heavy and hard. The long line of cars arcs around the bend, curving into sight. The night train is moving slowly, like an animal sniffing a subtle scent that is hard to follow.

There is blazing light in every window. Usually the train speeds across the flats, making good time between Winnipeg and Calgary before the crawl across the Rockies. She has seen it flash by a hundred times, the blur of framed faces slipping past too quickly for her eyes to catch. But tonight the train floats in slow motion upon the snow, one foot above the earth, an easy invitation for anyone to climb aboard. She stands beside the fence, close enough to feel the train's hot breath, and sees inside the cars. There is a lady knitting something red and a girl kissing a soldier home on leave and a thin man trying to light a fat cigar. A girl with a blue ribbon in her hair lifts her face from a book and a little boy in a sailor-suit squashes his nose against the window. She sees grandmothers and gamblers, farmers and businessmen, nuns and thieves. The 8:19 is stitching across the white cloth of the country, a multi-coloured thread embroidering a thousand pictures into one large design. During too many long, silent evenings the girl has forced her eyes to stay fixed upon white cloth spread across her lap. She has insisted her restless limbs stay still, commanded her boiling blood to slow into a simmer; and now, finally, she watches herself sitting in the dining-car of the 8:19, poised before a cloth of snowy linen and a silver pot of steaming coffee, sewn into the tapestry of the night train.

There is a call for the last sitting of dinner, and passengers stand and stretch and move carefully down the aisles. The tables fill and faces turn to menus. Few eyes look out at a sky falling into a million pieces upon the ground, and only several sharper ones observe what appears to be one more post of a fence, blunt and shapeless with snow; for reflections cover the windows, mirroring what is inside the train and closing out what is beyond. Only the red eye of the caboose stares back at a world left behind scarcely seen, untouched, forgotten.

Every other time the girl has taken the baby from her coat and held him high in the air to show him the night train speeding by. The baby has cried because of cold so shocking that he will always remember a frozen vision. It will remain in some closed, dark room in his mind until an icy night makes him quickly turn his head to see a brilliant train slide past the corner of his eye, and to gaze into the distance where it has gone. But tonight the baby is invisible beneath a coat now coloured pure white as a wedding gown, as the girl moves down the narrow aisle, as she is carried away by her unsuspecting lover.

Her body has been still although she has travelled a distance down the line, and her feet have grown numb, her blood heavy. As she is taken by the train, pins and needles stab and sew her further into it. She shifts the baby slightly; it still sleeps within her arms. This landscape is unknown: there are hills where no hills were before, and valleys where the earth was flat as the old lady's singing. Abide with me. . . . Her mind sees the old lady wipe steam off the kitchen window and glare out into the night. The old man stares at a puddle of melting snow just inside the door. Then the window blurs again and the old couple are clouded from the girl's vision, lost in the darkness behind.

The train wanders through the new world, and the fence along the tracks drifts by. Her sweat is warm and wet against the girl's skin, and soaks into the cloth of her dress, although this movement requires no enormous effort. *One* two three, rocks the train, and she is gliding in slow motion one foot above the ground, waltzing in three-four time through the snow, twirling round and round with her baby in her arms. The front eyes of the night train peer into the darkness ahead, illuminating it. *One* two three, *one* two three, exalts her heart. She doesn't fall, she sinks into silken arms that hold her tight and never let her go. The sight of all her fellow passengers passes through her mind, like memories of everyone she has ever loved. The train rocks drowsily onward, the lullaby in three-four time lilts her to sleep, the old cradle sways beside the mother's bed.

The baby opens his eyes. He sees darkness. He feels a smooth, slippery surface on one side, a colder and rougher one on the other. He wriggles closer toward the warm, beating blood, presses his ear harder against the throbbing pulse of violins. *One* two three, *one* two three. They sing slower and slower, and more faintly. When the old man finds the body on the tracks, it's still warm against the crying baby. Lucky the 11:05's late again, he says.

The train makes a grumbling sound, then jerks reluctantly forward. Richard starts out of his long gaze at the window. He sees he has been drawing shapes and patterns upon the steam, but cannot decipher them now. They quickly vanish into the blurred expanse of the window.

It's about time, he thinks. We're going to be hours late. The carriage is cold and his feet are numb. I might as well be out in the snow, he complains to himself. If we're going to crawl along forever, at least we could do it in warmth. He remembers all the previous journeys he has made towards uncertain destinations and elusive dreams. All the erratic dashes to New Orleans and San Francisco, Albuquerque and Chicago, and points farther south. They were movements more away from somewhere than towards anyplace else, weren't they? He sighs. The train is slow to pick up speed, and it rocks gently, clicking over the rails. *One* two three, *one* two three.

I'm never coming back, Richard said the day before in rainy Vancouver, looking directly into his mother's eyes. The words were a warning, a promise and an apology. Footsteps and voices echoed in the big cave of the station. Confused, nervous sounds exchanged between the ones leaving and the ones left behind. His mother looked at Richard and pressed her lips together. When her arms wrapped around him, her body felt thin and light as a starved bird's. Then she turned and walked quickly away, before the train pulled from the station.

Richard considers the big, black trunk riding in a baggage-compartment a number of cars before or behind him. It contains nothing practical, he admits. None of the items necessary for starting a new life. Only scrapbooks and photographs and sentimental souvenirs. A yellowed clipping that has been folded and unfolded many times. The accident didn't make the city papers; it was described in seven lines and three typos in the local weekly. Of course my father couldn't see me off at the station, Richard says aloud. Of course something inside him protested at my going back in the direction of that cold night from which he fled.

The night train begins to gather speed. The drug of fast forward motion hits Richard's heart, and now he knows that all these journeys are equally away from and towards, simultaneously forward and back. In the dimness around him Richard's fellow passengers are shaking themselves back to life. Fresh cigarettes are lit, make-up compacts are removed from purses, and a few murmured conversations commence.

Still, Richard wishes a conductor or some uniformed figure

would enter the carriage so he could ask why the train stopped. Was there an accident, a mechanical failure, or was the snow simply too thick? He would like someone with some definite answers to come along. Richard wipes the window once more and looks outside. Snow is still falling, but its descent is steady and unhurried now; it wavers in vertical lines down from the big, black sky. The world has calmed as if it had never rioted. Is this all there is? A black-and-white photograph with no object of interest focused cunningly in the foreground? Is there nothing the eye can seize upon with relief to save it from a vision of light and dark stretching unbroken to the horizon? Richard smiles. The train picks up speed until it seems to fly, and then it is rushing steadily forward through the night, towards the east where soon the sun will rise again.

Similkameen

Similkameen

There isn't all the time in the world. The cold winds are blowing from the east and from the west; and before the bombs begin to fall, I must rush to the bank, the post office, the cleaner's. I will run with the others to catch every subway-train as if it were the last, and we will press together, shrink apart, in the swaying body that hurtles us beneath the ground, through all the dark tunnels. In our arms we clutch packages of things we have bought to make it through this day, and perhaps the next. Yes, I must re-join the throng, after being away so long, and there isn't enough time to sit here, drumming my fingers against the surface of the desk, waiting for the piano-tuner to arrive.

He is late.

I feel him moving through the city, drawing away from the last room where he has done his work and coming closer to this one. My new room. They took away the previous place and it was necessary to find another one quickly, for winter and cold and darkness were coming fast. I was lucky to stumble onto this address: hardwood floor, oak mantel, many panels of dark, old wood. A strong, solid place. I'll take it. The acoustics will be perfect. Sound will strike these hard, wooden surfaces, and return to me clearly and brightly. I will not be surrounded only by drywall and plaster, or the cheaper materials so often used these days, the kind that suck up sound, muffling it like a voice sinking in a swamp. And the piano will fit beautifully in that corner.

What piano?

You no longer have an instrument. Remember? You haven't had one for years. Whatever happened to that old one? And what could have happened to the mother and father, to all the childish possessions...?

Well, things become left behind, lost. Not everything will fit into the suitcase and it's as simple as that. No, there certainly weren't many practical or sentimental objects to unpack and fill this new room. But seven days ago two men rolled a piano off a truck. They wheeled it down the sidewalk, up the stairs and into the space waiting for it. I signed a document, testifying to its safe deliverance. Yet in the cold air outside the strings of the piano's heart shrank, and its travels from one place to another disturbed it, unsettled it. Before I touched the keys I knew how they would sound. Too much cold motion has shrunken my own strings, and I sing flatly, nearly a whole tone too low. Far off-pitch.

The piano-tuner is late. I called a number from the Yellow Pages and a voice told me someone would be sent to help. He would arrive at two o'clock on Wednesday. He is nearly ten years too late. . . .

The instrument has sat almost untouched this past week, as dumb and lifeless as any piece of furniture. Leave it alone until its pitch is corrected and it can sing with its true voice once more. Anyway, I am frightened to touch it. I know my fingers will be clumsy and stiff, there are muscles which have gone unused for too long, they have nearly disappeared. But as soon as I make a bit of money, I will buy a few folios, and again learn to play the old, beautiful music, and to discover new notes as well. As soon as the piano-tuner arrives.

The windows at one corner of my room form three sides of an octagon and look out on the intersection of two streets. Cars pass up and down, back and forth. The ugly sound of engines wounds the ear, like gunfire. A few people hurry by with collars turned up and heads bowed down. They do not flinch at the explosions around them, though sometimes their eyes jerk up and look with puzzlement to both sides. At the corner they pause. A figure dressed in a fluorescent coat, and bundled up against the cold to the point of appearing sexless, steps bravely off the sidewalk, holding a stop-sign up high. The crossing-guard herds the waiting people across the street like cattle, then stays behind as they go on their way.

One man walks slowly, his eyes looking straight before him. A white cane tap, taps the sidewalk, like a divining-rod. His other hand holds a black case resembling a doctor's bag. He is growing old and his body appears shrunken. His hair is short and thin, and looks less white than drained of colour. Maybe to his eyes his drab clothes are vivid, his pale skin glowing. Perhaps he is able to imagine the grey street a shining path of light, stretching forward through the darkness, without end.

He knocks on the door. I let him in. This way, to your right. He sets down cane and case carefully, removes his coat, waits. The piano is right before you, I say.

He reveals no curiosity about me or my room. I am grateful. This is a time when any eyes are spies and my curtains are usually closed. I remember too clearly the gaze that moves steadily up and down my body, measuring what might be taken from it against what that might cost. This man does not ask my name or age or place of birth. The piano-tuner does not remark on the bad weather, the hard times. He wants to know what kind of piano this is, where I got it, how much I am paying. Striking the keys with disgust, he insists upon their discord, harps on their wrongness. This piano is nearly a whole tone flat, you shouldn't rent a piano like this, it will have to be tuned twice, he says.

He takes out his tools, takes the lid off the piano. No fumbling. Across the room I sit and watch. When one sense is absent or destroyed, others become more alert, alive, to compensate. In the spreading darkness we must sharpen our ears to hear the sound of others who also stumble without light. Their tuneless cries. The piano-tuner tightens the strings with his tools. He plays thirds and fifths and eighths. Listening, adjusting. He works quickly, as if in a hurry. The hammers hit the pads and there is the sound of nails being driven through one surface, into another. Something is being held together, constructed.

Six feet away I feel the sense of peace, or release, that can flood you when after so long your pitch is made right again, and no one asks you why it ever went wrong.

The cabin was on the shore, down the curve of the bay from the Reserve. It was a windy place. In winter waves splattered against the front window of my room, which was a lean-to built onto the cabin like an afterthought. In the unheated room I bundled up in sweaters and struggled with exercises until my fingers burned with warmth. Then I raised music into the air, filling the room with notes that trembled in the light like motes of dust before they fell back to the ground. I could play as long as I liked without disturbing the others inside the cabin proper, and more often I practised upon the instrument rather than attend high school in the next town, until my absence was almost as marked as that of the kids from the Reserve, who worked out in the boats all salmon season. After midnight I still bent over the keys, and in their room at the cabin's centre my father and his new wife heard the music faintly, as sound from another country, a language not understood. Much later at night the cat walked along the keyboard, playing strange songs that woke me and made me listen to the strong, persistent wind that howled in from the sea.

Quickly carved from the forest by people in haste to take the fish and timber and minerals from that place, the nearby town appeared raw and unplanned. It was small, and contained no music teachers; so every second week I had to be taken two hundred miles down the long island for lessons. My father drove grimly, determinedly. Even after I was licensed to drive, he wouldn't give up the wheel to rest for fifty miles. My father didn't understand music and often said so, but he came from people who silently assumed every burden that came their way, no matter how heavy or mysterious its weight. In my father there was pride in facing squarely what had to be done and stubbornness in doing it.

We set out early on Saturdays, first making good time on paved road. The north end of the island was scarcely settled, and the empty highway led mile after mile through woods, sometimes passing shocking squares where the trees had been brutally taken, and all the roots were torn. Then the paved road abruptly ended. The highway wasn't completed, and for forty miles there was only logging road — twisting and turning, dusty in summer, potholed or washed away in winter. The rain forest was dark and thick on either side, and the silence of the north pressed against the car and filled it. These trees had been growing for years, unwitnessed by any eyes and indifferent to human approval; these hills had not the slightest intention of shifting themselves to make passage through them easier. My father and I rode in obstinate silence, each believing the other's concerns less important than his own. He didn't wish to listen to me speak about music; I had no desire to hear him describe his latest battle with the neighbours, the branch of government he worked for, or his first wife, my mother; and we refused to admit we had any subjects in common. We stonily met huge logging-trucks that swerved around the corners, their enormous loads balanced precariously on top, red ribbons of danger trailing merrily behind. The car was forced off the road time and again.

Its wheels seemed to sigh in relief when they touched pavement again, and then the car glided smoothly and silently south. The island became more settled and cleared, and the traffic grew heavier. My father and I looked at the signs of civilization around us as if we had been away a very long time, and in spite of ourselves we spoke about recent changes and things that had stayed the same. When we reached the music teacher, I had a marathon lesson, bringing forth music like golden apples carried long and far, and learning new ways to polish them more brightly. Meanwhile my father shopped for all kinds of things which could not be bought in the small northern stores.

We turned back in the loaded car. My father was anxious to get in as many miles as he could before dark. It was difficult for him to drive at night, even without rain or snow. Lights of another car would seem to weave as they approached, and he wasn't sure if the other driver or he had trouble keeping a straight course. The centre line blurred. The road seemed to become dangerously narrow, the earth on either side to fall steeply in a vast drop down. The pain started in my father's eyes, travelled through his neck and shoulders, then rolled into his stomach in wild waves. He pulled the car sharply onto the shoulder of the road, and I looked away as he leaned out the door to vomit. Without comment, he drove on. His eyes seemed to refuse to work any longer, and each trip down and up the island was more difficult than the last. He wouldn't go to the damned doctor to find out what was wrong, the name for it, if it could be fixed. The trouble would grow worse if that's what its mind was set on. He chewed aspirin and codeine, and gripped the wheel tighter.

For part of the trip back, I sat in the front beside my father, believing my eyes and will could assist in keeping the car on the road, even if this help were rejected. We each had secret, silent thoughts; but there were times when it almost seemed they joined together of their own accord and crossed the three feet of distance between us, to lie there like a huge, heavy rock that separated us further. I turned my head and looked at the woods rushing by. They were darker than the sky, and from their deep, private heart deer would sometimes venture, hesitating in the brush along the road. For a split second their eyes would catch the headlights of the car and glint madly. There was no way of knowing if they would leap toward or away from the light. In the darkened car I turned over the things the music teacher had told me, feeling them with my hands, as though I were reaching into a black cave and by touch discovering what was hidden there. The car suddenly swerved; I started. My father swore, rubbed his eyes with one hand, then hunched more closely over the wheel. The radio signal of the southern station had long since faded into static, and now only the CB carried sound, voices of men away on the boats or in the woods, calling home.

Later, I stretched out on the back seat, the humming of the engine beneath my ear. My father really preferred it when I wasn't in the front to witness the near accidents, the small mistakes. The chances that had taken us this far. He didn't speak about the past, in the way that people who have lived long and thoroughly through a difficult time do not talk about it when it ends, as though the better present were a fragile thing that words could easily erase. The time before my birth was mostly a blackness to me, and my father may have intended this blankness as a great gift; for if I did not have a sense of the limited circumstances from which I had come, then I might not conceive boundaries around where I could go. He can no longer see a great distance in the dark, I thought again, feeling the slight hesitations, the subtle uncertainties in the car's forward movement.

My father forced his mind to turn from the dull ache that spread behind his eyes and concentrated on the new, clean scent of the car's interior. This was the first new car he had driven. It was issued to him by the government for his travels around the north of the island to inspect the small schools. He saw the children of chokermen, with their wary eyes that had viewed one logging camp after another, that mistrusted the transient present. His own parents had settled in an interior town for no clear reason except that perhaps they had travelled as far west as their energy or imagination allowed. He had studied, received scholarships, and become the bright but poor local boy who went to university at the coast. This quite recent move to the north of the island had been the latest in a long series of small steps forward in position and salary, but it was clear that there would be no further steps, except possibly in a sideways direction. For years he had been stubborn, difficult, prickly, and now in bitter moments he accused the present government, which he opposed too openly, of sticking him in the north to rot.

The body of the car vibrated tensely, seeming to gather momentum and speed, to hurtle itself forward without regard for those it carried. My father drove silently. He didn't hum or sing to himself. The family joked that he had a tin ear. I inherited a feeling for music from my mother, they said. Sometimes she would call from the city. I listened to distance humming across the wire. I pictured my mother wandering the rooms of her apartment, the receiver cradled against her ear, the long cord trailing behind, the fourth glass of wine spilling on the carpet. Is he still taking you for the lessons? she asked at last. I had my father's ear, really, no sense of pitch at all. Music teachers wondered that I played the way I did. I wasn't yet able to explain that to me sound was shape and line and colour, and could be drawn as surely as any image with chalk or paint.

The canvas air stretched all around, taut and empty and waiting. The car quivered through the darkness, its bright lights piercing only a short distance ahead. My father calculated the number of miles to go before home and let the weight of his foot fall more heavily on the gas. I closed my eyes and listened to the turning wheels. They revolved from the past to the future, leaving the present behind too swiftly, illuminated too briefly. I felt pressing upon me, like a heavy blanket of cold earth, the knowledge that a note can travel only so far. It vibrates through the air. An arrow. People turn their heads to watch it pass. Then it loses force, thins, dies. The car rushed through the night, leaving behind an immense silence, and then only falling branches disturbed the dark woods at the north end of the island.

The notes pierced several thousand miles of air to reach me in places where I did not understand the language. His sight is failing him, they said. He would like to see you again while he still can. Like his sisters, my father suffered pain that doctors could not explain or relieve. I had come to believe the family unlucky, and hoped to move beyond reach of the mournful song in their blood. Behind me I felt a long line of people who accepted as their lot a life of little joy spent in a cold, grey climate. With a new name and a new colour of hair and skin, I carried tokens of great luck from one place of colour and warmth to another. I left behind letters that said: the doctors are trying a new treatment, but it doesn't seem to do much good. You know he won't write to you himself, you must remember how stubborn he can be. Like father, like son.

All around me voices murmured foreign phrases that echoed inside my tin ear. I could not hear clearly enough to comprehend. He's learning to get around in spite of it, of course he won't admit it poses any problem at all, they wrote. I closed my eyes and listened to the whispering sea, the music sighing from the depths, and blocked out the sound of distant voices that said: it's a shame you gave up the music, all the miles your father drove you. I didn't give up a single thing, I insisted to myself, playing the keyboard of the typewriter, shaping lines and phrases that curved from diminuendo to crescendo, then back again. I don't care to understand your language and I refuse to translate, I said in my father's wilful way. And I don't know why the shells I gather from this Mediterranean shore insist upon singing such old and faraway refrains.

When we pulled up before the cabin on the bay, I would carry inside my music books and the purchases from the south. My father stayed in the stilled car; its engine would remain hot for a long time. Maybe he was contemplating the sun porch he was going to build on the east side of the cabin. It will run out to here, he would say, gesturing largely with his arms. Though not a big man, my father paced off feet and yards with very heavy steps, like a giant who could shake the earth. He never built the sun deck or the greenhouse or the swimming-pool, but these things were definitely planned in exact, complete detail. He would not consider them unrealized. He could see the blue water in the pool, the lush growth in the greenhouse, the yellow sun on the deck; and anyone who could not even glimpse these sights suffered an unfortunate lack of vision.

I went down to the beach. There were three dots of islands some distance from shore, with beaches of white shells. The shells were broken and polished and smoothed by the rough waves, and across the dark water they gleamed in slanting moonlight. No one but I troubled to go to the islands any more, as far as I knew, but once the Nimkish had brought their dead there. They placed the bodies on platforms high in the trees, along with treasured and lucky things.

Recently, I had discovered beneath the back porch an old kayak, left behind by the people who had lived in the cabin before us. Its joints were loosening, its shell cracking, and it took on quantities of water which formed a puddle I had to sit in while paddling out to the islands. Increasingly, I would leave the piano to go skimming across the bay, separating myself from the land and everything on it. Sometimes a wind would rise from the north, and I would have to keep the nose of the kayak pointed into the waves that also rose, to avoid being swamped. I couldn't paddle straight to the islands, but had to tack back and forth, and so reach them indirectly. When the bottom of the boat scraped upon the shore of shells, I would pull it high out of the water, then hesitate at the edge of the wild, tangled growth that loomed forbiddingly beyond the beach. Once feet had made trails into the centres of these islands, but that was long ago; now they were dark, mysterious graveyards of a past so distant it seemed a world that could be discovered, explored and named for the first time. I would turn my eyes back to the land I had left, to the cabins along the bay that appeared so small and insignificant from this distance. Often, when wind turned into storm, I was forced to wait all day on the islands, before the wide water calmed and I dared cross back to the larger land.

Now I stood poised on the dark home shore, as exhausted as if I had walked the great distance down and up the long island. Behind me were the cabin lights. My father's second wife was standing in the open door, letting in the cold. Mitch, she called. He was still sitting in the car. She saw his face behind the glass windshield like a moon beneath water. His hands were pressed tightly between the warm seat and his thighs, to keep them from shaking. My father had taken me as far as he could, and already I was planning to make my own journey, to go further alone. It would be next month or next summer or any time soon. Closing the lid of the piano, I would build parks for the town during daytime and wash dishes in a restaurant at night. With red and blistered and callused hands I would count my money, and when there was enough I would mention to my father that an airplane with me on it was leaving the next day. I never thanked him for the miles he had taken me, and for a while it seemed necessary even to abandon that distance, to lift my hands from the keyboard believing it was for good and to start alone on a separate journey.

His eyes have grown dim now, he cannot see where I have gone. He is living on a farm at the edge of another small town, this one inland and by chance near to the place where he grew up. The towns seem to grow smaller and smaller, or maybe it is the same town shrinking from sight. He has retired early, because he refused to adapt his work to his failed vision. He says he is glad to be out from that pool of sharks and brags about the fat pension he receives. For years he has yearned for a climate and place and time to grow things, the way his mother used to do. She could make anything rise from the ground, and as a boy during the hard times long ago my father went from house to house around the town, knocking on doors and selling her vegetables. Now he digs his hands into the dirt. It is dark and dank. He feels for the bulbs, presses them into the earth, sets them in the place where they will grow.

A wind travels through my father's valley, whistling among the apple trees. The name of the valley is an Indian word which means the meeting of the winds. Similkameen. I pass the corner of the house. It looks old and poor, with flaking paint and grimy windows. No matter how much money my father has, he will never live in a beautiful home; he could not see himself in such a place, and resists the vision. I know the inside of his house must be cluttered, filthy. Three wives and four children have left him, and now he lives alone. There is no one for him to clean for, no one to clean for him, and he cannot see the mess anyway. He collects old newspapers and pieces of string, tin cans and milk cartons. Some day all will have their use, he firmly believes. He plans to build a time machine with them.

The ground outside the house is strewn with bits of broken machinery and useless tools. The wind is stinging my eyes, they blur. I trip over a length of pipe hidden in the long grass. I rub my throbbing shin and swear. How can he manage to walk here? How does he make his stubborn way, still?

The wind rises, crescendos, as if it would lift everything from the earth. As if all things will be carried in the air, to be set back down in the place where they belong. The wind pushes me forward and blows me back. When I used to stand on the shore, after the trips down and up the island with my father, I felt myself placed on the point where the air from the land met the air from the sea. The opposing scents of salt and pine collided, but both were dark and cold. I breathed deeply. In my lungs the warring winds mixed together, and were exhaled as one.

The wind is loud. My father cannot hear me coming closer. I could now shout to him and ask him why he has ended up in such a God-forsaken place, this valley enclosed by a ring of steep hills infested with rattlesnakes. My father would quickly answer that the area is actually a semi-arid desert, and it gives him hope in the future of mankind to see potential wasteland converted by the modern miracle of irrigation into acres of useful, beautiful orchard. Or he would throw his arms expansively toward the twigs stuck in desolate rows in the large field before his house; they look as if they would long ago have snapped in this eternal wind, but in fact, I see, they are growing in a sturdy, slanted way, leaning stubbornly against the wind. Were there such perfect peach trees in Paradise? my father would demand. Or to my question he would reply simply: Similkameen.

I stand at the edge of my father's garden. It is enormous and chaotic and crowded. The strawberries are running into the cucumbers, which threaten to invade the neighbouring potato plants. The tall corn is waving. I wipe my eyes. A map of lines is drawn around them from squinting too long at the southern sun. They are like my father's. I have grown exactly his height, though he would claim a quarter-inch on me. His body is heavier than before, his shoulders hunched as he gazes intently into the earth. What does he see? I can see my father bowed upon ground, his tools and seeds scattered around him. I can see him clearly, but he cannot see me.

He is done so quickly. The piano-tuner has finished his work already and he is in a hurry to leave. Not yet, I want to say. Stay a little longer. Play something for me. Anything.

The piano-tuner puts the lid back on the piano and replaces his tools in the black case. He puts on his coat and picks up his cane. Here are three twenties, I say, placing the bills in his hand and wondering if he has a secret way of feeling their denomination. Or does he simply trust?

A minute later he passes before my window, returning in the direction from which he came. Night is pouncing like a black cat upon the city. The day of work is done and the traffic is heavier in the street. People are hurrying home, anxious to get back. Is the piano-tuner returning to his rooms? I picture objects arranged carefully and neatly, so everything can be reached for quickly and without fumbling. So nothing is lost. Or does another person wait with an instrument that needs to be set right?

I close the curtains and turn on the lamps. The wood in my room glows richly, the piano shines in golden light. The precious ivory. I have travelled south to learn new ways to polish the golden apples more brightly, and now in the north I can begin to make them shine. The instrument is ready. It is in tune, correctly pitched again. The notes already exist, they require merely my touch to lift them into the air, to send them soaring and scattering like seeds.

Not yet.

Outside the cars speed north and south. The distant sound of weapons draws nearer. Overhead are blinking lights of airplanes and satellites and space stations. I think of my father and all our fathers, and how they have taken us as far as they can, and what strain has been placed upon their vision by peering forward into the darkness. We must light the lamps and there is not much time. The piano-tuner hurries down the street, rushing from one room to another, setting our instruments in order. Winds blow back and forth across the planet, meeting, colliding, mixing. From north and south, east and west. From the past to the future and back again. Where have we come from and where are we going? The question looms large and black in the night beyond. The answer lies inside. Similkameen. In my room I touch the keys, turn the locks, open doors long closed to me. All across the city mysterious music is rising. It is borne rippling on the wind to the children who dance on the new moon.

The End of
Orphans

The End of Orphans

They told us our parents were dead, but Frances and I knew it wasn't true. "It's a lie," she informed me upon my arrival at the Home when I was six, one year younger than her. She had already been there three years, and swore she didn't care if she ever left or not. "All this," she declared, waving her long hands in the air, "is immaterial to me."

Frances? She was very thin and pale, and her hair was long and thin and light brown. The first thing she told me was that her mother was named Greta Garbo and her father a man called Montgomery Clift. They were busy making movies; that's why they had to leave Frances in the Home with Fat Annie and two dozen orphan brats. "They'll come and get me when they're ready," said Frances coolly, chewing the ends of her hair with an absorbed expression. She showed me pictures of her parents, both so young and beautiful. "Of course, I take more after him than her," Frances pointed out, and I looked between her face and Montgomery Clift's until I saw what she meant. Frances had a large scrapbook full of photographs she'd cut from the old movie magazines Fat Annie collected, and during Free Times she could tell long stories about every single one. "This," said Frances, "was taken during the time I had measles. That's why my mother looks so sad. She would sit up all night beside my bed, singing lullabys until I was better. She knew a million songs, and every one was different."

You want to know about Fat Annie. Well, she was the Matron and she was in love with Tyrone Power. Everyone knew. The only reason she and Tyrone Power weren't married was because they had never met. "If he had seen me just once on one of those wide streets in Hollywood," Fat Annie would begin, causing Frances to roll her eyes and puff out her cheeks so her face was soft and sad as Fat Annie's. Who would go on about how she and Tyrone Power would have lived in an extremely large mansion in Beverly Hills with many servants who did all the work when she and Tyrone Power threw grand parties for a thousand stars, after which Tyrone Power would beg her to act with him in his movies. Every one of their kissing scenes would be real.

When Frances asked who my parents were, at first I couldn't answer. I had been living with someone named Sally, who said she was my aunt, along with different men who liked her for a while. She called them all Daddy. I couldn't remember my mother and father until I looked in Fat Annie's magazines. Then it was easy to recognize them at once, but don't ask how: I just knew. Their names were Marilyn and James, you've heard of them. "Were they nice?" asked Frances. Yes, I said. But at the beginning I couldn't recall much about them, however hard I tried.

The main thing about Frances and me was that we were always together, except at night when she slept in the Girls and I in the Boys. We liked best to discuss how it had been before, in a corner away from the orphans. They were quiet and mournful, not knowing who they were or where they had come from, and frightened of Frances who could pinch very hard. She could also steal. For instance, a Junior League Lady would come by to pour pity on us, and the minute she set down her white gloves they were gone for good. Likewise, Fat Annie's lipsticks and Day Workers' nickels and dimes. Our parents had millions of dollars and sent some of them to the Home for us, but we were robbed. "We have to take what we need," Frances whispered fiercely, bending her sharp, white face near to mine.

The orphans came and went like identical afternoons, while Frances and I stayed. Now and then Fat Annie would waddle into either dormitory, Boys or Girls, and announce that a Prospective

Parent was waiting in Reception. "I'm giving you a chance for a Real Home!" she would cry, swooping down upon a chosen child. "Your own pink or blue bedroom, a dog named Spot, a father who reads the newspaper after work, wearing the slippers you bring him, and a mother who tra-la-las in an apron in the kitchen, preparing nutritional, economical casseroles for suppers at the dot of six."

With compassion Frances and I watched Betty or Bobby being led off by Fat Annie, who hissed: "Smile, look endearing, bat your eyelashes. Think! A Real Home!"

An hour later the kid would return from the Interview with a weak smile or the same lost face. Sometimes they went away and we never saw them again. We forgot them, as if they had never been.

Fat Annie couldn't understand why Frances and I were never chosen for a Real Home. She became blue because we drooled and stuttered and crossed our eyes when Prospective Parents looked us over with narrow, measuring eyes, like we were a pound of steak on special at the supermarket that week.

Frances and I hated dogs named Spot and smelly slippers of faded fathers and mousy mothers who sang in thin, flat voices. We had spent our first years dining on caviar at the Ritz and champagne was what we drank from our baby bottles, and there were only movie-queen mothers in our earliest memories.

"I'll tell you what!" Fat Annie would exclaim, wagging her head like one of those grotesque dogs fake fathers put in the back windows of shapeless station-wagons. "I'll tell you what! I make this place too homey for you Poor Dears. Other matrons slap and starve their charges, so naturally the waifs will do anything under God's sun to escape into a Real Home. I'm too sympathetic, knowing what it's like to be a Homeless Child."

Fat Annie had been an orphan brat herself once upon a time. "It's easy as pie to know why *she* never found a Real Home," said Frances. "Just look at her, or close your eyes and listen to that voice."

In evening, when the Day Workers went home and left Fat Annie alone with us, she was always tender and sad. While we pretended to sip lumpy hot chocolate, she would hover heavily over us, feeding us visions of a Real Home. Speaking of suburbs and station-wagons Fat Annie was passionate, and mention of

Mothers' or Fathers' Day caused tears to turn the thick powder on her face into a kind of glue that would stick a child to any unrelated stranger who came along and asked for one.

I don't know. Tyrone Power was still alive because every evening Fat Annie put lots of colour on her face, swathed herself in pink or purple, and sipped a drink while waiting for him. I waited too. Any minute the doorbell would ring and Marilyn Monroe and James Dean would burst in, asking me if I was ready to leave with them. And it was immaterial to Frances and I that we waited dressed in the same clothes as the other kids, which Fat Annie called Perfectly Decent. Boys had blue pants and white shirts. Girls wore dresses made from unpatterned material coloured halfway between grey and brown. You see, we were in disguise, safe from Nosy Parkers who might otherwise recognize us as the children of our true parents. Who might wonder how we had ended up in this Institution, so far from Hollywood, our Real Home.

That's how it was until I was eleven and Frances was twelve. As time went by, Fat Annie gave us fewer chances for a Real Home. We had missed too many Excellent Opportunities, she said. To tell the truth, Frances and I were relieved. The more we spoke about our parents, the nearer they came to us; that's when I discovered that words, like these ones, can make anything more real, almost true. And we didn't give a single damn about birthdays with broken toys any fool could tell came straight from Sally Ann. We pitied children who had parents that grew old and ugly and feeble, we with daddies forever handsome and mothers all the world yearned to kiss. "Foundling!" Frances would say to an orphan when she wanted someone else, not her, to cry. The world was far away and we didn't have many chances to go into it; even now, it's a place that puzzles me. Inside the Home we wove our famous histories upon the stinging scent of antiseptic and ammonia, gilding the Serviceable Furnishings with glitter and gold, always hovering an indefinite time in the past, when things were different. People looked at us curiously and called us quaint. "Don't listen to their lies," warned Frances, who was turning thinner as she grew older. "They aren't dead."

At night we took turns being the Little Baby who went into Fat Annie's big bed, where she would dress us like dolls and arrange our limbs to suit the endless similar stories her hot breath muttered. We were her little babies, we drank mama's milk, baby likes that, don't he? If I were in the bed, Frances would be free to press her face close to the television and watch her mother or father act out scenes in black-and-white, or brilliant Technicolor. And she would do the same for me. I remember this scene, I would think, I was sitting right there, just behind the piano my mother is playing, that's why you can't see me. We saw our parents still alive, always dazzling, forever young. They looked at us and spoke to us, and their smiles and gestures and words were very familiar, like anything inside your heart.

Until one day Frances went away. "They must be crazy!" she told me after her Interview. "They must be searching for the worst child ever. My parents would have been ashamed to see how I acted towards those strangers." Fat Annie was sadly triumphant as she packed for Frances. "What's this?" she asked, holding up her old map, missing all winter, that showed where all the stars lived in Hollywood. Then her face quivered, and she closed the suitcase that held Frances's few stolen things. Frances and I promised each other that we would meet on the corner of Hollywood and Vine in exactly five years' time. Then they dragged Frances off, kicking and screaming all the way.

After that it wasn't so good in the Home. There was no one to talk to about my mother and father, only poor orphans who waited patiently for anyone at all to come along and claim them like a piece of lost luggage. "You've still got me," said Fat Annie, but there was no Frances to laugh with over what happened in the big bed. How Fat Annie liked different things now, how she would whisper the name Tyrone while she did them to me. And there was less chance to see the TV screen, to touch it and feel my parents' skin, glowing with heat.

Frances sent me three postcards, addressed c/o James Dean Junior. *SOS! They make me call them Mom and Dad! Help! I have to mention them in my prayers! Save me! They like me to kiss them good night!*

Although I wrote back to Frances, I never heard from her again. I wondered if her new parents had taken her somewhere else or if they had changed her name. Maybe she had forgotten Greta Garbo and Montgomery Clift and stared suspiciously at their pictures, like she would at any strangers. It could be she believed them dead and gone, so she would just settle for

second-best parents in their place. Later, I got to thinking how
Frances would often look into the mirror with frightened eyes
and touch her sharp face with doubtful fingers, her last months
in the Home. Like she was turning anxious about who she really
was. I couldn't blame her if she cried crocodile tears during her
Interview, instead of acting mean. Did she sign her name Susan
Smith now, without thinking twice? Perhaps she pauses in the
middle of a minor scale, when a certain note makes her remember a voice from long ago. What's wrong? asks the music teacher
by her side. Finish the scale, Susan. And then she watches her
fingers crawl up and down the keys, like they belong to someone
else's hands.

See, I got very weary too, waiting for my mother and father to
finish making movies. They might at least come to visit for one
hour once a year, I thought. If they really loved me. I became
quieter and people looked at me funny. I'd try to remember,
nights in my bed at the end of the row of twelve, how it had felt
when my daddy's arms wrapped tight around me as we rode
together on his big motorcycle, going so fast. And the sound of
Marilyn's giggle when she blew champagne bubbles into the air to
make me laugh. Baby, don't call me mother, she would say. It
sounds so *old*. Then her voice grew fainter, until all I could hear
was the kid in the next bed whimpering in his sleep. I put the pillow over my head and held my breath until morning, when
Mother Marilyn would come for me.

But she didn't, and neither did James Dean. I gazed at pictures
of their smiling faces. I felt afraid I'd grow old and change so
much they wouldn't recognize me when they finally arrived. They
wouldn't see how my eyes were just like theirs, and how if you put
his smile on top of hers you would have a picture of my mouth;
when I remembered those days when they took me to the Santa
Monica Pier and we went on all the rides, except Marilyn was
always frightened of the roller-coaster and stayed on the ground
combing her yellow hair while Daddy Dean and I rode round and
round, screaming all the way to God.

Wake up! said the teacher who came five days a week to the
Home. I saw his lips move but couldn't hear his voice. I was listening to my daddy drawl and my mother whisper, somewhere
inside my hopeful heart.

One day some men came to see me in the orphanage, but they

weren't there to maybe take me to a Real Home. They wanted to hear how Marilyn Monroe used to rock me in a cradle while singing Frank Sinatra songs and how James Dean took me to the circus every afternoon. After the men left, Fat Annie was quiet and looked at me often when she thought I didn't see. They didn't ask me about Tyrone, I told her, staring at her big bed. She looked relieved and started speaking quickly. She said I had to go, but not into a Real Home. I was too old for the orphanage and they were putting me in another place, except mothers and fathers didn't come searching for children there. On the last night Fat Annie cried that I was her First Failure, but she would always be my mother. My eyes looked away from her while I packed the scrapbooks and the teddy bear that still had Marilyn's perfume on it, smelling sweet.

I don't like discussing the new place, it's none of your business why. Bad things happened there. In the night the others would catch me and it hurt. They were mean because they had parents who didn't want them; they were a different kind of orphan than the kids in the Home. I kept trying to remember how Daddy's blue eyes would look down on me when he believed I was sleeping and how Marilyn would always say it was going to be OK whenever things went wrong. During those bad times I could picture my parents best. After the big boys left me alone, I'd hear them crying for me, Marilyn and James. They wished they could help me, but they couldn't. They couldn't. And then the Warden came along and told me to stop that blubbering.

Day-times they made us sit in rows while they told us things we were supposed to remember. There were lines and shapes on a blackboard they wanted us to see and understand. The teachers liked me because I was quiet and stared straight ahead. They couldn't guess that what I saw was Marilyn Monroe and James Dean in the sunshine of a land called California, ambling along a big, wide street that led all the way to the Pacific Ocean. They were holding hands, they were whispering words to each other that only they could hear. Sunglasses were on their faces so no one could know who they really were or see how their sad eyes were always searching for me.

By now I knew that they couldn't find me. Or they would never have left me here, where at night the old pipes gurgled and wheezed, and boys smoking pot coughed. The stinking smell curled around my head, the boys' low voices rumbled in the room, and more distant voices called me home. On every windy night they called and called, and I listened hard as I could so as not to think about some sudden bad thing springing at me in the dark. Creeping to the window, I twisted my neck to see the sky above the wall beyond. There were bright stars up there, shining. I could see them.

I shouldn't say how I escaped in case someone wrong reads this and tries to take me back. But one night their voices told me to leave. So I did. I came here to this city, though it's not in California and no wide street stretches clear to Santa Monica. Only, it seems to me, any place you run to can be called California because that's what the word means. And they're here, my mother and father. From the first day I saw signs of their presence everywhere.

I have my room to stay inside, my locked door to wait behind. It isn't near like how Fat Annie described a Real Home, but their pictures are on the walls. They watch over me. When I bring the funny men back, they see the things that happen on the bed; and remembering Fat Annie we smile, the three of us, in a way no one else can notice. They also see the needle enter my arm, bringing me nearer to them. And, you know, their expressions never change no matter what happens in this room, but remain the same, like mine. They watch over me with eyes I can't describe, but I bet you can't tell me how your own mama's and daddy's eyes look either. You only have a kind of feeling.

Call me Rickie if you want. It don't matter, I won't tell you my real name. You can see me wandering in arcades, where machines flash and ring and cry in the dimness. I don't understand the games, I only like the patterns of light and sound and how everyone is crowded together like they all belong. When it's dark you can find me waiting on the corner, spelling the word patience with my body. My eyes look at the sky, except they've put big buildings in the way so it's hard to see. There are some stars up there I always notice; if you look carefully you can make out a tightrope stretched between them. I am balancing between my mother's and father's bright eyes, always moving back and forth between them, with no net below. Their shining gaze keeps me steady, I never fall. The most important thing, they tell me, is not to look down.

I look up to the lighted windows of the towers that rise high above the city, up to the big clean rooms where the funny men sometimes take me. There I feel closer to the stars. Everything looks like it costs a lot of money, they like to tell you how much they paid for this and that. It's easy to know they are lonely, it's hard not to wonder where their parents are. I stare at the large prints on the walls. My mother and father are trapped behind glass and inside frames, waiting to be freed. If I were Frances, I would steal them away once the funny men fell asleep. But I was taught that we must all wait to be released. I see Fat Annie patiently sipping her drink at night, still expecting Tyrone Power to stride through the door. I see you reading this, then moving from the circle of lamp light, crossing the dark room to the window, looking out. I look between the prints on the walls and the stars beyond the window, puzzled. What is it? ask the lonely men, coming close with their empty hands. I know them, I say, those stars. What else do you know? the men wonder, their voices turned thick, their fingers fumbling. Taking what they need.

Look, I'm trying to tell you what I've learned. How the lonely men make me think that there are all kinds of orphans in this world. Old people and married people and people who have taken any of a hundred different paths that lead them farther from the one warm touch they can't forget. I put on the sunglasses that hide my eyes and walk through these streets, watching. I see your fast steps and your quick glances away from anyone who looks familiar: you don't look through windows into lighted rooms, you hurry by my corner, you don't see me.

In the dark places where the pounding music never stops, there are only black shapes drifting towards and away from one another. Or maybe I sit in similar darkness at the movies. One of those places where they show old pictures from the past. Way up front I watch, right inside the bright colours and the music. The stars say over and over what I know by heart. I hear their words before they speak them, I see them watching me there in the darkness with you, with the others. All of us crowded together like one big family who have forgotten each other's names. The throng of related strangers gazes at my mother and father; everyone wishes to belong to shining stars that appear in every night of clear sky, and do not go away, or only fall to slide inside our eyes, illuminating us for good.

I see Frances sometimes just before I fall asleep or as soon as I wake up. The time has come and gone for us to meet on a corner in Hollywood. Often I guess she has forgotten. I see her in college, quickly writing down everything they say, then with a strained expression reading it over and over, until she believes it is true. Other times I see her waiting on a corner. Her face is still sharp and white beneath the red she's put on it. She watches everyone who walks towards her from all directions, she keeps turning her head quickly. A plastic purse swings upon her arm and the toe of one shoe kicks the sidewalks gently. If her hair were still long, she would chew its ends. Finally Frances grows tired of waiting; she was always less patient than me. A strange man comes along and she goes off with him, laughing. He doesn't look like Montgomery Clift or Greta Garbo. Or me. She doesn't glance back once to where she waited. Where I or Greta Garbo or any other dream might pass by tomorrow.

It was Frances who taught me not to believe everything people say. They tell me they both died young and that's why I'm an orphan. They say her cold hand still clutched the telephone when too many pills were inside her. They say his body was torn and twisted within the smashed car. There are a lot of lies in this world, but I go on looking like I believe everything. Whatever untruth you tell me, I'll nod my head and say: yes, yes. It's easier that way, people don't look at you so funny. I keep quiet and feel the print of her fingers upon my cheek, smell his smoky kisses on my forehead. Yes, yes, I say in the secret place inside myself. You'll never find it.

Now is my tomorrow. I return to the room. Back home. I am wearing blue pants and a white shirt, still in disguise. Outside the light was bright, and I take off the sunglasses so I can see better in the dimness. So I can see them waiting for me in the room. She is sitting before the mirror, with one hand moving the lipstick around her mouth in the most careful way. He is standing by the window, making three fresh drinks. The ice chimes like bells. They have stopped making movies so they can spend more time with me. We need each other. Their old words will keep speaking to you in your darkness; these words I am writing now will still talk when I have left you. And I won't tell you where we are, Marilyn and James and I. You must find your own home.

They were both orphans, or almost, themselves, you know.

Even when they are laughing there is something sad in the sound: listen. We have given our love to many strangers, to you or to anyone at all, because there was a time when we were alone, and lost from each other. Maybe we received something in return that helped us hold on until this day. And didn't we give you some small thing that strengthened you to wait until your day? Today the three of us are laughing and laughing in this room, though it is small and dirty and the bugs won't go away. We laugh and laugh like all the world is a Real Home called California, and if you listened to us you might believe someday there is an end to being orphaned.

Other Voices
and the Real World IV

One writes of scars healed, a loose parallel to the pathology of the skin, but there is no such thing in the life of an individual. There are open wounds, shrunk sometimes to the size of a pinprick but wounds still. The marks of suffering are more comparable to the loss of a finger, or of the sight of an eye. We may not miss them, either, for one minute in a year, but if we should there is nothing to be done about it.
— F. Scott Fitzgerald, *Tender Is the Night*

scar 1. the mark left by a healed wound, sore or burn 2. any lasting aftereffect of trouble 3. (botany) a mark indicating a former point of attachment as where a leaf has fallen from a stem 4. to leave a scar upon 5. a precipitous rocky place, cliff 6. a low or submerged rock in the sea
— *The Random House College Dictionary*, 1973

When people think their lives devoid of meaning or when they find themselves in oppressive and despair-inducing poverty, they may turn to drugs or reach out for short-term physical intimacy. . . .
— from the U.S. Catholic Conference Administrative Board's AIDS Statement, 1987

He [William Holden] didn't make it through the tunnel.
— Faye Dunaway

A Child of Man

A Child of Man

Once I was walking down a hallway in the hotel where I lived. One of the other prostitutes or addicts had stolen the bulb from the light socket in the ceiling, so the hall was dark. The closed doors on either side of me were chipped and scratched, but unmarked by numbers. No sound issued from the rooms, yet I sensed people sitting very still inside them until I passed, then continuing some painfully private act. Turning a corner, I heard the sound of crying. One door was open and I could see into a room. A small child was sitting on an unmade bed, his legs dangling over the edge, not long enough to reach the floor. He was naked and alone. He wept the way people do when their tears have been flowing for a long time and have no hope of being dammed soon. It was a dull mechanical sound, like one of those toys that keeps making noise until its spring winds down. There was a bottle of bourbon, one third full, on the floor beside the bed. A peach-coloured satin slip was thrown over the back of a chair. Although the boy saw me look at him for one long minute, my presence did not alter the sound he was making or the expression on his face. I walked quickly away, down the maze of halls and stairs, and out onto the street. I went to the corner where I stood every evening. Above me, the small boy I had left behind was wishing to be re-born.

Up in the attic the black trunk exhaled a sharp, strong odour when my mother opened it. The trunk was filled with dresses, blouses and skirts packed in neat layers and protected by mothballs from decay. There were clothes for girls of all sizes. Disregarding me, my mother's eyes focused sharply on the interior of the trunk. She dug through cloth, disarranging the careful order. She found a pink dress with ruffles of white lace around the collar and sleeves. She pushed and pulled the cloth on me, I couldn't do up the buttons on the back of the dress myself, I hadn't learned the special way of reaching behind and seeing with my fingers to fasten the row of little pearl buttons. My mother thrust me an arm's length away and examined the effect through narrowed eyes. The smoke from her cigarette unwound in the air between us, curling into the corners of my eyes. They blurred as my mother's face softened, then hardened again. Don't just stand there, she suddenly said. I skipped awkwardly in the dusty space between the rocking-horse and the dresser's mannequin and the sporting trophies of my father's youth. The loose folds of the dress floated around me. Released from the tight, binding cloth of my pants, I felt a curious unfamiliar sense of freedom. The empty air between and around my legs made me feel very light. For a moment it seemed possible to rise easily above the earth. My mother ground her cigarette beneath her heel. Take it off, she said shortly, a curtain closing across her eyes. She wheeled from the attic, shutting the door behind her. I fumbled with the buttons of the dress. When I returned to the attic in my chafing trousers, a week or month later, I tried to open the black trunk, but it was locked. A layer of undisturbed dust covered it again. Peering down, I searched the attic floor until I found the place where my mother's cigarette had burned it, marked it.

On my corner of the street a woman wearing thick glasses presses a pamphlet into my hand. On the cover is the word "murder", the red colour of blood, a hand wielding a scalpel that stabs a fetus. I feel the cold air of the northern city around me. A car pulls up to the curb beside me, its door opens in invitation. My blood keeps the metal blade in my shoe warm. I feel the coldness of jumping from bed to bed, like a child playing leap-frog. The shock of slipping suddenly and too soon from warm, wet darkness. Sucked into a vacuum of chill daylight.

This time the father must be strong, handsome, intelligent. He must be warm and caring and full of constant love. Like a dream that doesn't end when you wake at morning.

As a child, I played the imagination game. You look at something you love, then close your eyes and try to picture it in complete, exact and vivid detail. When you open your eyes, you compare how closely the imagined picture resembles the original. I played the game until the time I looked at my father, closed my eyes, then opened them to find him gone. The picture never really matches its subject very well.

I search for the father in the most unlikely of places. In the bar only young men hover in the darkness, only male bodies move anxiously to the loud music. Eyes strain to pierce the shadows, as though scanning the far horizon of some sea for sight of a white sail. Smoke curls like halos around heads and hands clutch glasses tightly. The lonely little boys are growing older. They gulp poison thirstily, swallowing the night quickly to reach sooner the end of darkness, the morning that lies at the bottom of glasses. Solid, windowless walls press the bodies together, keep out a world that has grown bigger and bigger since the time the first and only home was lost.

I find him easily, at once. He is standing beside me, his arm brushes mine, he turns to me. His hands do not hold a glass of clear or coloured liquid, a smoking wand. His eyes are clear and blue. He doesn't smoke because his mother held a burning cigarette in one hand and a fork in the other during those long, endless suppers. He won't drink because he still remembers the taste of his father's sweet, bitter kisses. My blood stirs and calls to him, like the magnet of a child's cry pulling at its mother.

My father sits on the edge of the bed, part of his body pressing on mine. A light, heavy weight. He bends down to kiss me good night. His cheek is rough with stubble. I slowly say my prayers.

He breaks from me, twisting and reaching into the drawer of the night table. We don't need that, I say. Didn't I tell you? I'm barren. He hesitates, then draws me back to him, is naked inside me. Making love. For the first time I understand the power contained in the verb. The force of building, creating. Afterwards, I curl in a ball and feel his seed spreading through me, reaching towards the dark place where it will grow. He props himself up on one elbow, he leans over me. What loved subject does the picture of my face imperfectly resemble?

I dream the child inside me, as my mother once dreamed me. The dream unfolds in secret, uncurling as it reaches towards the light. A light, heavy weight. The size of my heart. I do not ponder its exact location inside my body, my mind skips hastily over this unimportant point. Beneath my skin is a dark, unexplored world. A labyrinth of tunnels and dim hallways wind between mysterious caves, empty rooms. The fetus floats in my salty blood. Invisible from the outside.

The small boy sitting alone in the hotel inside my head stops crying. He senses the approach of someone who will stay by him, not leave him, and he licks his salty tears. The sound of his sobbing fades, and I can hear the voice of my child's father. Why don't you stay around? he says.

His name rhymes with pain and rain, train and stain, and Cain.

I planned to leave immediately after being given what I need. But at once I feel the desire to be protected while I protect the seed inside myself. An eviction notice was slid under the door of my barren, empty room a week ago. I want a nest. Shane is startled at the ease with which I pick myself up from one place and set myself down in another. You learn to pack quickly when the police are on the way, and there isn't time to look beneath the bed or in the closet for things you might be forgetting, leaving behind. I have taught myself to make any place my home for a day, a week, a month. I come and go, I warn him. It's only fair.

Shane has been living alone for several years, nursing the wound left by the last hurtful lover. As soon as I share his bed, he cannot imagine lying alone in it again. He is cautious about introducing me to his friends, in case I leave and require him to make sad explanations. I am a secret he keeps inside his rooms. I stay in the

apartment nearly all the time, and he likes it that I am there when
he leaves for work and there when he returns. I work at home, I
say, spreading pens and paper over a table in front of a window.
He picks up a page, reads it, sets it down without comment. I am
hardly aware of him now, he is a blurred shape hovering beyond
the focus of my vision. I peer through the telescope of my mind
in search of growth inside myself. Through the stethoscope of my
ears I listen for the sound of a whisper from behind the closed
door. In bed Shane's body looms over me. I am indifferent, such
motion is superfluous now.

During the day, while Shane is at work, I wander the rooms of
the apartment. It is on an upper floor of a tall tower. From the
balcony I watch the world far below, it is silent or its sounds do
not carry up this high. I can see all the way to the lake and sometimes imagine I glimpse the farther American shore. Another
country. The rooms behind me are very neat, clean, sterile, like
many of the places where young men live alone. Expensive
machines and articles of furniture and pieces of art, carefully
accumulated, fill the space. I lightly touch objects which hold no
meaning for me and wonder what memories they recall to Shane.
I do not answer the ringing telephone. Sometimes I pause by the
table and peer down at pages covered with unfamiliar handwriting. I am surprised, I have not noticed anyone enter the room
and sit at the table, I must have forgotten to lock the door. I look
at the words not to discover their meaning, but to see their shape
on the page. Rorschachs.

I won't smoke or drink, the space inside me must be kept clean
and free of poison. But I eat ravenously. Enough for both of us,
Shane laughs across the table, scarcely touching his food. I'm not
hungry, he quickly says, watching me eat with his starved eyes.

My mother didn't want more children, but my father insisted in
the dark. He wished for a dozen children in the same way he later
desired, and obtained, enormous gardens, vast orchards, huge
houses. But he doesn't have enough time or energy to take care
of all the necessary pruning, spraying, thinning, weeding, housekeeping. His farm grows beyond his control, half wild. When one
of his grown children pauses from wild wandering to visit, my

father will give his son or daughter a single, sideways glance. I
have to get these tomatoes set today, he will say, looking quickly
away. You can sleep the night in there, he will say, pointing to
one of a dozen spare rooms. They are overflowing with junk:
stacks of unread newspapers he plans to look at one day, projects
he has begun but will never finish, tomato seedlings started early
indoors in milk cartons cut in half. He doesn't have time to trans-
plant them into the garden, their roots grow too long for the milk
cartons, they wither.

When her last child was still a baby, my mother stopped eating.
For several months she lived on coffee and cigarettes. In the
front seat of the car, beside my father, she watched mile after
mile unroll between Lake Manyara and the Serengeti Plain. She
picked constantly at the left corner of her lower lip, tearing the
tender flesh with her fingers, not allowing it to heal. In the
crowded seat behind her, too many children dozed in the dusty
heat. My mother asked my father to stop the car. She disappeared behind a screen of grey thorny bushes of the same variety
the Masai use for building circular walls around their camps, to
keep out lions at night. What's she doing? asked my sister in a
loud, sudden voice. My father didn't answer, and in silence we
watched the bushes for a long time. Just when I thought my
mother had decided to walk away from us, to cross two hundred
miles of hill and plain until she reached the Indian Ocean, she
reappeared. She strode quickly and firmly as always. One arm
was held straight down along her side and ended in a fist. The
other swung back and forth to the strong, steady rhythm of her
step, like a pendulum. She climbed into the car and my father
drove on. Leaning forward, I looked into the front seat and saw
blood on my mother's skirt. She lit a cigarette and exhaled a luxu-
rious stream of blue smoke, pursuing a private pleasure. The
filter of the cigarette was red where it touched the corner of her
lip. Mixed with the heavy smell of smoke and dust and approach-
ing rain was a darker scent that lingered in the car, all the way to
Arusha.

I pick a doctor's name from the Yellow Pages and make an
appointment. I would like a set of X-rays. I feel there is something wrong inside me, I partly lie. A growth, perhaps a tumour.

The doctor is reluctant, she believes this just imagination. I insist, and leave the clinic with four sheets of transparent plastic contained inside a manilla envelope. In the apartment I hold the negatives up to light. There's nothing here, the doctor said. I see vague patches of darkness, swirls of light. Indications of absence and presence. I am reminded of the craters, deserts and lakes of a lunar landscape. A glimpse of the distant heavens brought near by the eye of a telescope's lens. I strain to see signs of another form of life beyond me, while a planet slowly twirls inside my body.

I begin to waken in the night to study Shane's face, which appears like a countryside of shadowed hollows and hills sleeping beneath a dark sky. A place known to me only dimly. I examine his face to find clues of what the child will look like. Sometimes I try to imagine his features superimposed on mine, and to picture what face would emerge from such a combination. As if we were one person. I look at Shane, close my eyes, and conjure his face in the greatest possible detail. I open my eyes and see the face I have imagined, still there.

Finding Shane, I find the courage to play the imagination game again.

When my younger sister grew older than a baby, I believed all the dresses my mother put on her came from the black trunk in the attic. I thought I recognized them from the single glimpse of several years before. The sharp stab of desire when my sister wore a pink dress with white lace around her throat and wrists. The clear memory of floating like risen dust around the attic. I followed my sister with hungry eyes.

You're clumsy, she said when I fumbled with the row of little pearl buttons. The curious, unfamiliar sensation of soft, smooth skin against my body, where I had always felt something rougher, harder, hairier before. I melted with longing into my sister, until I could not feel where her softness left off and my hardness began.

Shane is a number of years older than I, although usually he looks younger. He dresses like a teen-aged boy. His closets are filled with immaculately preserved clothes dating back for years. Many no longer fit him. Although his body is more solid now, when my age Shane was as thin as I am. I have so few clothes of my own, I begin to dress in his. He is surprised to see his old clothes on my body, but says nothing. There is a curious expression on his face, a mixture of nostalgia and longing, when he undresses me. As though uncovering someone he used to know. Who went away and did not return. I feel a layer of skin is peeled from me and someone almost forgotten, almost a stranger, exposed. My new flesh is tender, it shivers at his touch.

When Shane returns from work and the gym in afternoon, his skin cold from the winter air, I am absorbed in feeling my way through the dark places inside myself, searching for the cave where the fetus is curled. I carry blankets in my arms, I must keep it warm. (Why do I say "it"? A human's sex is determined at the moment of conception, every mother knows from that instant whether a male or female body hides inside hers. This belief is so strong and clear that, when a mistake occurs and the girl is born a boy, the mother will unlock the black trunk in the attic, if only once.) He. I must cover him with blankets, the winter is cold, I must keep him warm.

Slowly I sense the careful, ordered routine that Shane developed while living alone, to give structure to the empty hours of evening. Shower, shave, cook, clean. On the corner of the couch I sit outside the set circle of his movements, feeling them wash against me as a shore feels the disturbance of water by a boat out on the sea. Shane often glances at me with puzzlement because I sit so quietly for hours. He does not know I am reluctant to stir for fear of jarring the baby awake. He needs this first long sleep to grow. Sleep, sleep, I murmur, while Shane describes his day, offers details concerning people I have not met. The telephone rings often, and I hear one side of long conversations without troubling to piece together the other, unheard side. Gradually I grow aware of the different tones of voice Shane speaks to different people, and notice that none of them resemble the way he speaks to me. I hear various topics of conversation that I have not realized are of interest to him. I learn, without conscious effort or study, the vocabulary of a foreign language simply because it fills the air around me. Sonar, radar.

He shows me a photograph album. Contained inside neat borders and arranged in chronological order are images of a series of lovers. Shane describes each one in terms vague enough to make them all seem the same. There is Shane, as a beautiful boy. Before my face had character, he laughs. Then comes a gap, a number of blank pages where the photographs have been removed. On the other, earlier side of this empty space are photographs of a very large, fat boy. Watching through layers of puffy, swollen skin are Shane's eyes. At fifteen he looked like a man of late middle age. Extra layers of skin enfolded him, to protect him from the cold.

The father would be gone away a long time, until his face was almost forgotten. Then he would suddenly appear in the bedroom door. The father would bend over the fat child, breathing fumes of poison in his face. He kissed the boy good night, leaving a sweet, bitter taste on his son's lips. Where is he? asked the boy the next morning. His mother was sitting before the mirror, patting cream and powder on the bruised flesh around her eye. She couldn't hear the boy, her lips were moving quickly, whispering a steady stream of angry words. The boy walked heavily around the house, hunting through rooms, beneath beds, in closets. Where is he? the boy asked again. Twice was too often, and his mother lifted the stick. Stop whimpering, she said later, when they sat before full plates at the kitchen table. As soon as he finished his food, his mother gave him more, but he could taste only the smoke from her cigarette. Smoke always rose from the green glass ashtray, smelling like incense and forming shapes that wavered away before the boy could see what they were. Where do you think you're going? his mother asked, spooning another mound of pale, puffy potatoes onto his plate. All evening a heap of food stood before the boy, like a mountain he could not hope to climb over or tunnel through, no matter how he tried.

I feel something stir. What's wrong? asks Shane, closing the album quickly. For the first time I feel movement inside me. Let's go to bed, says Shane, placing his hand on the back of my neck. A light, heavy weight. The baby has wakened from his first long sleep. He uncurls his fingers slowly, then uses them like sticks to swirl my blood. The waves of the waterbed lap and slap. Shane carries me on his tide, in and out, in and out. The three of us are rocked to sleep as the water calms. On the smooth sea we float towards the shore of morning.

The temperature of Shane's blood is unusually low, he tells me the medical term that describes his condition. This is the reason for the special, expensive down-quilt upon his bed, he explains. To keep him warm on winter nights. In the coldest hour before morning, I waken. The baby is restless. Shane stirs, turns towards me. Cradled in my arms, his incubated body burns with heat.

I have not seen my sister for many years. She has been living in Africa with a husband and small child, I have heard. She married a man who came from the same small town as my father and who is, also like my father, a teacher. In both cases, it was my mother and sister, rather than their husbands, who wished to move to Africa. My sister returned to the heat and dust, where in afternoon the air throbs like a pulse. My sister sat on the veranda of her house, next door to the nuns. Sometimes she thought it was her brother, not her son, who was digging a hole in the dirt of the yard. She watched the little boy poke his stick into the ground. He was trying to make a tunnel, or a wishing-well.

For ten years Shane was not in contact with his mother. She sent him the ring that his father wore before his early alcoholic death. Shane changed his name. In the gym he pushed masses of hard iron, lifting heavy weight off himself, peeling away layers of flesh. A handsome face and strong, hard body slowly emerged. When she would no longer recognize him if she passed him on the street, Shane began to send his mother cards for Christmas and her birthday. Not a nice woman, he tells me, struggling for fairness. She telephones from New Brunswick in the middle of the night. Shane's face is frozen as he listens to her cry. I have to work in the morning, he says, hanging up. He moves away from me in the bed and lies shivering. The smooth, firm skin on his upper thighs is streaked with pale, wavering lines that resemble stretch marks.

I read medical books and first-hand accounts of pregnancy. The development of the fetus, the corresponding changes in the body that bears it. Shane looks questioningly at the books. Research, I explain. I'm writing about pregnancy. It's fiction, but I want it to be real. You've got a lot done today, Shane says when he comes home from work. Seeing through his eyes, I realize I am sitting at the table. A pen is in my hand. The words on the paper form shapes which suggest a number of different possibilities, which call various pictures to my mind. I rise and go to Shane, reluctant to look further at the words, it is not yet time to reach a sense of final recognition. I feel the wavering, dark shape inside myself. Later, Shane wakens to find the bed empty of me. I look up from the lamplight and see his form as something darker than the darkness of the room. I cannot see him in detail, but I see the mass of his body, its blurred outline. I thought you had gone, he says.

A telegram is forwarded by the publisher. My grandmother is dying, it says. There is cancer in her breast. I haven't seen the quarrelsome old woman for ten years, and we have not written or spoken on the telephone during this time. She would not recognize me if we passed on the street. My old family believes I am living in another country, rather than this one. You should go and see her, says Shane. He touches my tattooed body. It is covered with designs, pictures, words I do not wish to remember. The scars won't fade. I think of the perfect, unmarked skin of my baby. I don't go to the distant bed on which my grandmother lies dying. Instead, on our bed I show Shane the scars that cover my body, like a map of where I've been and what has happened to me there. The small marks of needles on the insides of my arms. The traces of a broken arm, a split skull, a knife wound. All the accidents we survive. I thought you would never tell me who you are, says Shane.

On my rare walks in the street I move slowly, heavily. I find myself cautiously avoiding places of danger, such as the old corner that I used to run towards carelessly. My eyes stab every stranger whose approach makes my baby cry in fear. Everyone is a potential murderer of my child. I carry a blade in my shoe, as I used to do when I worked the corner. The metal is warmed by the blood in my foot, reminding me of the two times I had to use the knife. Cutting a stranger before he cuts you.

I have always been thin, with small, slight bones. My mother was anxious and tense while carrying me, and too nervous or unhappy to eat. When I was born, there was no milk in her breasts. Later, for supper she would serve one bowl of soup, one slice of bread and one glass of milk to each member of her family, stating that this was, nutritionally, quite sufficient. Now, for the first time since running away from home, I gain weight. Shane is pleased. I am a more solid body to hold in the dark. Before, he sometimes felt he held something nebulous as air. He feared that when he woke at morning he would find his arms embracing emptiness. And then he would have to hunt through rooms, under beds, in closets, until he found no one was there. You feel good, he says. You're here.

Our child has been growing for three months. I want to share with Shane the secret inside my rooms. But I am afraid. Dreams are creatures shy as deer, and you must allow them to make their own hesitant way out of the dark forest. You must keep perfectly still while they look at you and smell you and learn you mean them no harm. Then you can touch them and feel they are really there, the dreams that don't end when you wake at morning. In the dawn Shane's touch is light and tender, and I stop trembling. When his head rests upon my body, I sense him listening to the sounds of life inside.

The books inform me that the baby is at a certain stage of development, that growth happens in a stated, unfailing sequence through time. I disbelieve the charts, diagrams, statistics. There is no precedence for this particular miracle, no documentation can describe it. This fetus is growing far more quickly than would be believed. For instance, his eyes have been open for some weeks already. I sense his curiosity at the first sight of many things. Objects I would not normally notice jump out at me as I feel his eyes narrow and widen in wonder. Passing playgrounds, I must pause while he shouts with joy and longing at the sight of children swinging high into the sky, touching the sun with the tips of their toes. He has developed, too, tastes which are not my own, and for his sake I wade through dishes of chocolate ice cream, strawberries swimming in milk. He licks his lips and asks for more. I love to indulge him, this will be the only time that I can satisfy his every wish, and shield him from all pain and hurt and disappointment.

You spoil me, says Shane when I rub his feet at evening. The heavy weight he carried for half his life has left his feet always sore. I rub cream into the skin, watching his toes curl and uncurl at my touch. He stares at me through half-closed eyes, like a cat in ecstasy. This is as good as making love, for him. For me.

I feel him growing moment by moment, his size swelling the space inside me, filling me so completely I gasp in a kind of pain. Are you OK? asks Shane.

I wonder how long I can contain this child inside me. The books say that the last months of pregnancy can seem endless to the waiting mother. Time refuses to move forward, despite her longing to see the face of her child, to deliver it to the world. For me, however, the days and nights are whirling by like leaves, and I want to feel the texture of their skin, to see the patterns of their veins, before they twirl away down the street. I fear the moment of birth intensely. I dread that the light will be too bright for my baby's eyes, that it will blind him and prevent him from seeing me. I fear the cold will shock his heart to a halt. I worry that the temperature of his blood will be unusually low, and freeze outside the warm chamber of my body.

He will be a good father. His hands will throw the ball to our child, then will catch the round globe when our child throws it back. He will look steadily into our son's eyes until the fear leaves them. He will not leave suddenly and he will keep his promises, and when the boy grows older Shane will teach him to swim, to drive, to shave. It will be all right if the boy is born a girl. Shane will be things to our child that our fathers were not to us, because

he feels so strongly the absences that were left inside him that
they have become presences.

Another telegram arrives. My grandmother is dead. Go, says
Shane again. I see fear in his eyes. I have confessed to him my
weakness for motion, how once stirred I keep going and going
without wondering why the miles are passing or where they are
leading. I have confessed to him my fear of new marks upon my
body, etched by sharp needles of eyes, questions, accusations.
Family love. The bubbles of blood that rise to the surface of the
skin, staining it. Go, he says again.

I fly to the west coast. They are waiting for me at the airport. The
child inside me sits up and stares through the wall of flesh. He
reaches towards these beings filled with blood that resembles the
red lake in which he paddles. You're lucky, I inform him. You're
very lucky to be still safe inside, protected from this brusque, difficult love that puts its arms around me. My mother thrusts me an
arm's length away and inspects me through narrowed eyes. The
smoke from her cigarette blurs my vision, I can hardly see the
small scar on the left corner of her lower lip. My father's hand is a
light, heavy weight floating on my shoulder.

The day after the funeral I visit my sister. What do you want? she
asks. Nothing, I say, staring at her child. I have not seen this small
boy before. He is six years old. He has blond hair and blue eyes,
like Shane. The boy doesn't look at me, he never looks at the
faces of the men who come to the house because the faces are
always different. Mark has bigger feet than me, says Gabriel,
looking at the ground. His mother pours something to drink, she
is always pouring something to drink in two glasses. One for her,
one for the man. Gabriel is always thirsty. Mark isn't here, says his
mother. Your father is in Africa, you know that. He stayed there
and we came here, you remember flying in the airplane through
the sky. Sometimes the men pick him up, as if they don't know
what else to do with him. They spin him around and around, so
that his legs fly straight out behind him. He thinks they will let go
of his hands and send him flying through the air, all the way to
Africa, where he will land at his father's big feet.
    I want to pick up the small boy and hold him in my arms. Smell

his hair, it will smell like hay, I know. His neck. He is my nephew and my son. I see my sister's face beneath me, her eyes are closed though the room is dark. The dark movements together, her dark hair scattered over the white pillow.

Her hair is longer now, falling loose around her shoulders. She flicks it away from one eye. Get out, she says. He'll have enough problems as it is. She fears I might touch the boy in the wrong place, the wrong way. Things I say might confuse him, make him wonder and ask difficult questions. Mark him.

Walking away, I hold my stomach in pain. The child inside me is kicking, with angry jealousy.

How did it go? Shane glances at me as he drives us home from the airport. The skin around his eyes is creamy and pale. His face appears puffy. While I was gone, he didn't sleep or slept too long. I feel invisible threads stretching across the wide country, reaching to me and holding me. I shift restlessly in the car. The threads will not break, but they loosen enough so that I can breathe freely again.

I missed you, he says, pulling me towards him. I feel his urgent need, for the first time it seems stronger than the baby's. He is surprised that I respond so hungrily to his hands. During this long, lasting moment I forget the baby, and afterwards am shocked by my neglect. I am wet. For a split second I fear the water has been broken by our urgent act. Then I see that the moisture is sweat, glistening on Shane's body as well as mine.

I know that some births are more difficult than others. But I have not expected this. I wonder if the price of my child's existence is my own life; if that is so, I wish his death. With my back turned to Shane I sit at the table and grip the pen tightly, forcing my mind from the pain to the marks I am placing on the white paper. I feel the presence of Shane behind me and hate him for the part he has played in creating this. I am angry at his ignorance of the reason for my pain and I resent the fact that he does not share it. Now I do not even care to see the face of my emerging child. I just want the pain to end.

I am empty inside. I could rise with ease above the earth, but there is something nearby that anchors me here, and I don't want to leave it. The story is done, and through the opened door a light enters my rooms, illuminating them clearly and brightly. Yet I see that some dark shadows still lurk in the corners. I hear my baby crying in the next room. He is cold and hungry and afraid. I put down the pen and look up from the lamplight. Shane is a black shape in the darkness of the room, yet at the same time I can see him standing clearly in all the revealing brightness inside me. He shines like a star. Come back, he laughs. I walk towards him, feeling I cross a vast distance with each step. I missed you, I say, reaching him. I stand before my child and the father of my child. I face him with love.

Every dawn is a new birth we conceive in the preceding darkness. Love has always been a dangerous thing, forsaking as many as it saves, and now during these times of plague it has more value, is made more precious by the surrounding darkness. This moment of creation lasts and lasts, until it becomes all the years that have gone before and all that will come. And when his seed spreads through me, it doesn't end, this love. There is only the briefest moment of sadness while the seed leaks from me and falls upon the barren sheets. Beside me, Shane's chest is rising and falling strongly, evenly. Wayne, I whisper. He stiffens at the sound of his old name, the name of the sad, fat child who with guarded eyes watched the world through layers and walls of flesh. He lies still as I reach for his hand and find with the eyes of my fingers the ring that was worn by his father. He is silent while I slide the circle of silver upon my finger, while I feel it wrapped around my flesh, and the bone and blood beneath. He stops breathing.

I pull him towards me. My turn, I say. My child's face turns to my smooth shaven chest. His mouth searches the rounded mounds of muscle. He suckles at my nipple. My milk flows into his mouth.

Another Accident

Another Accident

Abruptly, the darkness shrilly insists that it was never silent, mute, dumb. The voice pierces the room and enters his sleeping mind as a warning or an alarm. His eyes open and focus. They see the numbers on the clock radio beside the bed and register their meaning; a particular pattern of red glowing light places this moment precisely, etching it upon the black, blank surface of the night.

The sound repeats. Identical, anonymous, finely calculated to disturb the nerve endings in the ear. His memory informs him that it will continue. From beneath the blanket one hand reaches into cold air and gropes for the plastic object especially formed to fit easily within his grip. It feels familiar, and is covered with countless smudges of his fingerprints.

Hello?

A faint electric hum enters his ear, travels to his brain, sends off sparks of anticipation, irritation, fear. The thin wire descends from his telephone to the earth six floors below, where it joins numerous others to form a thick, clumsy mass. He imagines the subterranean world beneath the concrete skin of the city crowded with twisting, coiling strands. Veins and arteries that cross and tangle and lead in all directions. They are dormant and cold, but capable of suddenly wakening into a state of burning life.

He feels a prick of pain in his left leg.

I hear you listening to me, I feel your mind and body turned towards

*me. I have captured your attention, you are my victim. Your are not out of
reach, you are still there.*

Hello?

His voice conveys sleepiness, but is otherwise devoid of emotions which might, depending upon the ultimate identity of the
caller, prove inappropriate. He waits and listens, hearing no
sound of breathing at the wire's other end. No aural clues.
Silence.

The caller hangs up. There is a click of disconnection, then a
monotonous purring.

He replaces the receiver upon its cradle, returns his hand
beneath the blanket. His eyes close and see the front door of his
apartment. The double locks that carry an inviolable guarantee.
He hears cars moving north and south along the freeway to his
left; the sound never ceases, even when most of this half of the
world is sleeping. There is always someone awake, somewhere.
Before bed he usually turns down the heat in the apartment and
opens the window. The winter air is cold. He shifts his arms and
legs, arranging them in a more comfortable position. Beneath the
single light, heavy eiderdown his body burns with warmth,
though now he always sleeps alone.

It has happened once or twice each of these past months.
Except that they always come between midnight and morning,
there is little pattern to the calls. They have not occurred often
enough to keep him awake, on guard, waiting. Not often enough
to impel him to change his number again. In the space between
one call and the next, he can almost forget the whole thing.

He is presently unlisted. Disturbed by a previous series of calls
several years ago, he had his number changed to one unavailable
from Information. He gave this new number, one of an almost
infinite combination of digits, to a few close friends, a small select
circle, asking them to preserve its privacy. The troublesome calls
ceased. Until recently, he could know that only a limited number
of chosen voices would speak when he lifted the receiver. He
would have liked no more unpleasant surprises or unwanted
intrusions. No more accidents.

He has lived a number of years in this city and passed through
a number of other lives. Lovers, friends, acquaintances. Strangers. There was a time when he was less cautious, before he
became aware that relationships could end in ways that made him

remember them as unfortunate incidents, close calls with danger. Now it puzzles him that after a car has nearly left a road, say, either of its occupants could wish for both of them to peer down the edge they almost fell over. To stare together into the vast drop and determine who had been the driver of the vehicle, who merely the passenger.

It's over, he has always thought, shaken after each near miss, closing his door behind him. He would feel relief to see all the objects in his rooms in their usual positions. Although the apartment appears somewhat bare, he has inhabited it for six years; the rent is controlled and still fairly inexpensive, and recently the city has become crowded with people scrambling from one cramped, unaffordable set of rooms to another. It would be foolish for him even to consider moving. Inside this space he can regulate the heat and arrange the furniture according to his desire. He can turn on the television, selecting which scenes he wishes to see, which voices to hear. I'm safe again, he can think.

Still, even now that he avoids people or circumstances hinting however slightly of danger, he sometimes believes the scent of a past strewn with accidents clings to him, giving off a subtle perfume and attracting unbalanced people, unexpected events. No matter how he orders his life or appearance, it seems, some peculiar arrangement of atoms within him, some imbalance of positive and negative, creates a surrounding magnetic field charged with the unpredictable. Walking down Yonge Street, for example, he would probably be the single random target of a sniper or the only victim of a heavy object falling from above.

When this current series of calls began, he would casually ask his friends if they had phoned the night before, knowing their answers would be negative. He had chosen these friends with the certainty that they would not call at three in the morning, or ring his buzzer at the entrance of the building without prior notice, or visit drunk or drugged. They would not borrow money and they would never burst into tears in public, and on the telephone their voices would always sound reasonable. Like his.

Because he has filled his life so that there is little room for chance to enter it, he is unable to see his closest friends on anything like a daily basis; he finds the telephone a convenient and necessary form of communication, often joking that he could not survive without it. At home in the evening he holds long conversations with people who live perhaps on the other side of the city. The dialogues are comfortable and, though his eyes wander to and from the television screen, relatively intimate. He talks well on the telephone, not feeling deprived by the absence of his friends' eyes. On days after he has been awakened against his will in the night, he is especially likely to call friends. Feeling familiar voices and words slide smoothly into the grooves of his ear, he is reassured that the world can be controlled by means of traffic signals and other apparatuses.

The next night it seems he wakens a split second before the air is broken by waves that crash against his ear, as though he heard them just in advance of their rising from the flat, silent sea. For several moments he considers not lifting the receiver. Let the caller believe him not at home, or too deeply sleeping to be wakened. Nonetheless, his hand insists on reaching into the cold darkness once more.

As always, the caller is silent. There is no noise of blurred music or voices in the background. He imagines the caller within a room bare of clues that might suggest the kind of person who inhabits it. A blank space devoid of photographs, books, pieces of art: indications of preference, interest, taste. Or he imagines a payphone. A receiver chilled by winter air pressed against an ear warm with blood. An unknown woman's perfume lingering on the plastic. Numbers and initials, meaningful only to departed strangers, scratched into the surrounding surfaces. Beyond the transparent substance, neither plastic nor glass, infrequent passersby disappear into the darkness, unfollowed and alone.

He imagines he hears a distant heart beat at the swifter pace of fear or excitement or love.

I feel your hand holding the receiver as it once held me. Strong, square fingers, neatly clipped nails. A sprinkling of dark hairs just below the knuckles, just like mine. Your other hand presses against your eyes, which ache from staring at the illuminated screen of the computer terminal. (I saw you enter and leave your place of work today.) Now the hand massages your right bicep. (I saw you go into and come out of your gym, afterwards.) I know the pattern on the eiderdown that covers you, I remember how it also covered me. I feel your body near me, I feel less cold.

He realizes the sound of beating blood is his own quickened pulse.

He wonders who it is. Despite the discretion of his friends, over time the number of his telephone has unavoidably become less secret, and perhaps has been obtained by certain people with whom he would rather not speak. His eyes travel down a list of names imprinted upon the disc of his memory. He enters data pertaining to actions and words into a program, then considers possibilities, judges probabilities. Several names are eliminated, but there are too many unknown factors, too many dark places inside every heart, to determine conclusively the identity of the caller. No, not that one. Not him, either. Him? Or could it be him?

In the morning his face is slightly puffy. He rubs a small amount of expensive cream into the flesh under his eyes. The mirror states that he looks far younger than his age, scarcely the survivor of thirty accidental years. He shaves with special caution because he is haemophiliac.

No doctor has been able to explain exactly why his blood refuses to clot on occasions when it clearly should. Various conflicting theories have been proposed and a score of drugs and diets been unsuccessfully administered. In memory his childhood consists of one long dark drive of panic to an emergency ward, with an unwilling neighbour at the wheel — his parents did not own a car, and in any case his father was never around, his mother never in any shape to drive. The most innocent scrape would set off the most painfully repetitive process: the haemorrhage staining an infinite amount of white cloth red; the loss of blood making him dizzy, weak, pale; the transfusion of blood leaving him dull, heavy, hopeless. The repeated warnings to be more careful in the future. Now sight of the smallest drop of a stranger's blood nauseates him; he feels his own interior ocean yearn to escape and join it with one final, unstoppable gush.

Over time he has concluded his condition to be a simple statement that accidents pose a unique threat to him; for some unknowable reason he has been marked as one at the worst odds with fluctuations of fortune. As a child he enviously watched friends fall off bicycles and down stairs with little consequence; now he views, from a distance, people skip in and out of

relationships, slide easily away from emotional messes, slip free
from the grasping hands of love and hate. He ponders whether
misfortune knows to follow the ones who attempt innocuous am-
bles down the street: unable to resist glancing nervously over
their shoulders, they walk straight into a lamp post.

An hour later he is feeding numerical and alphabetical symbols
into a computer terminal, subtly affecting a complicated system,
with light touches that ultimately create lasting and significant
changes. One ear listens to the office girls discuss dates and diets;
it is almost too easy to charm them, requiring only minute movements of well-exercised facial muscles, speedy summons of
selected expressions. He performs his duties flawlessly and feels
impatient at careless mistakes of colleagues, even when these do
not affect his work. Perhaps he is slightly irritable; occasionally he
uses Benzedrine to control his weight. For this same reason he
skips lunch and works straight through the day. Leaving the
office an hour earlier than the others, he walks quickly to one of
three weekly appointments with a doctor.

Two years previously a car hit him while he was riding his bicycle. In addition to minor injuries and complications of bleeding,
the cartilage and bones in the area of one knee were shattered to
such a degree that doctors advised amputation. This counsel he
refused, and a metal plate was set into his left leg, with warning
that he probably would not walk again; certainly, there would be
considerable painful difficulties for an indefinite time. During
some months he was confined to bed in his apartment, and then
transported himself first by wheelchair, later by crutches. The
physiotherapist congratulated his grimly determined efforts, and
expressed amazement at his progress towards recovery.

Now he walks with no sign of lameness. The accident was not
his fault, and he is involved in a legal suit to recover a large sum
of money in damages — a case that promises to drag on at length.
He was not compensated completely against the long absence
from work; his financial situation remains tenuous and is one reason for the quiet quality of his present life. Although he has
begun to attend the gym once more, rebuilding the aesthetically
pleasing body achieved through years of constant care, he is limited to what exercise he can undertake, and often his leg is too
painful to permit any. In the future there exists the possibility
that his body might reject the metal set into it, and further hospi-

talization if that occurs. Presently, a doctor must, by injection, freeze the leg three times a week. Without this treatment he would feel constant pain, and he still finds need to take frequent pain-killers. He realizes they affect his mood, inclining him to react inappropriately to certain situations.

While largely confined after the accident, he felt isolated. His telephone did not often ring and friends visited seldom. He believed most were uncaring and unconcerned, and regretted being caught in a position where this could wound him. Upon resuming his normal life, he stopped seeing nearly all of these friends; the few that remain close from before the accident remark that now he is quieter, more serious. Lately, he has been prone to stress that he has a positive attitude, as if repeating a line of litany.

He convinces himself that there can be no more accidents. He sees his life as a series of progressively dangerous mishaps, and fears he will not have strength to survive a future one: it will be the final one. He is more careful than ever, making no more flying leaps through the air, no more flights across dark, unfamiliar terrain. He slips on the jeans that so seductively cover the scar. Heads turn to look after him in the street. He is conscious that the more control he exudes, the greater number of unsteady people who will be attracted to him as their opposite, as their anchor. He senses that calmer hands are also tempted to touch his body, as if a fire. He has felt their fingers travel across the map of his skin, seeking the cities and towns where catastrophe occurred. While repeating his tales of narrowly averted tragedy, his lips have brushed their sleeker skins. Now he walks on, telling himself that while recovering from this latest accident he grew used to being alone, and to like it that way.

The ringing seems louder and more demanding than before. Commanding. Listening, he almost believes each signal has greater volume than the previous one. He imagines the sound swelling until it deafens him, making him unable to hear whispers of love, murmurs of desire.

It is only several nights since the last call. Will they occur at increasingly close intervals? Will the telephone soon scream constantly? Will there finally be a ringing always in his ears, whether he is strolling down a street, swimming in a lake, climbing through thick green pines far from any voices except natural ones?

He lifts the receiver at the tenth ring. This time he does not say hello. His silence is met with silence. He feels chained by the mute wire to an invisible fellow prisoner.

You thought you could touch me, then take your hand away forever. You thought you could open your arms to me, then lock your door against me. You can't erase me from the program in your heart, I won't let you forget.

He is the one to end the connection on this occasion. Replacing the receiver, he gets out of bed, puts on a dressing-gown, goes into the living-room. He turns on the television, but at this hour no programs are broadcast. His eyes move to the video cartridges lined along one shelf and are wearied by choice. He watches the blank screen and listens to its mechanical whine. He flicks past squares of interference, static, electrical confusion. Test patterns: shapes and lines and colours whose meaning is not clarified through constant repetition. The curtains are drawn across the windows, closing in the room. A circle of light around the lamp is given definition by the darkness. His apartment is more or less soundproof: he can hardly ever hear neighbours on either side of him, above or below him. Anyway, they are surely sleeping now.

He stares at the second telephone, placed for convenience in the living-room. It is a newer model, small and light and neat. It looks as harmless as a toy. An innocent plaything meant for pleasure.

If he complains to the telephone company, a bland voice will inform him that it is very difficult and also expensive to trace calls; normally this is done only in extraordinary circumstances, as when police are investigating a serious crime. He will be advised to remain silent, then to hang up — this being the course of action most likely to discourage a bothersome caller, as several studies have shown. If he wishes, naturally, he can have his number changed again.

He does not want to change his number again; he dislikes being forced into any action against his will. Already he has obscured his presence in this building by removing his name from the list of occupants, arranged beside apartment numbers and corresponding buzzers at the front entrance. Already he has changed his name and altered his body and reincarnated himself from too many pyres of ash. His leg hurts too much for him to be always on the run.

He knows who it is. Of course. Really, he has known all along. Yes, it's him.

They met purely by chance; statistically, it should never have happened. It was not a case of their being introduced by mutual acquaintances or often having seen each other in some location frequented by them both. Their lives had never intersected at all. There was no context to this connection, no outer grid of people or custom to which the relationship could be referred. No varying points of perspective to lend it even a degree of objectivity.

He would never have let it happen except that he was somewhat exhilarated at having recovered so successfully and against such great odds from the most recent accident. In his excitement over walking again, he allowed his newly re-strengthened legs to carry him into a situation he should have avoided. He was celebrating the beginning of another life by a rare night of drinking, and perhaps his hope for an improved existence spilled from him to include this boy.

Afterwards, he could see very clearly that it could never have worked, and the reasons for this. He had tried to proceed slowly and with caution after the first meeting. He had investigated the boy through questions, observations. Yet, finally, it was the body of a stranger he pulled across one foot of space in bed. He had no way of knowing what emotions his lightest touch could raise to the surface of that smooth, unmarked skin. How a casual caress could be misinterpreted and answered by an intense one. How words could bend into the shapes of a foreign language as they travelled through an arm's length of air. He held himself responsible for entering the relationship, but did not blame himself for his actions once inside it. Anyway, how long did it last? Four months? How much shared life, emotional or sexual, could accumulate over that amount of time? And he had been right to end it quickly, abruptly. Far better to leave the scene of an accident at once, than to lingeringly inspect the stains of blood upon the road, splinters of glass and shards of metal strewn in confusion across a large, undefined area. The evidence. The clues.

The object three feet away explodes into life. He leaps up, at once feeling his left leg grown stiff with sitting motionless in the chill room: it will ache by morning. He picks up the receiver at the second ring. No, he replies to the query that follows his hello. You have the wrong number.

A finger, or the mind that moved it, made an error while dialling a number. A small accident. One that anyone could make, one that anyone could be affected by.

He smiles to himself, goes to bed, falls asleep at once. It is nearly dawn. The hour when it is impossible to discern if the sky is filled more with darkness, or more with light.

Work is difficult the next day. His head pounds dully, the pain in his leg increases. He must force his mind against its will to concentrate on the tasks at hand if he hopes to avoid mistakes; as it is, he nearly makes several small slips. Expressions of the office girls indicate he is curt with them. It is not a day for his leg to be injected, so he takes a pain-killer in early afternoon. On the way home from work he buys a new video cassette for his VCR — the only real luxury he has given himself since the bicycle accident. Shop-therapy, he thinks, hearing the click of his credit card against the cashier's counter.

By night his leg is throbbing; he can almost hear its persistent voice complaining in the darkness. Although he takes three more grains of medication than usual, he lies awake. His mind is groggy, and normally sharp, straight lines of thought waver and blur. Memories of past unlucky episodes twist and turn him upon the bed. He feels himself fall onto a point of iron, feels it enter his back. He watches his father stab his mother one New Year's Eve. He is left on the street by a betraying lover without money, a job or a home. He falls through a pane of glass. Early one morning three men break through a door to slice his lover's throat, and to break his own arm, fracture his own collarbone. . . .

His hand moves wearily across his warm flesh, searching for scars. Souvenirs of disaster. Mementos of misfortune. Luckily, the sharp point of iron did not penetrate vital organs. Luckily, his father did not murder his mother. It was also fortunate that he was miraculously rescued from the street, that no splinters of glass entered his eyes, that an unusually prompt ambulance arrived before all the blood flowed from his lover's throat. Survivors are the truly lucky ones.

As he is floating nearer towards sleep, the telephone rings. Yes, its voice sounds more urgent when it calls in the dark; this is the hour for sleepers to be roused by fresh news of calamity. He listens to ten rings, observing that they seem to carry now from nearby, now from a farther distance. The sound suggests, by turns, anger, fear, desperation.

Immediately he recognizes from the quality of his mother's voice, reaching him across several provinces, that she has been drinking and crying for some time. In silence he listens to the sound of her words and the shape of her sentences — rather than to their meaning; this story, or a slight variation upon it, has been sobbed often enough into his ear before. He hears an accent belonging to a region to the east and a pattern of speech suggesting little education or money. He has methodically erased these indications from his own speech; only at rare moments of heightened emotion do they escape from cracks as minute and many as the pores of his skin. Still silent, he hangs up the phone.

After several seconds of deliberation, he unplugs the cord from the wall. He reaches for the bottle of tablets on the table beside the bed, shakes one more into the palm of his hand and swallows it with a glass of water waiting for that purpose.

The sound travels to him from the other room. He has forgotten to unplug the second telephone. His body screams with frustration and discomfort. The ringing continues.

Listen. I know you hear me. Mine is not the voice of vengeance, mine is the voice of love. Do you remember?

In his mind he sees the boy's face. Recently he has looked at one or two photographs he has of the boy. An attractively appealing face. He gave no photographs of himself away, and the boy's memory of him must have grown faded, false. He watches the face and sees it strain with longing and hope and determination. He sees it shift, alter, then change into another face. Which melts into another face, and another, and another. All faces of strangers. A crowd of unknown bodies presses against him, a thick, breathing mass of flesh keeps him in place, blocks his escape.

The sound still echoes through the dark space. He leaves the warm bed and manoeuvres through the bedroom. His left leg bangs against a chair that is out of place. He swears, then cries out in pain.

Bending over the instrument, he lifts the receiver.

It's you, he says into the wire.

There is an immediate click of disconnection.

Among other things, he has always taken pride in his ability to accurately remember numbers; they remain in his mind a long time after entering it only once or twice. He turns on the lamp and dials a series of seven digits. He hears a tone stop and start at intervals of one second. In his ear the sound is as loud as the ringing of his own telephone. He continues to grip the receiver and to listen to the insistent voice he has caused to cry. He stands naked and shivering in the cold room.

He misses the following day of work. It is morning by the time he finally falls asleep, and when he wakes at noon his head is heavy, his mind is cloudy. He calls work to explain that he is ill, but will be better by the next day. With methodical motions he showers, shaves, deodorizes. He blow-dries his hair, rubs cream into his face, dresses. Both telephones are unplugged. When he leaves the apartment, he is a very attractive young man. However, he favours his left leg slightly.

At the local office of the telephone company he has his number changed to another unlisted one. He insists the new number be functional by the end of the working day. Told this is impossible, he demands to see the clerk's supervisor and refuses to leave the office without assurance that his request will be carried out. Afterwards he visits his doctor to have his leg frozen. At a pharmacy he has a prescription for a stronger brand of pain-killer filled.

Early darkness is falling as he returns home. He prepares and eats a meal of carefully counted calories. There is no pain in his left leg, and he feels relaxed, switching television channels by remote control. With satisfaction he has picked up the telephone and heard it purring with new life. He considers employing an answering-service to intercept any troublesome calls that might occur in the future. Or he can buy an answering-machine — he has had one before — and force a recorded message to deal with all calls. He can choose how he uses the telephone.

It will not ring tonight, he is certain. He hasn't yet informed his friends of the changed number; tomorrow they will say they tried to call him, but reached only a recorded voice stating that his number was no longer in service. He feels inclined to call his friends himself and share the details of this latest unfortunate episode, which he has so far kept private. His friends will laugh, and their light, reasonable response to the story will make it less disturbing.

He abandons the thought. This will be one evening free of all communication.

When the telephone rings, his brain swiftly releases chemicals through his body, and his muscles seize, his pulse slams. He recognizes the particular character of this sound, its persistent, stubborn spirit. After a dozen signals, the sound stops. His body relaxes, and he is able to hear the knocking of his heart.

Let me back inside your room.

A moment later the sound recommences. He listens to its inevitable, eternal tone. He feels the blood foaming beneath his skin, searching for a way out. His head is lifted and his eyes turned towards the window. He forgot to draw the drapes upon returning home. He gazes above the flickering images on the screen to the night outside. Darkness pours through the glass, licks the edges of the lamplight, sniffs the vibrating telephone. Later, when they find the body, they will say that he was always unlucky, it was just another accident.

After the Glitter and the Rouge

After the Glitter
and the Rouge

"At least it's only the one side," said Diamond Lil, appearing out of the pale Portland daylight to take Frances from the hospital. The doctors had only been able to do so much, the grafts hadn't taken as they'd hoped; there were certain complications, they explained. The marquee outside The Golden Arms made a promise that got bigger as the cab drew nearer: *Live Entertainment!* Frances watched the driver try to keep his eyes from the rearview mirror; before people had stared for another reason. "Everything heals," Lil, the last of the old-time strippers lied later, expertly packing feathers and boas and fans, preparing to follow the Jupiter Circuit on to Eugene one more time. They drank a last champagne toast, then to the tune of shattered glass Lil vowed they'd work together again, Hell or high water. "Maybe a mask, a bit of classy kink," she mused, snapping her make-up case shut, again hardening herself to the fact that she was pushing forty like it was a boulder you had to heave uphill or else be crushed. The Circuit's orbit was unaffected by accidents, it would bring Lil back this way again; Frances would always know where to find her. *Dancing Nightly!* red neon stuttered outside the window of the room where Frances stayed on with her costumes and her Camels through May. One night she tried to see what she could do with make-up; it only made the left side of her face flame. Out in the hall complaining batches of new dancers trooped down to the Showroom; she knew their dissatisfactions off by heart. Rain dropped in straight lines along Centre Street and traffic lights changed colour. Then quarters fell into a phone booth slot during the northbound bus's ten-minute stopover in Tacoma. "I'm coming home," she said, after Bea's voice needled through a bad connection. "Frances," she said, knowing then she'd have to forget being Blaze and Star and Crystal.

"Well, it's not pretty," was Bea's greeting at the screen door Frances had last slammed nine years before. "It's not like he was your real father," she added to news that George had passed away in '79. There had been no other changes, according to Bea. She glanced at the single cardboard suitcase, pushed at her wig, went back into the kitchen. For a year after they'd taken her in at twelve, Frances wondered why George and Bea never talked; after that she wouldn't have heard them anyway. The same furniture was in her old room above the porch, but some of the things she'd left behind were gone. She unpacked, then sat on the edge of the bed until Bea called up that some supper was ready. Soon it was clear Bea still went out only to shop at the Safeway or to stop at the bank. The house was paid for, the plant gave her a part of George's pension: everything was settled for good. "The same ones as always, I guess," she replied impatiently when Frances asked who lived next door these days. She'd heard the plant had been laying off the last few years, people had moved away.

Frances walked downtown, past the old high school, over the bridge, and through East Brale. There weren't many people around, nobody she could recognize; the place itself appeared the same. She didn't take more walks after that one time. The doctors had told her to stay out of the sun from now on; she spent the days inside with the TV. Bea cleaned. "Dirty Italians," she muttered in the midst of frying meat and boiling potatoes. "Filthy Wops." They ate early, with the afternoon still hot, food steaming the kitchen damp. Afterwards Bea went up and closed her bedroom door. Frances sat out on the deep front porch; the boards were warped, the grey paint was peeling. *I'm your private dancer*, moaned radios of cars cruising Columbia Avenue those summer evenings of '84. Drivers were boys with grandmothers who'd never learned English; they had last names like Lorenzo or

Catalano. Maybe they were heading down to Gyro Park with gallon jars of papa's homemade wine. After, they'd get brave enough for the cold fast river, try to make it to the flat rocks midstream. That last summer, when she was sixteen, the boys didn't call her Little Orphan Frannie any more; four years in town wasn't long enough for girls to trust her. The wine was red and rough, their clothes made shapes on the bank, a moon turned the current white. The first time she reached the rocks, Frances knew she'd be gone by fall. "It was an accident," she finally said in September, when Bea still hadn't asked.

First the doctors, then the police explained that he must have planned well in advance. The acid was quite rare, difficult to obtain, something used only in specific laboratory experiments. He'd been someone unseen beyond the pink and purple boring into her eyes, one of the hot angry men sending up smoke to cloud the lights, waiting for her next move. She'd felt him out there for years, ever since Lil had found her strung out on speed in Seattle, table-dancing in the rough Red Room whenever she could get herself together. "Honey, there's more to this business than young pussy, those little girls burn up in a week," said Lil, teaching her costumes and music and lights. Soon the two of them were trading off the headline spot on the Jupiter, doubling up in the hotel rooms, living steady and straight and sober. "I come every time I'm on that stage," said Lil, always staying in the room after work, her eyes hungry insects crawling over pages of books, going through one after another like a chain-smoker. Frances would sit by the window, all those nights in Salem or Olympia or Spokane, sewing on a million sequins. Wondering which of her moves would make something click in his head, tell him she was the one who had to wake up in a motel room with fire feeding from her face. He'd stop her dancing, he'd make it so the hot lights never dimmed. They'd still sear into her head as on all those staged nights, burning pieces of before into ash and cinder, current like something white wiping away what had made her restless. "I don't remember," she said when they asked who he was, how he looked, what took place that night she'd become tired of waiting for it to happen. By then she was always calm, always peaceful.

She went up to the room above the porch as soon as night cooled. The pear tree she'd once used as a ladder at midnight was gnarled and bent outside the window now. Waking with steady heat on her face, she was still on stage, her shadow kept moving on the wall. By the end she could pick up her cues blind, close her eyes and feel the difference between red and blue on her skin. *When a man loves a woman* and *Misty blue* and the one about the rain against the window: she moved to them all. Downstairs in the dark her fingers found the old piano hadn't been tuned since that last time she'd played. She'd forgotten how the songs went, or they'd flattened into something else. Behind her a black shape loomed in the doorway. "I always knew you'd be back," said Bea. From now on everything would be quiet and slow.

Dying to Get Home

Dying to Get Home

So soon it is midnight again, and time for children grown old to dream themselves back home. They tremble inside the big belly of silver steel, as the machine clumsily crosses dark runways, searching for the particular line of blue lights that leads to the sky. Some passengers press their faces against transparent squares, looking out; some sit with closed eyes, murmuring prayers and charms of good luck; and motionless others stare straight ahead, anxious or frightened or tensely concealing these emotions. The machine decides to leave the ground. With a roar of engines it rushes forward, gathers momentum and speed, then angles upward, defying gravity one more time.

There is a tangible sense of relief inside the aircraft. Passengers stir and light cigarettes and look curiously at fellow travellers. The million lights of the city left behind are spread upon the slow, dark curve of the earth below. Then the airplane cuts into cloud, and all sight of the world is lost.

Quickly, youthful and attractive women mime accompaniment to an audio/visual display of the aircraft's safety features and its emergency procedures. Their faces smile and say such an accident could never happen. They distribute cushions, blankets and drinks, and then headphones which enable the passengers to listen to music and later the soundtrack of a film. Trolleys of carefully prepared and packaged food roll down the aisles. There follow coffee, after-dinner drinks and the film. It is recent, and seems at first to be a mild, harmless comedy. The passengers smile and laugh at the same places, as though buttons were pushed in their brains. When the film turns disturbing and dark, it is still met with shrieks of laughter. The spectators' lips open wide to reveal large, dark caves of mouths. Facial muscles pull to narrow eyes that glint with terror. The cabin is filled with howls and moans and screams of laughter.

Light hits Richard's eyes, beating them open. He finds himself still on the ground, lying on a mattress on the floor of a very small room. Its walls are bare of photographs or prints or other decorations. He is naked and cold beneath a thin, small blanket he once stole from an airplane. Another sweet dream, he yawns. His head hurts, his eyes ache, and his body is unrested. What did you do to yourself last night? he wonders. Never mind, I don't want to know. . . . At least you could put curtains on the fucking window, he informs himself, dressing in clothes heaped beside the mattress. Manoeuvring with difficulty around books, papers, shoes and more clothing that litter the floor, he plugs in an electric kettle and makes a cup of strong instant coffee. It shouldn't be too difficult even for someone of your limited intelligence to know some kind of cloth over the glass would shut out the light. Then you might be able to sleep a few hours past dawn, genius. Then you might not have to look at that marvellous view outside.

Richard turns and glares out the window. Twelve feet away stands a large, old house. It looms there, blocking sight of anything else and later, in afternoon, casting shadow into Richard's room. A number of windows face his direction and in one of them a figure watches Richard. Fuck, he fumes. That's all I need at this unholy hour of the morning. If they're going to die, at least they could do it out of my sight.

Richard has been living in this room for three months. He did not plan to stay in it even this long, but he is broke again. Caught. He hasn't bothered with any of the little efforts he usually makes to turn these traps into some kind of a home. It is a small, dirty space. In the main room, besides the mattress, there are a scratched, beat-up chest of drawers and a small refrigerator that drones loudly and monotonously. A few clothes hang in a closet which could not hold many more. The only other room, smaller still, contains a toilet, a shower and a sink that doesn't work. My little cage, Richard calls it.

He has lived brief periods before in this large city, in rooms more or less similar. For reasons he cannot clearly recall, he recently returned here from an equally small room on another continent. There is a severe shortage of housing in the city, and being without money or friends Richard knows he should be grateful for any roof above his head. Still, he feels tricked at being stuck beside the house next door. Of all the million possible holes, of course I'd crawl into the one with such charming neighbours, he rants. Such delightful people to whom I can run when I need to borrow a cup of sugar or any of the small things neighbours are so overjoyed to lend each other. Give and take, it makes the world go round. Or is that love? I wouldn't know. . . .

Only after moving into the little cage (a mere question of rounding up one battered trunk and several cardboard boxes scattered in obscure corners across the city) did Richard learn that the house next door was being set up as a hospice for people infected with a virus without cure and always fatal. A place to die peacefully. Perfect! Beautiful! Just my ambiance! chortled Richard. It was started as the first of its kind in the country, funded by various government, corporate and private grants. For a time the building stood empty. Then, over one or two months, workmen occupied it, making extensive alterations to its interior. From what he observed through his window, Richard presumed these changes were to make it more comfortable, warm and home-like. Come over and fix up my place when you're done here, he suggested to carpenters lounging with coffee on the sidewalk. I need more help than them. He watched men spray the outside of the building with powerful chemicals that stripped away a layer of apple green paint, exposing old brick. Later, when furniture was carried inside, Richard eyed several pieces he wouldn't mind having — an easy-chair to feel easy in, a lamp to be softly lit by, a bed to gently float upon. What appeared to be an office, equipped with desks, telephones and filing cabinets, was set up in a room facing his. One morning at the end of summer he awoke to notice that, sometime in the night, the people for whom the house was intended had moved in.

While the place was empty, Richard grew accustomed to knowing there was no one to look at him through his window. He felt

safely hidden from the world, and stumbled around naked or
barely dressed before carefully showering, shaving and putting
on clothes that would make him anonymous in the street. There's
no one there, he told infrequent lovers (to use the word loosely)
who felt exposed before the uncurtained window. There's no one
there, he told himself on more typical nights when he clawed
through the disarray of the empty room, searching for pills or
powders or anything for an aching heart. No one.

I watch him. There are other windows of that house to look into,
but he is home most often and he doesn't draw his blinds. I wait
in this place that even now in early autumn is kept well heated, to
lessen the risk of pneumonia our bodies could not battle. Behind
me are the quiet sounds of sickness. Sudden outbursts of crying,
swearing, screaming. Efficient footsteps of medical workers move
quickly towards moments of crisis. Voices of volunteers, well-
meaning and full of false cheer, bring news from the healthy
world beyond. Calm words of counsellors are meant to smooth
our journeys into darkness.

Often the others move towards me, wishing to draw me to
them and to make this process they call dying less lonely. Leave
me alone. I'm not dying. As long as there's breath to speak, I say I
am living.

I stay silent by the window. Sometimes he turns and sees me.
His face flashes with annoyance. I am rude, I am sick of being
polite. There have been too many civilized good-byes and courte-
ous murders and pleasant stabbings of the heart. I will take what
I need now. No more patient waiting. I suck the sight of his life
greedily into my eyes. He doesn't draw his curtains against me
and I'm grateful for that.

For several hours the passengers are distracted from thought of
the enormous dark vacuum in which they are precariously
poised. Then expressions of worry, fear and uncertainty appear
on a few faces, to spread swiftly as an uncontrolled virus through
the compartment. The intricate manipulation of physical laws
that allows this ton of dead weight to soar through the air is not
clearly understood by most of those who burden it. They do not
know, either, why they are on this flight they did not wish to take.

The air inside the cabin is pressurized and controlled at a comfortable degree of temperature. Through the clean, thoughtfully appointed space arise murmurs of discontent. The young women who are to make the journey more pleasant fail to respond to buttons that are pressed to call them. The confused babble of voices grows louder when watches seem to have stopped. Attempts are made to calculate how long the plane has been in the air. Are we flying east or west? North or south? Darkness presses thickly around the brightly illuminated aircraft on all sides. The earth cannot been seen, and there are no clues to hint how far below it might be. It is impossible to discern even if the plane flies through clear or clouded sky. The engines hum steadily.

Although the light that enters his room is pale and white, Richard puts on sunglasses before descending stairs to the street. This damned ghetto where you're constantly on display, he swears. *He's* looking a bit used up, my dear. Not quite so young and gorgeous, hmm? Richard knows his face is pale and drawn, his body thin and weak; but he believes he can transform himself within several weeks, with aid of a gym, a tanning salon and beautiful clothes. He is confident there is still a choice.

On the corner he drops a quarter into the slot of a metal box containing newspapers. Baby got a smoke, baby got the time? inquire the girls prowling there. They are the only people Richard feels comfortable with in this city, and the only ones he speaks with daily. You getting off shift or just starting? he asks the TV who is really Diana Ross's younger sister. Behind them the hospice is silent. The girls pointedly ignore it. Their corner was famous long before it came into being, and they aren't going to move nohow for no one. This is an excellent spot on a fairly quiet street that is densely populated and therefore as safe as any corner can be, Richard's practised eye perceives. When we gonna team up and don't give me that retirement shit, says Diana Ross's younger sister. Once a who'e, always a who'e.

Right, agrees Richard. He returns to the cage to spend the morning brooding over descriptions of accidents, statistics of disease and death, bland pronouncements of doom by the puppets in power. He is hunched on the mattress with his back to the window. There is a dime of dope to drift on.

Noticing his hands have become stained black by the ink of the newspaper, Richard gets up to wash them clean. Someone is still in the window across the way. If I were dying, thinks Richard, I'd find better things to do than peep like Tom all day. He stares blackly at the figure, trying to drive it from the window.

The watcher remains motionless, as though painted on the window, frozen within its frame. Two panes of glass separate Richard and the watcher, and these distort the light, play tricks with vision. Does the same person always watch? Or have the eyes that looked at me last week suddenly been closed for good? The figure lifts one hand in a gesture of greeting or recognition, then backs away, sinking into a pool of shadow. Richard still stares, straining his eyes until they tear. It can't be possible. If so, where and when and who? No.

He doesn't remember me, and why should he? I hardly recognized him, and wouldn't have except that I've been staring at all the images that ever touched me, so that even when death wipes his dark hand across my mind, I will still remember them. Strangers in the night, yeah, and life is just one long Tony Bennett song. I knew he was a little high, but that was OK, you know. A film across his eyes he was watching, I don't think he really saw me at all. Give me a warm body in a bed, please, and can I ask you to wrap your arms around me until morning? If it's not too much trouble. . . .

He stays up late. I know what it's like to be frightened of sleep. Beneath his naked light bulb I can see him more clearly. How on his mattress he frowns into a book, anxiously turning the pages. With a purely unconscious motion he reaches for another cigarette. Sometimes I see him looking a long time through some cardboard boxes, but he never seems to find what he's looking for. He shuffles photographs like a deck of cards that will turn out lucky one day. He walks quickly back and forth across the room. Five steps, turn. Five steps, turn. I guess he takes something at night, because he seems unaware of his surroundings then. Far away. He never sees me at night. But, of course, the hospice lights are out and I am sitting in darkness. The fool, I think. Forgetting it is just as hard to live as it is to die.

The flight is crowded, there are few empty seats, and the cabin feels more confining with time. When it seems they will go unanswered, the complaints of the passengers die down. Slowly the lights dim and silence spreads. Some seek sleep, reclining their seats and arranging pillows and blankets to suit themselves. Others smoke in the darkness or sit quietly with hands folded upon laps. They think about what they are leaving behind and feel strong emotions of longing and love for people they previously regarded with calm. Pictures of faces and places slide across their eyes. When they struggle to see visions of the future, their minds become empty caves without light or sound or smell. The plane drones onward.

There is too much time, and Richard does little except wait wearily for several cheques to arrive by mail; as soon as they do, he will buy an airplane ticket and get the fuck out of this sick city. Occasionally he bends over a sheaf of papers, moving his lips silently. Where did the person go who wrote those words, and what was he trying to say? The telephone rings often, always suddenly. Richard never answers it. After four signals a machine connected to it switches on automatically and Richard's recorded voice mumbles a message. He hears the caller leave a message in return. Usually these concern the business connected to Richard's art. Several friends wonder where he is and what he is doing. Former lovers feel nostalgic and suggest one more rendezvous for old times' sake. Richard returns none of these calls. Like the cheques, the one call he awaits will never come until tomorrow. Take another pill, kid. These ones are good. You don't feel a thing.

I come under attack of infection and, while drugs are pumped hopefully into my body, am confined one week to bed. This is one more time I survive, one less time I will survive. When my condition stabilizes, the faces of those who treat me are relieved and disappointed at once. My eyes wander slowly around this pleasing room. Tasteful décor, soothing colour scheme, neat and clean. A far better place to live than his.

There is not endless time. Reluctantly I write several letters to be mailed after my death. Dear Mother, I begin. Ten years. She must believe me dead and gone already. And don't come back, she said. So I didn't. Now what is there to say? I forgive you and hope you forgive me? Or: you killed me. Or: I love you, I hate you, maybe it's something in between.

The others here are composing similar letters. We have no home to die in, or we do not wish to inflict our death upon our families, or we are selfish beings who cannot bring ourselves to share this experience.

I destroy the unfinished letter. She has buried me once. Surely that's enough.

In a brightly lit kitchen a woman of fifty looks out a window. She must bring her face very near the glass to see beyond her own reflection and into the darkness stretching before her. This is one of many thousands of isolated houses scattered across a sad, lonely land, and no lights of other kitchens are visible from her window. Her husband snores before a television in the next room. There is another room containing a single bed, a desk and chair, a closet filled with musty clothes, with pictures cut from magazines upon the walls. It has been empty ten years. Once she tried to use it as a sewing-room. She set up her old Singer on the desk, removed ancient school books, report cards and diaries from the drawers, replaced them with patterns and prints and sewing tools. She found she didn't get much work done in there, though, and gave up the idea. Now they call it the guest-room, although there is never company. Still, she vacuums and dusts it on the same days she does the rest of the house. As if it were just another room.

She would never mention it to John, but now and then she's thought about buying a plot behind the United Church and setting a small stone there. A short, simple inscription. Name and age and place of birth. And death. Something to visit on Sundays and his birthday, that's all. A memorial.

The darkness lies unbroken before her eyes. Suddenly, she lifts her head at a sound above. She moves quickly to the door. Outside the air is a crisp, clear shock. Her face turns towards the sky; although the night is unclouded, she can see no blinking lights at the tips of wings. The sound of engines grows faint, is gone. She stands a moment longer there, then returns inside.

Where did you go? asks John from the other room, hearing the door. Nowhere, she calls back. After the darkness, the kitchen light seems brigher. She shivers, drawing the curtains across the window. That's what they're for. To shut out darkness, to hold in light.

The leaves on the few trees along the street have turned colour overnight and the air is suddenly cooler. Richard shivers, thinking of winter that always comes so quickly. Darkness, cold. As his quarter drops into the slot carefully formed to receive it, a young man rises to his feet on the hospice steps. Feeling someone behind, Richard turns sharply away with irritation. Aren't you even going to say hello? asks the man. Hello, snaps Richard rudely, then with his newspaper walks quickly away, not glancing behind. He stops to check his mail box. Empty. Fucking publishers. He pauses there, trying to place the voice. His mind is heavy and empty; the previous night was spent mechanically inhaling acrid white powder through his nostrils. A small token of affection from Diana Ross's younger sister. The lining of his nose is irritated, and he sneezes pale blood. Looking back towards the corner, he sees it empty except for a few girls.

The stairs are difficult. Which voice? On the answering-machine, which Richard ignored the night before, green light blinks in a pattern of seven. Richard flicks a switch and hears seven voices, each separated by a piercing tone, speak seven messages. Familiar voices, all but one. Come on, pick up the phone, says the voice of the unknown man on the street. I know you're there, talk to me, please.

Richard returns the switch back to its previous position. The machine becomes silent. He disconnects the telephone from the plug on the wall. The empty refrigerator hums a third of a tone flat. The shower drips. Flicking a switch in his head, Richard listens to a long tape unwind between the distant past and the present. He listens intently, replaying certain segments to hear certain voices again. Parts of the tape are silent, blank space where Richard has accidentally or deliberately erased. He doesn't hear the unknown voice from the street and from the machine. You're lucky you can remember yesterday, he reminds himself. The way you're going. Which way is that?

The window facing his has been empty for a week. For good, he has hoped. Turning now, he sees two unblinking eyes focused upon him. I've got to get the fuck out of here, he thinks, sliding his eyes away. In the corner beside the refrigerator is a heap of dirty cloth coloured bile green. Drapes that were hanging in the window when Richard moved into the little cage. He took them down immediately because they were filthy and ugly and the last straw. There are such things as dry cleaners, fool. Some mysterious method of removing stains and dirt to make the dingiest material look brand new.

Something inside him resists the idea. If he hangs curtains on the window, he will close them and never open them again. He will bolt his door and not unlock it. He will curl into a small ball in the darkness, playing over and over in his mind a film that is old and scratched and nauseatingly familiar. Scenes acted out in a brilliant light that suddenly expired.

When he stumbles from the room, the curtains remain in a messy pile on the floor.

Although they frown at me when I leave the house — the day is chilly — I follow him. The sidewalks are crowded with people rushing to catch subway trains that will take them home from work. He wanders slowly and without apparent direction. At first his eyes are fixed down at his feet; after nearly bumping into several people, he lifts them and looks straight ahead.

I haven't been outside in several weeks. These streets and many of the people who frequent them are familiar to me. A number of heads jerk in my direction, and startled eyes look as though at a ghost.

We turn down the main artery of the city, moving with many restless others. So many who have fled numerous small towns to this place where they will be unrecognized, one more insignificant figure in a crowd. We see ourselves in strangers' glassy eyes, in mirrored expressions of loneliness and fear. He turns and sees me out of the corner of his eye, walking just behind his shoulder. His face hardens. Perhaps I only imagine he slows his pace slightly. I feel the cold touch my bones, which are covered with less flesh these days. Neon is switching on all the way down Yonge Street, bright and gaudy rags of colour fluttering in the wind. It is growing dark earlier and more quickly now. We walk side by side, headed in the same direction.

"It should be getting light soon," one passenger says to another. "How many hours have gone by, do you think?" asks someone else. There is the sound of a man weeping softly in the darkness. Cries for help are directed towards God. Several people take initiative and leave their seats in search of someone with explanations; they find the doors at either end of the compartment locked. Fists bang against windows made from a thick, strong substance that is neither plastic nor glass. Disagreements swell concerning the probable hour of night, the possible place of destination. Intermittent fights occur, with fists thrown and bodies rolling in the aisles. As the aircraft continues to be surrounded by darkness, it almost seems to have stopped moving, despite the passage of time, the sustained throb of engines. It could be hanging motionless in space, suspended by a single very strong wire. Connected to what place above?

Well, what's your problem, kid? Richard demands of his shadow on the wall, pouring more poison from the bottle into the glass. Self-pity, self-indulgence, self-destruction. Pay less attention to yourself, turn to those with worse problems, Ann Landers would wisely advise. Visit the sick, chat with the dying. An easy way of feeling you are lucky and blessed. A simple cure.

Shut up, he says to the damned voice that keeps whispering in his ear. I'll stop you talking now, he threatens, taking out his outfit. Words of dead love echo mockingly inside Richard's heart, scratching his memory. Do you like it when I do this? Or do you like it better when I do that? I'll never leave you, I'll always be right here beside you, lies the voice.

No, it's more than another banal story of a broken heart. Something went wrong long before that, almost at the beginning. It wasn't one thing, it was a slow process, an accumulation of many minor injuries that left him broken here, too far from any place resembling home and with no means of going back. If too many things go wrong for too long. . . .

If you can't explain it, just do it, Richard interrupts. You are boring yourself, not to mention others, with the same sad stories, the endless examination of old scars. The marks are there, my friend. Look at them, try to understand how and why they got there, make an effort to live with them and to move beyond them. Otherwise, choose one of the time-honoured methods, quickly. Is it going to be ten too many pills or opened veins in a warm bath or what? Choice is luxury and time is money, so hurry up with it.

It is long past midnight, and the other cages around Richard's are quiet. When people are poor, they are also meek. They cringe to avoid notice of the ones with money and power, whose heavy sticks can descend without warning or reason, sending multitudes of minute, pale bugs swarming in all directions, frantically in search of another place to hide.

Richard presses his thumb against the base of the syringe, forcing a little liquid to squirt through the top. He fixes, waits for his slamming heart to slow, looks up. The house across the way is dark and silent. Is everyone sleeping? No, they can't sleep either, the ones stricken that way. They lie awake and sweat. In the opposite window is a shape blacker than the night. Darkness made solid.

Richard picks up the telephone. His finger dials a long, intricate combination of numbers, and clicking sounds connect him to places further and further away. A different time zone. Is it earlier or later there, at the other side of the country? The ringing stops, a voice thick with sleep speaks. Hello? A woman's voice. The timbre and pitch and tone expressed through a single word send a million memories rushing through Richard's blood, crashing into his heart. Quickly he hangs up.

He turns off the light. Move forward, not back, he thinks. In the darkness he can now see the fellow across the way more clearly. It doesn't matter who he is, or when or how he was known. Someone to watch over me. When Richard lights a cigarette, another match flares across the small gap of empty air. A second point of red light glows steadily. Richard watches someone who watches him. In their separate rooms they keep each other company until dawn.

Another crisis. They tell me I shouldn't have gone out in the cold. I should have stayed safe inside the warmth. I should have remained inside my mother's womb. I should have. . . .

This time I will not likely live to leave my bed. There is a clear progression of steadily decreasing odds that could be charted on a graph with different-coloured pencils to make its meaning more distinct. Pneumonia again. If it doesn't do the trick, then quickly forming and unchecked cancers will take care of me. Parasites will come along to help, invading my brain, destroying memory, thought, sight, consciousness. An ugly death. Who wants a pretty one?

Here in bed the drugs that ease the pain sing through my blood like some kind of choir. I close my eyes and turn the pages of a photograph album suspended in the darkness inside my head. I ponder images that move forward through time, from the beginning to the end. Faces I have loved. Like bright coins, shining treasure. Which one was it? Him or him or him? The question is purely academic now; but I am still a living human being and therefore curious. Who gave me the kiss of death? Who had the soft lips of Judas that brushed mine and started me on this journey? An act of love or hate?

Although I can't go to the window any more, I see his face. One of the volunteers would be only too happy to take a message next door, asking him to visit me. I could pick up the telephone and call him again.

No. I have said all I have to say to him. My face was the only message I had to give, and he saw it. OK.

Time drags. Seconds become minutes, hours become days. It seems this flight through darkness will not end soon, or at least there are no indications of this. Like an old sore, however, hope still itches that suddenly the plane will begin to slope downward, commencing a smooth descent that will end with a graceful landing back upon the earth, in a place of warm, brilliant light.

Richard slowly transforms himself through the afternoon. With painstaking effort he makes many small changes in his appearance, until he resembles only faintly the person he was that morning. Yet it is a flimsy disguise, one he will barely be able to maintain until midnight, when it will certainly crack. His eyes glance into the mirror, then to the window. It has become a habit. During the past week the window opposite his has been empty, and Richard feels some important part of his landscape is missing. Some landmark that told him who and where he was has vanished, leaving him slightly more puzzled than before.

He makes a token effort to tidy the room, then leaves it. At last he has accepted one of the tempting offers of his friends. An introduction to a beautiful body, intelligent mind, and dazzling charm. The whole bag of tricks. The sure antidote to anything.

"Where's Diana Ross the Younger?" he asks a girl, passing the corner. She rolls her eyes upwards. Gone.

Several hours later two bodies are moving together and apart on Richard's mattress. They create changing patterns and shapes, smoothly rearranged lines. Prearranged, carefully rehearsed motions.

Richard breaks abruptly away. I'm sorry, he says, dressing again. In offended silence the beautiful body belonging to the intelligent, charming young man covers itself. His back facing his room, Richard looks out the window. He hears the door open, then shut. He gazes through glass into dark, empty glass.

Sudden light blazes in the hospice. Richard sees figures move quickly through its rooms with the force of finality. The third time he has seen this happen. Several hours later the hospice lights are extinguished, and the building settles back into uneasy silence.

Richard waits for morning. When it arrives, he walks down three flights of stairs and takes two cheques from his mail box. He goes to a bank and leaves it with a bundle of travellers' cheques. He watches his finger dial a telephone number, then listens to his voice reserve a seat on a flight departing that evening. He moves steadily around the room, packing papers into a shoulder bag. His eyes do not turn to the window. As darkness falls, he leaves the little cage, carrying only the small flight bag. Leaving everything behind for whoever will pass through the place next.

I fly through darkness. Travelling forward or back, quickly or slowly, for a short or long time. There are others flying with me. We look at each other curiously and wonder what we have in common. Are we going to the same place?

Each passenger peers suspiciously through the dimness at his neighbours. All believe they themselves do not belong on this flight and have no connection to their fellow travellers. There is a steady wailing in a very high key, similar to the sound made by a pig being slowly slaughtered. Sudden screams slice the darkness, and also shrieked pleas for the aircraft to crash, to catch on fire, to explode. Then the cabin grows silent again. The passengers become dull with lost hope, drugged with dashed expectation. They accept that this plane will not return to earth. They concede that it will not reach any place of light.

A red sun is lifted over the eastern edge of the horizon, filling with light a sky that seemed pitch dark moments before. The pas-

sengers open, blink and rub their eyes. Richard listens to an am-
plified voice say, in fluent Spanish, broken French and incompre-
hensible English, that the plane will soon land. A city spread
upon the shore of the Mediterranean appears below. The airplane drops through blue sky to meet the earth; there is a bump
as wheels hit pavement, then the rumbling of resisted speed and
intense friction. The machine of silver steel idles to a stop before
a terminal.

Richard descends to the ground with the other passengers. He
heard their restless, disturbed voices and movements during the
flight. They appear tired and worn from the journey, as if it
lasted many nights and not just one. The air is soft and warm.
The brilliant, clear light is peculiar to this place, southern California and certain parts of Greece. Pausing, Richard looks south
towards nearby Africa, where it all began. His eyes turn north,
and see a hundred miles away a small town of white houses clus-
tered upon a hill rising from a coastal plain. There is a castle at
the top. Halfway up the hill is a large house. One of its small
white rooms is filled with books and music, papers and clothes
belonging to Richard. A narrow bed. A small table. A hard chair.
Clean, simple.

He travels north.

I do not pass through gates of pearl, and no trumpets ring a
brassy welcome. This place is familiar. Its paint has faded to pale
green, but otherwise the house appears the same. I push open the
rusty hinges of the gate and walk through the yard. There are
red and yellow flowers blooming by the front steps. I knock on
the door. It opens, and my mother's face peers through a crack.
She opens the door wider, and I see my father standing in the
shadow behind her. "It's you," she says without surprise. "You've
come back home. Did you have a good trip?"

Several hours after separating, the passengers have scattered in
all directions across a great distance. They have forgotten each
other and the flight. They look with new eyes at another world.
When darkness falls, the outlines of all living and inanimate
forms blur, then vanish. Night blends the world into one.

Richard pushes through a curtain of beaded strings and enters
the house. "It's you," says the woman. She kisses him and gives
him a key. He climbs stairs, unlocks a door and passes through a
small, white room. Another door leads onto a terrace which is
surrounded by a wall the height of Richard's waist. He leans
against it, looking towards the Mediterranean on one side, the
inland mountains capped with snow on the other. The afternoon
shades into evening. In the streets below people stroll through
shadows. Their ringing laughter rises to Richard's ears. Lifting
his eyes, he looks across dark fields of sugar cane to the next town
along the coast. It shimmers. There is a *faro* whose light turns
away from Richard, back towards him, away again. The stars
above are very hard and bright.

He looks into the darkness beyond the light and feels the magnet of America pull him. Home? That hungry child of a continent, always wanting more. There is always more, always more,
Richard's blood insists. More than old homes and ancient scars
and ageless ghosts.

A star falls at the end of the sky. Richard grimaces. Who do you
think you are and what do you think you're doing here so far
from home, foolish child? He breathes deeply. He feels the air of
a land that has been newly freed from years of darkness enter
him. You idiot. You are home.

Rorschachs V:
Serving Sentences

Rorschachs V:
Serving Sentences

My new case has endured ten years of solitary confinement in a small room with white, unmarked walls. Only a severe sentence handed down for obscure, terrible crimes could freeze a human being within such a fixed setting for so long. At times, his skin has been darker and his hair more blond, depending on the amount of sunlight outside the cell. (He allows himself one hour of fresh air and exercise each day.) Sometimes his face has been more lined and drawn, according to the amount of poison he has put inside his body to ease the burden of imprisonment. The dimensions, furnishings and appearance of the room have also varied from time to time, and every so often it has shifted itself from one place upon the planet to another. But, like its prisoner, the cell has remained essentially the same.

Until I come along. We'll have you out of here in no time, I say most briskly, rolling up my sleeves. He stands at the window, straining to see through the curtains he has closed.

No names, please. Strict anonymity is essential in my line of duty; for its sake I erase the outlines of my personality, blur the contours of my character. (Oh, you would be startled and perhaps shocked by all my little quirks, eccentricities!) Call me an artist or an alchemist, a psychotherapist or a scientist. I must employ many methods in my work; sometimes they conflict. In any of these roles I am committed, both professionally and morally, to my subject, and may turn from him only when it seems the job is done. When he himself lifts his self-imposed sentence. However, the arts I practise are sadly imprecise, and it is not always clear when a cure is completed.

Especially at the beginning, when my patient appears hopelessly trapped within himself, the impatient artist in me longs to transform him and his setting in some miraculous, dramatic way. Wouldn't it be fascinating if the young man were a young woman, or if he were old? Mightn't he be illuminated with more powerful light if placed in another context — say, on a yacht, in a castle, amid a crowd? Certainly it would be easy for me to wave my magic wand and conjure into being an entirely different character, who breathes and thinks and acts with the kind of vividness that resembles reality. But such is not my purpose here, alas. Not yet. Despite my wizard's wand and crystal ball, and all these exotic alchemist's airs, I am less free than you might suppose.

Let's begin. First I encourage the young man to spread documents upon his bed. He possesses three passports. One is legally valid, two are excellent forgeries. All are real in that they allow him to cross borders without incident. Corresponding papers permit him to drive a car, accept employment, transact business in a bank. Each document defines him in the most obvious ways — by height and weight, colour of hair and eyes, name and age and place of birth. They attach arbitrary numbers to him: you are represented by this series of digits and no other; don't question this, please. Yet the documents contain conflicting information, throwing into question the concreteness of facts. Was I born on an island off Spain, in a small Canadian town or in the heart of Hollywood? he wonders. Is my name Richard, Rick or Reeves? Isn't my weight greater now than those figures suggest, and aren't my eyes sometimes more green than brown?

For ten years he has been fascinated by the possibilities of choice and by the concept of self-creation. He can be a hero, a lover, a winner; he can be anything at all. A common fantasy of people who yearn to escape defining marks placed upon them before they were able, by themselves and in their own time, to discover who they might really be. Erase the old definitions, search for new ones, test them out to see which define most truthfully, according to character, ability and scope of dreams. The time has come (and long overdue, I can't help adding silently) for this young man to define himself clearly in one way or another. To make a choice. Certain primary things must be stated exactly before less tangible ones might be pursued, I prod him to realize.

Although he freely elected to enlist me and my methods, he regrets the step already. I prompt and push; I am alternately gentle and harsh; I horrify myself by stooping to the most unscrupulous devices to serve his — and my — ends. There are frequent scenes, tantrums, tears. Who knows me better than myself? the young man demands at every stage of this exploration. I answer only with one of my wise tolerant expressions.

I watch him somewhat wearily and with a degree of despair, wishing he would hurry up and complete these first steps of self-discovery, and then embark upon the fluid, stormy seas of living, where the strength of any boat is really tested. (I won't describe the long tedious hours he spends staring at his blank walls, lying motionless but awake on his bed, doping himself into oblivion. Be concise! my brilliant teachers drummed into my head.) I remind myself that the verb *to fix* has several meanings: 1) to mend, 2) to set something in place, to attach it to something else. My client must fasten his nebulous spirit to something concrete in order to be repaired. I burn for him to dance, to laugh, to make love. But first it must be resolved who is going to do the dancing and laughing. And can we be loved if we are not known by ourselves, never mind by others? (I skip hastily past this point, feeling my heart clench into a tight, hard fist.)

He studies the documents carefully and at length, as though intense scrutiny would reveal more elusive information: size of heart, power of mind, depth of imagination. I glance often at my watch and sigh. Taking a bottle of ink, I splatter black liquid upon the bare wall; before it dries, it runs and dribbles to form an amazing, mysterious shape. A subtle hint for my patient to start moving beyond bare facts into more complex worlds. Association, memory, imagination, dreams. He appears shocked at my sudden action. Good! Assuming a stubborn expression, he keeps his eyes fixed upon dates, measurements and definitions.

It is the next day or the one after. (I confess! I do not observe my subject continually; he is an obsessed, static character, and constant study of him would bore me to death.) He picks up a ruler and measures his room. With very neat, clear handwriting he painstakingly records figures. Some of his findings are:

1) The room is 280 cm by 255 cm from wall to wall, and 268 cm from floor to ceiling.
2) 42 brown tiles, each 44 cm square, cover the floor.
3) The single bed measures 100 cm by 182 cm and stands 48 cm above the floor.
4) The only window is 117 cm by 61 cm and faces northwest. It forms the upper half of a door made of metal and painted a shade of tan that leads onto a terrace.
5) Another door, directly across the room, is made of wood and painted grey. It opens onto a hallway lined with similar doors and is labelled with the digits 10.
6) The room's sole source of electric light is provided by a bulb of 100 watts screwed into a socket at the centre of the ceiling.
7) The walls are made of plaster and painted white.
8) The bookcase is formed from wood stained chocolate brown, and holds five shelves.
9) The bureau has five drawers made from the same substance and stained the same colour as the bookcase.
10) The sink has one tap; cold water runs from it.

I touch my young scientist's shoulder. Enough! I cry, exasperated. He grins and appears foolishly pleased with himself, as if he has discovered the secret of gravity and now knows why hidden things float to the surface from the depths. I believe he would like to figure out the number of cubic metres of air inside the room; fortunately, he never paid sufficient attention in school and is unable to make the calculation. It is all I can do to stop him from running to the store to buy a thermometer that could measure the temperature of his room. Of his thawing blood.

Sometimes I am filled with doubts. I question the importance of my work, and weigh the personal sacrifices it entails against the rewards it offers. In my most optimistic moments I like to believe I am dropping a few pebbles of knowledge into the oceans that once covered nearly all our earth. Or have I forsaken the joys of marriage and children, the comforts of home and family, merely to free a handful of human beings to battle countless others in the name of vanity or envy or greed? I would like, just once, to liberate a spirit capable of journeying to the moon, or of diving to the bottom of the sea, where more sunken treasure than can be imagined awaits discovery. Failing that, I would settle for a simple handshake, a few mumbled words of thanks, when the wounds are healed and my patients leave me. Always they are exhilarated by the strength of their new wings, and soar away from me without looking back. Without glancing down to where I stand, fixed firmly upon this earth.

I notice you haven't tried to wash the ink blot from the wall, I mention with false surprise. (All of us devoted to this work are superb, frustrated actors.) What an interesting shape! I say in my most suggestive tone.

I think about the story of the wise teacher who asks his eager students to define an elephant. One student responds with a description of the animal's ear, another with a detailed account of its trunk, and so forth. Each pupil believes he has captured the essence of an elephant; each of their separate, limited truths excludes the others. The teacher rewards his students unanimously, with the same degree of ironic praise.

What the hell is he up to now, my stubborn specimen? (Last night I danced and drank at the Discoteca Cosmos until dawn. My head hurts, I am tired, I have little patience with his nonsense today.) With an irritatingly absorbed expression the young man places the fingers of his right hand upon the veins that run beneath the skin of his left wrist. His eyes are fixed upon the second hand of his watch. He counts and notes the pulses of his blood over one minute's time. Then his hand rests upon the flesh that conceals his heart and feels for the number of beats it strains to make in thirty seconds. (I refuse to record all these calculations; I take great pride in my clear, uncluttered reports; my favourite fantasy is a description of personality through a single, ultimate word both perfectly precise and infinitely expansive. You can see how discouragingly distant I am from such a dream.) Unscrewing my bottle of ink, the young man dips the pads of his fingertips into the black well, then presses them onto paper. They look like this:

I remind myself that I am not writing this record only for my own purposes and pleasure. There is an audience to consider. True, an annual convention of dull, dreary scholars is not the most inspiring forum for my thrilling findings. (I, of course, with my twinkling eyes, flashing wit and seductive body, am not in the least like my bland colleagues.) But still. While my young friend is sleeping, or sitting still and sedated, I muse upon the many alternate ways his story can be told. All of them are aesthetically and scientifically correct, if employed carefully. I can view this case history from a near or far distance. I can select certain incidents one time, radically different ones another, and shade whichever ones I choose with varying degrees of darkness or of light. Chronology can be manipulated; narrative made linear or circular; rhythm jarringly broken, lullingly seamed. One loaded word thrown into a smooth sea of sentences will disturb the surface over an infinite distance. (Artistic or scientific objectivity is essentially a metaphorical definition.) Sentences serve me. The tricks of my trade are endless, and enable me to fashion any number of meanings from the same series of events. And all these accounts, however conflicting, are each the true story.

I believe in the usefulness of self-exploration. Obviously. To know ourselves is to heal ourselves. However, I feel my client is travelling blindly in a direction that leads only farther and deeper into a jungle of thick growth and twisting vines, where there is no sight of the wide blue sky in which we all long to fly free as birds. What a beautiful day! I comment brightly. Perfect weather for a long walk on the beach, and I believe the sea is warm enough for swimming. He pretends not to hear me. I skilfully take another tack. Doesn't that ink blot look like an elephant? (It looks like no such thing.) Scowling, he turns from me and with all his attention listens to the dull, mechanical beating of his heart. (If I allowed myself to become emotionally attached to my patients, my feelings would be hurt. Luckily I am scrupulously professional. Completely safe.)

The mysterious, unfathomable organism beneath my microscope eats, drinks, sleeps. He is almost unaware of the passing of day into night into dawn, and the river of hours and minutes and seconds is one which he refuses to battle actively or float upon. This seems to me an unusual case — but then every one of my cases seems singular while I am engrossed in it. I suggest he open the mail that each day grows into a taller pillar upon the chest of drawers. I advise him to look at the moon and stars, to take exercise, to chat with the good woman who lives downstairs. (She and I have become quite close through my frequent descents to seek refuge in her gentle gossip when my patient has infuriated me beyond all limits.) From long experience I know well that this kind of experiment becomes invalid unless undertaken with reference to the larger, outside world. While my back is turned (more and more I find myself studying the Rorschach on the wall, as if I were the lost soul in need of illumination), my young man leans over the wall that surrounds his terrace and peers down at the lively young people who every evening laugh and sing and promenade in brightly coloured clothes through the streets of this quaint little town. When he sees me glance towards him, he quickly bends his face near the palm of his left hand, pretending to scrutinize the lines etched upon it. You will live a long life, experience true love five times, and encounter fame and fortune within ten years, I inform him. (Yes, I am also a gypsy fortune-teller, and sometimes find it amusing to dress in scarlet robes and divine the future for desperate characters.) I modulate my tone of voice to wonder aloud: maybe it looks more like a lion than an elephant? What on earth are you talking about now? he demands rudely, without a hint of proper respect for me. There are no animals here, he snaps. Except you and me, I retort, equally curt.

Now he is cutting sheets of paper into small pieces, then inscribing a single word on each one. He tapes them around his room. They are labels, signs. On the wall is stuck the word *wall*, on the door the word *door*, on the window the word (surprise!) *window*. And so on. He makes other labels: *love, hate, pain, wound, birthmark*. He hesitates, unsure where to place them. Finally he attaches them by threads to the ceiling, so they dangle in mid air. Sometimes they stir in a breeze that enters the window, or in a draught that follows the opening or closing of the door. The young man paces the room, from various angles examining it and how he has defined it. His head brushes the words *love, hate, pain,* disturbing them. He fashions a label containing the word *me*, but doesn't attach it to any part of his body. Instead he carries it around with him, in his pocket or in his hand, wherever he goes. He sets the label upon a beach, on the empty seat beside him on a bus, beneath a coffee cup on a table in a café. He tries to discern if *me* appears different according to the shifting of context or the changing of light. (I sit in the empty room, waiting for him to return with flushed cheeks and sparkling eyes. Almost absently I note that I have begun smoking again, and also to sip steadily from the bottles he no longer touches.)

I try to conceal my pleasure and pride. (Perhaps I should consider employment as a gambler; my poker face would surely win me countless millions, or earn at least a larger income than this present occupation does. A limousine, a chic Monte Carlo apartment, champagne and caviar breakfasts . . .) He's coming along nicely, I tell myself modestly. Not bad, not bad. There's hope yet.

Night falls like an enormous blot of ink spilled from heaven upon the earth. For once the young man neglects to turn on the light in his room. We sit together in darkness. He moves his eyes in all directions around himself. The fixed and suspended labels, as well as the concrete or intangible things they describe, vanish beneath the pure, single, smoothing element of darkness. The young man tries to remember exactly; he has already forgotten much of what appeared clearly and sharply before his eyes only minutes ago. Is the glass of the window streaked? Exactly what does the crack in the wall, just above the bookcase, look like? And what about my own face? Excellent! Now he is beginning to see by the light of memory, or imagination. That dazzling light by which God created the universe. Well done, I applaud him, and am deafened by the sound of my one hand clapping. (My other hand tightly grips a glass of poison.)

He ponders the connection between what is real and what is unreal, and wonders if they are as opposite and complementary as, for example, red and blue. Is there a fine line between them which incorporates the essences of both to produce some kind of new, definite truth — just as red and blue can combine to create a new colour made from equal parts of each, called purple, that at the same time is an entirely separate, unique colour? Is memory or imagination another name for this fine line? And can we, stumbling outside our cages through dark, confused and undefinable worlds, employ our powers of memory and imagination to bridge the schisms between what is real and unreal? The schisms between our multiple personalities? Perhaps, possibly, we can even blend the disparate, conflicting colours of ourselves to create beautiful new shades of orange and pink and rose, such hues as man has never imagined before?

Keep going, keep going, I silently encourage him. He has forgotten I am in the room with him; I feel a stab of loneliness. It is time for me to leave him, and suddenly it seems the moment has come too quickly, before I am ready to depart into the night and wander alone, wondering who I am — magician, artist, doctor; cripple, child, prisoner. I quickly summon the blessed armour of professionalism and offer him my standard closing sermon: I have not given you any answers, only nudged you to ask the kinds of questions that one day will lead you to discover the outlines of the puzzles that haunt you — who am I? where have I come from? where am I going? I wish to warn you now that you will never be able to define the vague shape of yourself or others by kilograms or centimetres; if you are lucky, you may learn to interpret them by means of memory, metaphor, dream. One day, I know, you will burn two of your passports, and as a single identity cross all the boundaries we build to block our paths; and this single identity will shimmer and sparkle and dance like radiant light cast upon a sea always in motion and never fixed, and so elusive.

This moment before my departure is precious to me. What is love but a definition of the concern, care and courage two explorers offer each other during their brave, foolish attempts to cross high mountains or traverse burning deserts? He remains silent in this darkness we share, my fellow traveller. I try to think forward to my next case, but my mind trudges obstinately backwards to the beginning of my illustrious career, and stumbles over the hard fact that from the start I knew that only by assisting in the searches of others could I travel nearer to the discovery of myself, hidden in some small dark cave. Good-bye, I say to my companion, my friend, my lover. My voice trembles with an emotion that embarrasses me and would disgust my wise, stern teachers. He must be quite at peace, I think, he is breathing so softly now. No more angry gasps or choking sobs. (My own breathing sounds harsh and ragged to my ears.) I would like to see his face once more before I go, so I can remember him and add his image to all the others I have created. Hang it in the portrait gallery inside my head. I turn on the light. When did he leave? Why no farewell?

I go to the mirror and peer into his looking-glass. That is my face I see. Those eyes staring back at me, frightened and wide, are my own. Can't I see some echo of his expression in mine? Some similarity between the way his mouth curved and the way mine does? I turn from the mirror. His labels hang around the room. My blot of ink scars the surface of the wall. I settle into this cell, to start serving my long, hard sentence. I stare at the Rorschach looming before my eyes. What does it look like?

The Secret of
Perpetual Motion

The Secret of
Perpetual Motion

We arrange to meet in the Plaza de las Tendillas in Córdoba at a
certain hour of a certain day in December 1987. It takes me six
hours to travel there by bus from the coastal town where I presently live; according to the Koran, this is not a long journey. My
younger brother and I have not seen each other since his visit to
my home in the Hudson Hotel in Hollywood, and that was 1982.
Will I recognize him?

The bus rolls through the hills and plains of Andalusia. Gypsy
country. My fellow travellers have closed the curtains against the
landscape outside, creating a dimmer inner light which allows
them to view more clearly the motion picture playing on the
video screen at the front of the bus. As usual, it is a loud, violent
kung fu film — badly shot, amateurishly acted, and dubbed into
an excruciating Spanish. In the dim light I peer at snapshots
spread upon my lap and the empty seat beside me. I wonder if
anonymous photographs are as morally suspect as anonymous
letters. Holding them like a deck of cards, I flip the old images so
they seem to move. To live. Now, still, twenty years later.

David wrote to tell me he has been studying Spanish in Madrid.
He suggested we meet, then perhaps spend Christmas together.
The handwriting was jagged and jerky, with no smooth, flowing
lines. Although in his early twenties, David doesn't know how to

spell or how to form a sentence. He is unable to add two numbers together to make a third. The value of any currency, and measures of weight, time and distance have little meaning for him. If asked the cost of something, for example, David's body tenses and his face becomes anxious as with a poor show of nonchalance he struggles to guess wisely. The distance between this planet and the moon might be one hundred or one million miles — it doesn't really matter which. Nineteen sixty-eight might be the day before yesterday, not twenty years ago.

Of course, he may have changed. I may enter the Plaza de las Tendillas and fail to find a pale, thin young man with hunched shoulders and a caved-in chest, whose very pale blue eyes seem to look at a distant world through a film of distorting water. On a stone bench beside a flowering bush there may be waiting for me a smiling young man who exudes confidence, strength and physical well-being. Someone more like myself? Before my famous disappearance from home, people used to confuse us. Call me by his name. We aren't the least bit alike, I would snap. There's no resemblance at all, I would snarl, absolutely infuriated. During those years — the end of the seventies, the beginning of the eighties — I would give David my old clothes and he would wear them constantly, like a uniform. Returning home from another of my foolish journeys, I would find him reading books and listening to music, obsessively, that I had once enjoyed.

During the last five years he has written me several short notes, scarce on definite facts, which I did not answer. As far as I know, he has continued to live in my mother's house in Canada. There has been nothing to suggest that he has finally managed to form friendships or to complete the college courses our mother occasionally enrolls him in. (How he graduated from high school is a mystery to me.) I can't imagine that he has yet found any kind of a job, even as a dishwasher. He must still lounge around that Vancouver house — watching television, sitting alone and silent in his room, going for long, mysterious walks at night — until the sight of him fills my mother with frustration and prompts her to enroll him in some kind of structured program far from home, buy him a plane ticket, get him out of her hair for a few months. Like now. Madrid: perfect.

The bus arrives at Córdoba late. I must force myself to step from it and to shake off the passive lulling spell of being carried forward and further forward. Watch it, I warn myself, weaving through throngs of spitting soldiers on the Avenida de Cervantes and entering the Plaza. I see him at once. He sits alone on a bench, his head bent over a book resting on his lap. He doesn't seem to have changed at all, at first glance. Five years or five minutes?

"The Minster of York contains approximately half of all the stained glass in England; the Great East Window, itself larger than a tennis court, is the largest stained glass window in the world," I greet my brother.

David's head jerks up, and without missing a beat he picks up his cue: "The Duomo, standing in the heart of Florence, was begun in 1299, and its octagonal dome was built by Brunelleschi employing ingenious half shells."

We laugh painfully, realizing we still share a secret language; we will always be two spies exchanging coded information. "Let's split," I say in Spanish. I register that David hasn't learned a word of the language and, at the same time, remember how he is somehow, sometimes, able to touch the flat wall of existence and to illuminate it, in the same way that God once touched the blank heavens and created stars. As we walk towards the bus station, David tells me that our father, Mitch, is spending Christmas with our sister who lives in Zimbabwe and that our mother, Ardis, was last heard from in Nicaragua. He doesn't mention our older brother and I don't ask. "Then it's just you and me, kid," I say as we climb onto the bus. "Do you get off on kung fu flicks?"

As in our oldest recurring dream, we are passing through towns and villages we will never know except as glimpses through glass. "This looks familiar," says David. "Were we here in 1968?"

I say we never made it this far in Spain that year. David disagrees. Suddenly he rattles off a detailed account of a family in a white van passing from Barcelona to Valencia, Alicante and Granada, then turning into the heart of Andalusia. Where we are now.

I am astonished and outraged that there are no dark empty holes in David's memory. He is several years my junior; he should have forgotten more of the distant past than me. Why hasn't he? "Did we go to Switzerland for the first time just after my birthday in March?" I ask aggressively. "I think I remember us standing in streets of melting snow, then riding with wet feet in the van towards Italy. Didn't we all catch colds?"

David stares out the window. His silence annoys me, and his interest in a view I feel has little connection to ourselves. Sloping hills carved into neat terraces and planted with olive trees. What do they remind him of? Around me Spanish faces gaze intently at the video screen, where fight follows fight with brutal monotony. It could almost be the same fight repeated over and over.

"Why do you still go around looking like a refugee?" I suddenly demand. "They have lots of money, you should make them buy you decent clothes." Looking more closely, I see that my brother is actually wearing fairly new and expensive clothes. Somehow, whatever he wears appears old, shabby, ill-fitting. "Don't you have any money?" I ask. "I'm broke again. As usual."

He turns to me and smiles. "No caviar for Christmas?"

"There's always caviar for Christmas. Your big brother has more than one talent. I'll shoplift from the Supermercado Aldi. Of course. Champagne and caviar both."

The bus pulls into another little town. "Where are we?" asks David.

"Home," I grimace.

Our father grew up in a small interior town of British Columbia during the hard times. His four older sisters quit school early and took what work they could find in order to help him through university in Vancouver. His younger sister, Jeanette, was also able to get away; she attended nursing school in Victoria, where her roommate was an Island girl with dyed red hair. Ardis wrinkled her nose slightly when she first met Mitch, as though she could still smell the goats and cows he had herded for an uncle on the poisoned hills above his hometown for fifty dollars a summer. Later, when Mitch visited the nurses' residence more often than fraternal feeling might inspire, Jeanette would never forgive herself for not warning him that Ardis was the kind of girl who compulsively broke curfew to go drinking and driving with big Swedish loggers. She sat on his lap while the car went faster and faster, then climbed out of the wreck in the ditch to walk the miles back to Victoria, slipping into the first morning class just as a lecture concerning sprained, fractured and broken bones was commencing.

Immediately after Mitch obtained his teaching certificate, his older sisters broke their pencils and burned their steno pads. Joined by Jeanette, they were married in two sets of backyard weddings — one a double, the other a triple-decker affair. Mitch returned to the town soon afterwards with his Island girl. She endured the place for nine years. In between giving reluctant birth, Ardis scrubbed the walls of her new house with such fierceness that the paint came off and with her vicious vacuum-cleaning she wore the carpets bare long before their time — seeming to Mitch's sisters to make a mockery of their more modest housekeeping. The same day her fourth and last child, David, was born, Ardis sent away for an application form that might land Mitch a teaching job somewhere in the Third World. Clearly any world would be a marked improvement over one where the choice of social activity lay between bowling and bridge. "Sign," she said, handing Mitch a contract and a pen.

A photograph in the local paper, typically out of focus, depicted the family in the baggage compartment of the airplane that would "fly them as far as their dreams would soar," according to the caption below. In actual fact, the airplane flew them to Montreal, where they enjoyed a week of orientation, this term apparently an obscure synonym for food poisoning, if the fact that the entire shipment of Third World recruits encountered botulism at the opening get-together had any significance. Pink and orange vomit — the festivities had started with shrimp cocktails — spewed over white tablecloths just as the Leader's large-visioned remarks expounding fellowship, brotherhood and the global family were hitting stride. He managed to imply that this accidental illness was really planned, a subtle test of the moral, not to mention physical, strength that would be required during the time ahead.

Five years later Ardis sat on the terrace of the Morogoro Country Club, a name that always filled her with private amusement, washing down French, Italian and Spanish grammar with gin and tonic. She set out to master the subjunctive tenses of these languages with the same force of will she had previously mustered first to immunize the local native population against disease and death, then to conduct a series of moody affairs with the French Canadian Brothers of the Morogoro Teachers' Training College before their expulsion by the more powerful Dutch Fathers.

(Although the Tanzanian government had nationalized what had originally been a Catholic mission, it was sentimental as well as Marxist, and Fathers lingered on to pat with tender, pink hands the wiry heads of black children.) Ardis's favouring of the subjunctive tense indicated a preference for what might happen over what had or would definitely occur, and resulted in future conversations in these languages resting firmly in the domain of the indefinite, bending an inquiry into the correct road to Avignon, say, into a complicated dialogue exploring the questions of choice and chance and circumstance.

What had been definitely decided was that it was time for the family to return to Canada. For five years David had seemed perfectly content playing with sticks and stones in the red dirt of Africa; but now, nearly six, shouldn't he know the names for the colours of the hills and sky, and the number of fingers on his hands? And surely his pale blue eyes should blink more often? "Those damn small-town doctors with their clumsy forceps," Ardis began muttering in 1967, when postage stamps on letters from Canada reminded that the country was cautiously celebrating its centennial. The three older children were also inclined to stillness and silence — admirable qualities in the very young, but only to a certain point that in their case had long been passed. In Canada the children would learn to ski and skate, and they would join Boy Scouts and Girl Guides whether they wanted to or not. They would also attend school, an opportunity thus far denied them, unless one counted a single rainy season in the abandoned nunnery at the top of the College. There an American woman had carefully explained that Jesus was from Ohio, while in the dripping cocoa trees outside colobus monkeys screamed in shrill disagreement. After this teacher was stricken by a combination of malaria and homesickness and returned to the holy city of Akron, Ardis sent to Ottawa for correspondence lessons. With trepidation she read a guidebook vowing that "every Canadian child who successfully completes these carefully planned lessons, be it in the basin of the Amazon or on the peaks of the Himalayas, will have received the same high standard of education found in schools from Victoria to St. John's." Almost at once Ardis discovered that she could fill out the lessons much more quickly than her children, leaving them all long afternoons free for the Morogoro

Country Club. She was bitterly disappointed when she did not receive perfect scores in her Grade I and III examinations.

"We needn't rush back," Ardis suggested politicly to Mitch; he still harboured hometown feelings for the prison they were returning to. In addition to five sisters with dire fears that the family had turned black-skinned and foreign-speaking, a teaching job awaited Mitch there. "Why don't we look around Europe on our way?" wondered Ardis, suspecting that once more wrapped within his sisters' loving arms Mitch would never stir again. Already Ardis had managed to convey the family all over Africa and across to Israel, Turkey and Greece. Now she prepared for Western Europe with a vengeance that might have alarmed Mitch in the last months of 1967, if he were not consuming his time with ceaseless strides across the rough, ankle-length stubble that was called the Morogoro Golf Course in a desperate attempt to lower his handicap several more points, perhaps foreseeing that he would abandon golf as well as socialism upon leaving Africa.

Listening to the dull thud of tennis balls and the squealed *love* and *deuce* of British women, Ardis drained her drink. "God, I love this place," she declared to the waiter who was the only other occupant of the terrace and still the only black inside the Club. It had recently been closed several months by the government, until the board agreed to allow black to join white within its walls. At this point in history the indigenous population of Morogoro did not hold jobs which provided for long hours of leisure, and the only sign of de-segregation on the Club's re-opening was a portrait of Julius Nyerere on the wall behind the bar where Queen Elizabeth II had once bared her pearly teeth. Everyone agreed that Nyerere was much the handsomer of the two.

Ardis informed her children of the immediate plans in such a way as to suggest they were made principally for their benefit. They would have a first-hand view of what other children saw only in geography and history books. It was understood that Europe was to be an expansive school, with each country representing a different classroom with its own audio as well as visual instruction.

The house of cement blocks and tin roof was deeded over to the Morogoro Family Planning Association, as compensation for loss of its founding member, president, secretary and treasurer.

She distributed her children's clothes and toys and books among the unplanned ones of the shanty-town that straggled around the College, and gave her houseboy the furniture he had dusted and polished for five years in hope of saving enough East African shillings to afford marriage. Ardis's insistent efforts to have Rogacion perform his duties exactly made him decide against uniting with a woman who might turn out to be equally demanding, and the furniture was later sold to finance a three-day party in the village, during which several more unplanned children were conceived.

In the middle of January 1968 the family rode by bus to Dar es Salaam. Mitch caught a flight to Amsterdam, where he would buy the Volkswagen van that was to be the family's new home, then wait for Ardis and the children to join him. They caught a complicated series of connecting flights that took them, via Nairobi, Cairo, Athens and Berlin, to Moscow. Ardis had always wanted to see the Bolshoi Ballet, ever since she was a little girl.

The sēnora who owns the Pension Arnedo seems startled when presented with evidence that I have family. Her unmarried children are in their twenties and live at home. "Different customs," she has said, trying not to look baffled when I explain that I haven't seen my parents for years. Frequently she has urged me to watch television with her family in the evenings. I have always preferred to remain in my room on the upper floor, looking at old photographs, news clippings, letters.

Now David moves into the room beside mine. It's just as small and exactly the same shape, but not crowded with books and papers and less easily definable mess. "Can you believe it?" I say, seeing him look in bewilderment at my room. "Two years in this cell. I should transfer to Sing-Sing. They probably have more spacious accommodation."

"It's bigger than a van," says David.

I tell him I have to finish this damned book fast, if I'm to have a hope in hell of eating in three months. In the morning I make this machine click and clack, while one ear listens to my brother on the other side of the wall. He is fairly quiet, he spends most of the time reading the same few books over and over, he never seems to finish them. I suggest he sit out on the terrace in the sun. "Get a tan," I advise. "You'll look better."

"It always fades," he says.

"Not if you're dedicated," I say.

In the afternoons we sit in cafés. We walk on the beach. It is deserted and desolate and nearly ruined by recent rapid development. The wind is strong, the sea is rough; we watch a boat foundered upon shore being beaten apart by surf. "You should see the rest of this coast," I say. "Cement. It makes this place look like paradise."

"Don't tell me," says David. "That's what you're looking for."

"The word *hejira* has several meanings," I reply in my best lofty, older-brother voice.

The bars are dead, the people not particularly friendly, they don't speak English: it's impossible for David to meet anyone in this town. So we spend the evenings in my room. I light candles, turn on music, pour drinks. "Don't you like brandy?" I ask because I hate to drink by myself. David politely touches the glass to his lips once, then leaves it alone. I give him the pages I have written about 1968.

"Did you make this up?" he asks.

"What do you mean?" I demand.

Nineteen sixty-eight has expanded in my head like a balloon that threatens to grow larger and larger as long as I cannot divine its contents. As long as I lack the needle of clear sharp memory to prick it and to see that it contains only air. Nothing more, anything more. Nineteen sixty-eight is the year when Robert Kennedy and Martin Luther King were assassinated. Police battled riot crowds at the Democratic Convention in Chicago. Barbra Streisand made her cinematic début. You were born, or fell in love, or bore a child, or died in 1968. It is the striking of four different keys of this typewriter. A year the same as any other, except more than twelve months long and lacking Christmas.

"Isn't it true?" I insist.

David stares into his glass of fiery amber liquid. "Well," he says.

At the beginning we — Lily, my older sister; M.J., my older brother; and myself: David was always too young, and separate — play games. Mitch announces the time, Ardis states the number of kilometres until the day's destination, and whoever guesses the moment of arrival most correctly wins an ice-cream cone or a cup of hot chocolate. Or we play the game about the countries and the capital cities. The prize is not the point, nor is the destination, we soon learn. Sometimes Ardis opens the green oblong Michelin guide, which like the Bible contains all knowledge, and says that Köln was founded by the Romans in 68 B.C. or that the Strasbourg Cathedral rises 168 metres into the heavens. We recite the lesson until we know it by heart.

By June the van has already travelled north from Amsterdam, across the English Channel, through England and Wales, over to Ireland and back to Scotland, then south to the Continent again. Ardis and Mitch no longer lead games or even lessons. Mitch hunches over the steering wheel with deadly concentration, not turning his eyes from the road to the landscape it passes through. A flick of his wrist could kill us. His memory of 1968 will consist of two, three or four lanes of tarmac divided by solid or dotted lines. Beside him Ardis pores over maps; only she really knows where we are going, and she prefers not to divulge this information. Both our parents have grown steadily more silent, and their faces bear inward, faraway expressions; obviously, they are in the grip of a headache or a spell. They talk about gas mileage and currency-exchange rates, and they do not wish to be addressed by children. At first we asked where we were going a dozen times a day. "Home," replied Ardis and Mitch briefly. We stared at each other in silent disbelief. The map showed quite plainly that a large body of water separates Europe from North America. Although the van served as a home and a school as well as a means of transportation, it was clearly neither a boat nor a plane; not having attended church or Sunday school, we were not aware that seas could part. None of these roads led to Canada. We are going to Switzerland or we are going to Spain; we are going anywhere at all.

The van is camperized, and equipped with an icebox, a sink and water tank, and much storage space. It is an intricate puzzle of shelves that fold up, tables that fold down, beds that fold out. A family of four would find it ideal to camp in over one weekend; after six months its limitations become more obvious. Rain and cold heighten these shortcomings. Lily, M.J. and I squabble to sit nearest the front; where our parents are seems warmer. David lies in the back among the luggage. We pretend he is so still and silent because he is sleeping.

At night it gets dark. Mitch pulls into a campsite or a field, or beside the road. With an abstracted air Ardis prepares a meal over a small gas burner, while we help Mitch pitch the tent. It is a complicated affair of poles and pegs and flaps, and it is not supposed to leak in rain or collapse in wind. "We've come quite far today," says Mitch with satisfaction, and he is very pleased that each night we are able to raise the tent more quickly than the night before. "Seven minutes," he times us. "We can do better."

With Lily and M.J. I sleep in the tent, listening to the voices of my parents that murmur until I fall asleep, then whisper in my dreams. I cannot catch their words. Later I will presume that their conversations concerned whether to make an effort to return to Canada by the time school started in September. Possibly they discussed the fact that money was running low. Or they suggested names of places to each other, words falling like dazzling jewels from their mouths, filling the cramped van with the riches of choice. Nice, Venice, Monaco. Geneva, Naples, Barcelona. For years I could only believe they were blinded by the glittering light cast by these precious places, and could not see clearly a way to end their treasure-hunt quickly.

"What do they talk about?" I would ask David, whose bed at night was a hammock slung cleverly over the van's front seats. His hair is still the colour of straw; on returning to Canada it would darken quickly, as if from shock. His face is still soft and round, without a hint of its future sharp narrowness. He gazes at me from far away. Like a full pale moon in a deep blue sky, his face is nebulous and blank. He does not wish to answer my question, or he cannot answer it; and one day I will learn that photographs do not speak.

The small boy stands amid slender green shoots which rise above his waist. Their tips are tight clusters of seeds encased in thin skins of green. But some of the poppies have blossomed; scattered over the large flat field, their heads tilt this way and that. David wears a pair of blue shorts and a paler blue shirt with short sleeves. His skin is still faintly tanned from African sun. Mitch must have crouched low to take the photograph, because the small boy in the foreground appears taller than the distant line of low blue hills, and his head looms large in the sky. His body leans towards the bouquet of red poppies in his hands; he bends his face to see their black centres. Shadow covers a profiled eye, the curves of mouth and chin, but an ear and neck lie in clear light. The sky has paled nearly white during the afternoon of June 21, 1968 while David stands among poppies in Belgium. Today he has turned six. He does not know the names of the colours spilling from his hands, and he could not state the number of blossoms he holds. The scent of flowers sends him drifting deeper into the dream of Africa. Drifting like Dorothy. But there is no good witch to wave her wand and with sudden snow wake him from the drowsy drug of flowers; and David will never reach the palace of any wizard, true or false, of Oz. And he will not wake up in Kansas or Canada to be told that it was all just a dream. There's no place like home. No place.

The green-faced witch flew on her broomstick around the big back bedroom of the house on the Morogoro hills. While David lay sleeping a dark, indefinite distance across the room, I kept still, believing that if I did not open my eyes the bad witch might not see me. But, I thought, if I keep my eyes closed, I might also miss seeing the good witch. Anything was in the dark. There was no glass on the windows, only finely meshed wire screen to keep out snakes and insects. Fireflies could enter easily, and during the last weeks of rainy season they were always numerous. I could waken David with a sharp pinch or a soft slap and persuade him to play the firefly game. He always chose the red and green ones for his team while I backed the yellow and blue. We watched the specks of colour float through the darkness very slowly, very dreamily. Sometimes they would vanish out the window, or their lights would extinguish abruptly for no reasons that we knew. It wasn't much of a game. For every red or green firefly to appear before our eyes, David scored one point, while I counted blue and yellow ones. If you counted fireflies, you could forget about the drums that would not stop beating in the village farther up the hill. "Seven, green, three, eleven, red, blue, red," David mumbled like a prayer. He seemed to believe the names of numbers and colours applied only to fireflies and did not describe the miles and months we travelled in 1968, or the colours of Italy, France and Spain on the map we were caught upon.

My father takes the photograph, then returns to the van where I wait with Ardis and M.J. and Lily. David wanders farther into the field, holding his flowers high and at a distance from his chest. Ardis has told him he is lucky because his birthday is the longest day of the year. David turns six in Holland, Belgium and Luxembourg, where with wet feet and cold fingers we troop into a café to hold glasses of hot, sweet mint tea between our hands, while David darts from table to table and blows out candles that could have decorated a birthday cake. David blew out candles in Luxembourg and now his head becomes a singular specimen among many red poppies. He doesn't hear us call him and I run towards my brother, pushing through tall, thick stalks. Once we were riding in a taxi, trying to make a flight to Istanbul, for which we were typically late. Ardis looked around the cab, counting pieces of luggage and heads of children. We had forgotten David; the taxi had to turn back. We found him standing beside a rack of postcards in the lobby of the London hotel that for three nights had been home. He hadn't noticed we had left him behind because he was busy choosing certain cards. One depicted a red-uniformed guard at attention before Buckingham Palace, another the place in the Tower of London where Mary Queen of Scots was executed. He would never tell me why he chose those particular cards, and not others. There is a reason for everything. If I do not catch him, David will wander away from us through the field of poppies until he is lost, and he would not miss us. He would pick every red poppy, one million more than he could carry.

"Is this Canada?" David sometimes asks, opening his eyes and looking out the window. He has rolled onto his poppies and crushed them; there will be a purple stain on his blue shirt that Ardis will not be able to wash away. The smell of broken blossoms is dark and cold and heavy. It will always remain inside the van. David believes any country we are going to is called Canada. Sometimes Ardis wishes to see snow, sometimes Mitch wants to go where there is sun. The white van veers suddenly to the east or to the west. It rises north to Norway like a balloon; it plummets south like a falling stone. "Wake up, we're in Canada," M.J. says. David stares through the window and sees an Italian village. There is a fountain in the middle of a square, where our mother takes us to drink. The water is cold, and tastes of metal. It trickles from our mouths and falls upon the dust by our feet, making a sound like a sigh.

"Of course they're from him," I say bitterly, handing the photographs to David. I have received them one at a time, care of *poste restante* of this small town, of large American cities, wherever I happen to be. They arrive in envelopes lacking a return address, and there is never any letter or even note enclosed. They depict, all of them, scenes of 1968.

Although I haven't seen my father for five years, nor spoken to him through letters or telephones, I still know his ways too well. And it is easy to recognize his eccentric efforts with a camera. The horizon is often more slanted than it should be, and the central image is inclined to be part of an elbow resting upon a blank wall, a highway sign warning of curves in the road ahead, a stream surely too small to bear a name. There are no photographs of well-known buildings or monuments that might be easily identified. Children pose in elusive settings; they stare into the camera's indifferent eye, then keep staring after the eye has turned away.

David smiles at the snap shots. "Why does he send them to me?" I ask. "How does he even know where I live?"

"He'll always know where you live," says David. "Haven't you heard of radar?"

On the Costa del Sol my brother and I wait for Christmas to arrive, when we will separate. I have tried to ask David about Madrid; it seems his activity there was limited to watching *Rebel Without A Cause* numerous times in a cinema on Calle Princesa. When I asked if James Dean was still as great as ever, David replied that he preferred Sal Mineo. That seemed the end of that. Now we have given up trying to talk of anything except 1968.

There is M.J. lying near the top of a sloping hill, one arm thrown across his face. Scotland? There is Ardis tilting a bottle of wine into her mouth. Is the label French? And there am I as a small boy, the only passenger of a merry-go-round, sitting astride a very pink horse. My hands do not hold onto the horse; they are raised bravely, defiantly into the air. "Austria?"

"Germany," says David. "You wouldn't get off that merry-go-round when it stopped. Mitch had to pull you away. You wouldn't speak to any of us for days after that."

"I've always liked going round and round in circles."

"Join the club," says David. "Membership's free."

"Wake up, it's Christmas," Lily whispers fiercely one morning. Outside the tent is Portugal and our breath shows in the air.

"I want some presents," I say.

"Should we tell them?" Lily asks M.J., who is eleven and the oldest and able to remember Canada. He says he can remember the house on Aster Drive and what happens inside a school and the names of children who played hide-and-seek on our block on summer evenings.

"We were supposed to be back in Canada by now," says M.J. cautiously. From that Lily and I understand that the holiday will not be mentioned again. It seems that Christmas and New Year's are absent from 1968 and that the year itself has more than twelve months. Ardis and Mitch do not speak of a return; they no longer mention Canada. We watch their faces and know that the day after the thirty-first of December 1968 is not necessarily the first day of 1969. It is still 1968; it will always be 1968.

We end up in Naples without money. Mitch must go to Rome to sell the white van; he says he might be gone for as long as a week. Ardis has sent a telegram requesting funds from his sisters; it is phrased in such a way as to discourage a response. With her we wait in Room 17 of the Pensione Fiore. We know we are near the Piazza Garibaldi. Everything else is far away. On big, lumpy beds we sprawl and read old books we know off by heart. Unable to read, David curls into a ball by my feet. Ardis sits smoking in a chair before the window; it looks out on a grey dim courtyard haunted by hungry cats. February is rainy in Naples and I do not know what my mother can see through the streaked, splattered glass. The pensione is cold. "You have to buy us sweaters," Lily tells Ardis. She frowns, then leans closer towards the window. Rain falls into puddles in the courtyard and I can hear cats crying in the night. For five days after Mitch left for Rome we dined twice a day on bread spread with butter and jam, washed down with milk. After nine days we noticed that there was no jam on the bread, and six days later butter and milk were also things to be remembered. We cannot forget, now, that we have not eaten today or yesterday.

With one swift movement Ardis rises from her chair, throws around her shoulders a shawl which is black and stitched with shining scarlet threads. She places her cigarettes into a pocket of her skirt and leaves the room. The door closes carefully behind her. We look at each other at length.

"She's just gone to buy something to eat," says M.J.

"She always comes back," I say.

"David's sucking his thumb again," sighs Lily.

We know it is very late when Ardis returns because we have been drooping our heads and shaking each other awake for some time. We rub our eyes and fix them upon a long blonde loaf in our mother's hand. She digs through a heap of garments in the corner to find ones least patched and soiled. "Get dressed," she says. Then we are trailing out into the rainy night, floating in file down a street of shining cobblestones, drifting past dark doorways filled with lovers pressed close and dry together. Ardis pauses before a *ristorante*, then enters. We follow her to a table covered with heavy white linen. A candle rises from its centre, throwing a circle of orange light that contains us. We eat salad swimming in oil and vinegar, and hot rolls drooling with butter, and fettucine fat with clams and mussels and cream. Ardis drinks a bottle of red wine and smokes and ponders us. Whenever we set down our forks she asks if we're sure we don't want anything more. "Have it now," she suggests lightly. And so we melt gelato on our tongues and assume moustaches of hot chocolate upon our upper lips, while David sleeps against M.J.'s shoulder and Ardis plays with the candle, snuffing out the flame between her thumb and middle finger, then lighting it again. "Where's your wedding ring?" asks Lily, because according to the will we have drawn up to divide our parents' possessions between ourselves, the band of gold will be Lily's. Ardis lifts a lighter, naked hand into the air to summon the waiter. She takes a roll of brightly coloured lira from her skirt pocket and counts all the bills but one into the waiter's hand.

The next day, in 1968, our supper is bread that once upon a time was fresher. We chew slowly and listen to Ardis arguing in the hallway with the proprietor of the Pensione Fiore. She enters our room quickly, shuts the door behind her, turns the key in the lock. "Where's Father?" asks David dreamily. Ardis doesn't answer. She settles into her chair before the window and we watch her as we fall asleep.

"Brothers," says Señora María from the doorway of her kitchen. She's a fabulous cook, and tantalizing smells drift from the room behind her.

"She's invited us to eat with her whole horde on Christmas Day," I tell David.

"I'm going to Canada for Christmas," he says. "I have an open ticket back."

"What do you mean?" I flash. "It's only five days away. Why didn't you tell me before? You know I haven't got a ticket or the money to buy one. You can't leave me here."

"You were already here," says David. "It's for the best," he adds softly.

I wheel around and march to the señora's telephone. After half an hour I have managed to reserve him the last seat on a flight from Málaga to Vancouver on December 23. I climb upstairs and throw the piece of paper with his flight time and number at him.

"You need to be alone here during this time," says David.

"You're right," I say miserably. "You're fucking right again."

I don't know how it ended. Money arrived from Mitch's sisters or from the sale of the van, or it fell from the sky. I only know that in the spring of 1969 we flew from Rome to Montreal, then west to Vancouver. By September M.J., Lily and I were sitting among other children in straight rows of desks, fixed in alphabetical order. We learned to ski and to skate, but none of us mastered the fine art of making friends until we left home and lost each other. For years we huddled in the dim basement of the house on Aster Drive, listening to the sounds of the small-town subdivision outside, finding each other's company miserably unsatisfactory and painfully necessary. We refused to travel anywhere, even the few hundred miles to the coast; any time we stepped into a moving vehicle with Ardis or Mitch might mean the beginning of 1968 again. They went on far-flung holidays to China and Mexico and Ethiopia, sending us postcards which we burned.

Now we see each other seldom or not at all. After their rescue, fellow occupants of a lifeboat separate because they do not wish to be reminded of a time of shared fear and uncertainty. For ten years after it ended 1968 will never be mentioned, like any bad dream unpleasant to recall. Those months fall into darkness and become a black hole in space where concepts of time and distance and gravity do not exist.

I begin to forget, and then to believe that a family who journeyed with apparent aimlessness in a white van still does so, twenty years later. They ride over roads which always stretch a bit farther into the distance, and they have been in motion so long they could not dream of stopping. The brakes of the van have failed, and its motor no longer requires gasoline or oil. Whenever I am in any European city, such as Madrid or London or Rome, my eye is always alert for a 1968 model Volkswagen van, camperized and coloured white. I feel it pass through Paris and sojourn in Scandinavia. Of course, it will be battered by now, after so many miles and months. The interior will be scuffed and worn and dingy. Its body will be rusted, and there will be dents that mark the occurrences of slight accidents.

One day I will find it parked beside a road. A woman with platinum blonde hair will be breaking a loaf of bread into five pieces, then handing it with chunks of cheese to four children and one man. He wanders away with a gallon jar in search of water. The day is windy, and the woman ties a kerchief around her hair. She has difficulty lighting her cigarettes. The children wear odd homemade clothing many times patched. Their eyes are dull and their bodies listless; they will droop in the French field until it is time to return to the van and travel farther. When I appear over the curve of the horizon they don't recognize me because I am well disguised in beautiful clothes, brown skin and hair streaked blond by sun, and because my movements are quick and sure and vital. "Can you give me a ride to Marseilles?" I ask, remembering how the woman used to stop for soldiers on the road between Morogoro and Dar es Salaam when she was driving without her husband. The children would peek over into the front seat at the soldier with his black skin and the rifle resting between his legs. "Do you have room for me?" I will ask this family. Then I will travel down the road with them for the afternoon, observing them closely, noticing how every one of their words and gestures sets off a flash of light inside my head. When we arrive at the Mediterranean port I will leave them with the dazzling light of perfect memory flooding from my eyes and winding like a halo in the air around my head. It is always the dim, elusive memory that haunts and troubles and lingers eternally with the old sores we pick at compulsively and do not allow to heal. Only by recalling something with complete clarity and in exact detail can we forget it once and for all. Leave it behind for good.

While David is a teenager Ardis speaks more and more obsessively about his difficult birth. Some damage occurred, she insists. I have always believed him simply stubborn, refusing to learn to add or to spell for reasons of his own, which might involve a desire to remain helpless. In Canada David undergoes brain scans. Child psychologists interview him. He regularly suffers migraine headaches. While neurological and psychological tests reach uncertain conclusions, he is definitely diagnosed as suffering from a kind of curvature of the spine, a condition that will grow progressively worse until his body curls like a fetus — unless he commits himself to physiotherapy and performs set exercises daily. He refuses. His shoulders begin to hunch, his chest to hollow. He makes his way slowly and painfully through school with assistance from remedial teachers. He goes to bed very early and sleeps late. He becomes too excited too easily, and care must be taken not to upset him, for he will fly into blind rages and tears that leave the household frightened. The subject of 1968 is carefully avoided. I remember that my father took me to a bullfight in Barcelona for my birthday and that Lily caught measles in Lyons and that Ardis refused to climb the Leaning Tower of Pisa. But most of it is lost. There is only darkness inside my head, and for years I wander through it, bumping my shins against unseen emotions, tripping over hard facts lurking at my feet.

"La Catedral of Barcelona was begun in 1299, but not completed until the 1800s, and it rests on fourth-century Paleo-Christian remains," grins David, before walking through the departure gate of the Malaga airport.

"We should become tour guides," I suggest, and assume a bland, bored tone of voice: "Tintern Abbey is the majestic ruin of a twelfth-century Cistercian monastery and the inspiration for Wordsworth's famous poem, 'Lines Composed Few Miles Above A Tintern Abbey'."

My brother moves away from me down a clean, bright hallway of hard tiles. "Guides of inner or outer space?" he calls back.

On Christmas Eve I sit cross-legged on my bed with the photographs. First I arrange them in the order I received them. Then I push them together, shuffle them like a deck of cards, and lay them out so the last photograph completes a circle when it is set next to the first one. I shuffle again. I try grouping them in different piles according to their subject matter. Perhaps one day they will reveal some pattern, suggest some large meaning; I will not wait around to find out. I shuffle them again and lay out a hand of solitaire. Though I play for hours, this is another game I know I'll never win.

At midnight I step onto my terrace. A highway runs past the edge of town. Cars travel inland towards Granada, east to Almuñécar. Their lights move along in a file, now closer together, now farther apart, as though joined by elastic. I think of Ardis and Mitch moving through their own unfamiliar landscapes. Ardis rides battered buses crowded with Sandinistas; Mitch strolls beneath unique arrangements of African stars, which suggest different shapes than the stars I look at in this Spanish sky. In 1968 Ardis and Mitch stumbled upon the secret of perpetual motion, where laws of time and space do not apply. Sometimes I think David was born with this rare knowledge. It is the secret of gypsies and the basis for flamenco dancing.

Sevillanas drift up from the street below, like red carnations that in their scent contain the secrets of the future. I have little emotional connection to Spain. I am in this country because I am more useful here. In America I am overwhelmed by the forces of money and power. Spain has suffered its own double-lobotomy during this century: the first, Franco; the second, tourism. People here are trying to wake up. In cafés they watch me with clouded eyes, suspecting I will steal the silverware or make their children disappear. Gypsies never sleep. We live in secret and work in secret, and we will never tell you the true story of our lives.

I return inside this room. My work here is almost finished; soon I will be in motion again. I will take care to leave the old photographs behind in a place I will not remember. Travel light, travel right. One of many useful laws. It is time to return to Africa. I will cross the Strait of Gilbraltar and go deep into the desert, where there is sun and sand and little else. Where flowers and water and the slaking of thirst are consequences of miracle. Islam has told me that when a black shadow falls upon burning sand a new spirit is born. I reply that the secret of perpetual motion is not hidden in the Koran.

Compromise

Compromise

We have a big house surrounded by wild gardens and crumbling stone walls. On May mornings I watch you descend the cliff to gather feathers fallen from Icarus's foolish wings; now they float at the edge of the sea, now they fill the pillow upon which we no longer dare to dream. My arms can never hold you tightly enough and you will never look at me with Jesse's eyes. We have agreed not to ask each other for much; there is little left to give. Perhaps I offer you more coffee in the afternoon or you wonder if there is anything I need in town. During restless nights we refuse to hear wind stir the apple trees. At least it's peaceful, we think — while in the darkness beyond our walls crickets shrilly complain against quiet. A newspaper delivered daily to the door describes distant battles; our nearest neighbours are far away. Jesse sails yachts around Adriatic islands, or tosses lucky dice in Monte Carlo.

First he loved you, then he loved me; for a single season he loved us both. Photographs remain: Jesse always poses in the middle, his careless arms around your shoulders and mine, his eyes already shifting towards a summer absent of us. He strums his guitar on that Barcelona balcony, commanding an audience of other gypsies to gather in the street below, throwing red and yellow roses down through darkness, one false flower for each of his betrayals. He will leave no note behind, he will leave us to each other. This was an act of kindness, I finally understand. Now I pass a doorway and glimpse you sitting on the edge of our bed. Your arms emerge brown and veined from white sleeves, your large hands hold snapshots of Spain and also Andorra. No, we never stride into each other's secrets; we share the silent seasons, separate. You don't mention how often I call out in sleep and I don't ask if your lips upon my throat hunger for taste of him. Waking beside empty space on hot August nights, I am free of fear that you have obeyed summons to search for Jesse in crowded bars or on beaches of Mexico. I know you have only entered the orchard alone again, to shift sprinklers that can keep grass lush and green even when there is no rain.

On Monday I do the laundry and you steer the spitting iron through Tuesday and every Wednesday we wash the windows that stare upon the sea. Already another year has passed. Waves do not stop breaking upon the rocks below, the horizon has not neared. Sometimes town children come to play in these haunted gardens; their calls draw you out to wander through the long grass upon the rise. We can bear no heirs. So it startles me to notice that suddenly your Levis have faded like the sky before it dusks. I try to smooth away lines etched around my mirrored eyes. Aren't we still young and strong? And haven't older others survived defeat to continue fighting? I would tell Jesse that we do what we are able. We don't forget to wind the clocks or to split the wood for winter. Mail arrives at noon and supper is at six. In June we tread the dusty lane, our sleeves brushing lightly, to where the stream still rages with spring.